COVENANT

BOOK ONE OF
TERMS AND CONDITIONS

COVENANT

M. W. MCLEOD

Covenant
Terms and Conditions: Book One

Copyright © 2021 M. W. McLeod
www.beyondtheveilauthor.com

All rights reserved. No part of this publication may be reproduced, distributed, or transmitted in any form or by any means, including photocopying, recording, or other electronic or mechanical methods, without prior written permission of the author, except in the case or brief quotations for review purposes.

This is a work of fiction. Any resemblance to actual persons, places or events is purely coincidental.

Cover Copyright © 2021 by Andrew McCaffrey

ISBN (eBook):   978-1-7370310-0-0
ISBN (paperback):   978-1-7370310-1-7

Version 2021.04.16

Disclaimer: Do not make deals with demons, and, most importantly, do not trust demons, unless you summoned them in an annihilation ritual. Even then, you should NOT invite them to tea and scones. Be sure to consult more respectable grimoires than internet search browsers and videos made on a cell phone before using witchcraft.

For all the friends and family that supported me as a creator along the way, and to the child who grew up wanting to be an author.

We did it.

CONTENTS

- ARTICLE I 5
  - Wednesday, January 8, 2020 5
  - Thursday, January 9, 2020 14
  - Friday, January 10, 2020 43
- ARTICLE II 51
  - Thursday, February 13, 2020 51
  - Friday, February 14, 2020 57
- ARTICLE III 77
  - Thursday, March 5, 2020 77
  - Friday, March 13, 2020 85
  - Monday, March 23, 2020 96
  - Tuesday, March 24, 2020 103
- ARTICLE IV 115
  - Monday, March 30, 2020 115
  - Friday, April 10, 2020 119
- ARTICLE V 133
  - Monday, April 13, 2020 133
  - Tuesday, April 14, 2020 151
- ARTICLE VI 156
  - Monday, April 20, 2020 156
  - Tuesday, April 21, 2020 173
- ARTICLE VII 189
  - Wednesday, April 22, 2020 189
  - Thursday, April 23, 2020 207
- ARTICLE VIII 217

Saturday, October 31, 2020	217
Sunday, November 1, 2020	222
Wednesday, May 26, 2021	225
Thursday, May 27, 2021	227

COMING SOON ... 233
ABOUT THE AUTHOR ... 235

ARTICLE I

Wednesday, January 8, 2020

Ellyria looked up at the night's sky. The moon was nearly full and high. She stood in her fenced off back yard, arranging things for the ritual. A line of salt arranged in concentric circles. Charged stones for power. Protective sigils worked in. She kicked off her shoes, and stepped into the center of the circle. With a wave of one hand, five candles lit and flickered to life. Everything was in order. So, she sat down, closed her eyes, and started to channel power. She just needed a brief conversation with him. Even ten minutes would help. Hopefully, it would be enough.

As Ellyria focused on her power, all the candles began to dim, and the sigils started to slowly pulse with energy. The runes glowed brighter, and the pulses moved to a rhythm that was unnatural, to say the least. The moon grew brighter, and the stars seemed to disappear, not that she saw it; had she, she would have seen the blue light shift to a shade of red. The flames of the candles sparked up from their emberlike state to an inferno. The fire jumping and connecting to each candle formed a wall of heat that encased her within the circle. Finally, the circle she was sitting in seemed to melt away as the lines all moved to the outer circle, forming a wall as a tall, dark form emerged. Wings sprouted from its back, each as long as she was tall, and two ebony black horns protruded from its head, a tail swaying behind it. The fiend stood looking her over, let out a long sigh, bowing, and kneeling before her. "I am Zangrunath. How can I serve you, master?"

One of Ellyria's eyes peeked open to see the being before her and the fires surrounding them. She jumped, scooting backwards. "You're not my father!" She screamed in surprise.

The fiend's head rose to look at her eye level. "No, I am not." He replied with a curious look that bordered on annoyance. "You summoned me to be your weapon. Did you not?" He asked her, hoping that this was some sort of twisted trick.

She shook her head in a bit of panic. "No. I- I needed to talk to my Dad in the afterlife. I researched the ritual on the internet, and thought that this would work."

Zangrunath stood up quickly, now, looking around at the ritual they were both trapped in. "No!" He yelled before near instantly moving mere inches away from her face. "End this, now!" He ordered her as his eyes glowed red with anger.

Her lip quivered, but she saw the protective sigils pulsing lowly nearby. She looked him in the eyes without fear. "How do I do that?"

"Break the seal before the moon turns white. Otherwise, this is permanent." He growled.

She shook her head. "What seal?! Permanent?"

"The one you drew to perform this!" He fumed, glancing up to see the red moon starting to dim. "This ritual is meant to start wars! That is what an 'Annihilation Seal' is!" He yelled, the candles raging in intensity as he did so.

She nodded. "How can I talk to my Dad?!" She asked, starting to get angry herself. "He never got the chance to teach me this stuff. I need his grimoire." She started to look to the outer edge of the seal. As soon as she got the answer, she'd break it. It should make him go away. She hoped.

"An Articulation Seal!" He told her with a mix of anger and nervousness now as time was running out. "Now, break the seal, and end this! I will not be a tool for a child!"

"I'm not a child!" She shouted into the demon's face, and, with a huff, rolled over to brush some of the salt away to break the seal.

When she looked back behind her, though, as the flames faded, he was still there. "Uh, does this take a minute?"

As the red light of the moon turned back to the calming blue that it once was, there was an eerie silence that overtook the small yard. Zangrunath stared at the girl in front of him with seething rage just below the surface. "You were too late." He growled deeply, calculating the cadence of his words. "We. Are. Bound. Together."

She sat up, and brushed the dust from her leggings as she processed his words. "I'm- not sure what that means."

A look of unbridled frustration came across the demon's face. "Until all your enemies are slaughtered, their kingdoms razed, and their blood painted across the lands, We. Are. One." He told her simply.

"I don't have enemies." She deadpanned.

Quiet fell over the demon, and, as anger overtook him, he let out a corybantic yell, shattering all the windows to the teen's small house and the others nearby. He looked at the pathetic creature he was now bound to, and stalked up to her. "Then, you are a failure." He growled before turning around and vanishing into a wisp of black smoke.

Ellyria blinked several times, looking around the yard to find it looking, well, normal apart from the broken windows. She pinched herself. She wasn't dreaming. With a sigh, she cleaned up after the ritual, brushing away the remaining salt, picking up the stones and candles, and walking them inside. Next month, she would try again.

As she walked back into the house, she saw her mother's blonde locks splayed out as she was zoned out on the couch, and sighed. She averted her eyes and dipped down the hall, walking into her bedroom. What had Z- Za, whatever his name was, meant by them being one? She didn't understand. She scratched her head in confusion.

The light from the hallway and bedroom cast a shadow into the living room. Ellyria's mother opened bleary eyes to see her daughter's shadow, now with a pair of devilish horns gracing her head. Too stoned to call out in alarm, the woman succumbed to a fitful, drugged sleep.

When Ellyria got to her room and laid down on her bed, face buried deep in a pillow, a sigh escaped her. There was a twinge of pain that shot through her back, followed by a warm feeling. The warm feeling quickly became an intense burning, as an incredibly powerful seal branded itself onto her back. Ellyria grabbed her sheets, feeling tears fall from her face to the bed as pain lanced through her.

When the pain settled down, the demon appeared. "Well, I hope you are ready for a fun eternity together." He growled, glancing around her room. "We are now bound together, stuck this way until I help finish your task." He sighed deeply, and shook his head. "Figures that it would look like this."

The door to the room was closed, and, on the back of it, there were a couple of posters. The first was a poster with information on different gemstones and their properties while the other one was a poster for a local band called Omen. On the other side of the room was a window, which was covered up by a blanket with a black, white, and red evil eye design. Below that, purple and black bedding were thrown pell-mell across the bed, and, on top of a long, low dresser to the right of the bed, rested a jewelry box that looked like she might struggle to pick it up with her slender frame. Around the room, there were random items scattered all about, mostly planners or journals along with a few receipts. At the edge of one of these piles was a much larger pile of envelopes, which looked hastily ripped open, coming out of a few of them were yellow and pink notices, indicating Final Notice. Articles of clothing lay discarded next to the hamper instead of inside of it, and her backpack was tossed against the wall next to her bedroom door.

After a moment, the pain in Ellyria's back fully subsided, and she looked to the fiend. "Like what? This is what a normal girl's room looks like, you pervert. Get out of here."

Zangrunath shook his head. "I cannot do that." He told her simply, annoyance present in his voice. "Wherever you go, I go. That is what being 'one' is." He explained, picking up a magazine from her desk, idly flipping through the pages. He glanced up at her. "As for all of this," He replied with a flippant wave to the room. "I was hoping there would be more tomes, but, given your ineptitude for magic, it now makes more sense." He sighed, tossing the magazine back onto the desk and continuing to look around the room.

She looked away from him, laying down on her side. "I know." She sniffed. "I can't find them. My Dad's grimoires."

He rolled his eyes in annoyance. "Then, look harder."

She sighed, standing up, and getting into his face. "You don't think I've tried that?! I've doused the whole house. His work. Everywhere I could think of. They're either gone or hidden, and my one shot that I had to try to talk to him stuck me with you." She spat.

He effortlessly picked her up, lifting the slim girl back onto the bed, and glaring into her chestnut brown eyes. "Then, explain to me how in the Hells you managed to summon me with such little knowledge. Because the amount of power it takes to do such a thing shouldn't be possible by the likes of you." He bit back, looking her over before glancing at the door in the direction of her living room, and thinking about the woman with the glassy blue eyes. "What about the woman? Your mother."

"She doesn't know anything." Ellyria sighed. "My Dad was the caster. Besides, she's basically been zonked out of her mind like that since he died. I looked up the ritual on the internet, and it took me two months to charge enough crystals with magic to get the power level I needed for it."

He walked around her bed, inspecting her carefully. "Crystals would not help with the power that is needed for summoning someone like me. They only prolong the stability portion of the ritual, increasing its effectiveness." He corrected her.

She glared at him, and sighed with resignation. "Then, just call me an idiot savant. I don't know. I found the instructions, thinking I could talk to him for a few minutes, but, instead, I got you."

"Clearly." He grumbled, and walked to the center of the room. "Where did your father work on his spells?" He asked her, starting to grow curious about the man, thinking that he was the reason for her power.

She gave him a withering look, but silently walked him out of her room and into the garage, which shared a wall with her bedroom. She flipped on a light switch, and fluorescent bulbs lit the room with a bluish hue. She looked around the space paved with concrete. The walls were lined with pegboard, and tools hung on the walls. There was an old silver Pontiac Grand Prix up on blocks near a workbench with several lights and other tools nearby. Over on the other wall, a bicycle collected dust while hanging on a rack. "He used to work on cars in here, but I caught him a couple times casting when I was little. Never knew what for. When I got my magic about a year ago, he started teaching me how to cast in here under the guise of fixing the car."

"Then, he probably hid it in here." Zangrunath commented, melting into the floor as his shadow quickly encompassed the room, blocking out the light for all but a moment before reappearing next to the car. He effortlessly pushed the vehicle to the side, knocking it off its stilts, and denting the door slightly. He took a step back as he raised a hand, curling it into a fist and put it through the concrete below him, lifting the slab up, and setting it to the side. "You weren't looking hard enough." He grinned mischievously.

Her jaw dropped, and she did a double take between the car, the demon, and the hole in the ground. "No. No. I scried and doused this room a dozen times. It can't-" She grew very still and quiet for a moment. "I'm an idiot. The concrete."

"Wards can do wonders for things." He added, reaching down, and picking up a leather-bound tome before handing it to her.

"I'm not sensing a spell, but magic doesn't like to go through concrete that thick." She looked at the book, and brushed some dust away from its cover. Her fingers ran over the runic inscriptions in old, long forgotten languages, and the supple binding felt soft and pliable under her fingers. She unwrapped the leather strap, and fanned the parchment pages to see the old ink writings of her ancestors. Automatically, her nose lowered to the book, and she smelled the comforting scent that could only be described as a combination of a bookstore and magic. She looked to the demon, deflating a bit. "Thank you."

He shook his head. "I am a weapon of war. A tool. I am to be used as the- wielder sees fit." He sighed.

She investigated the space beneath the floor, and retrieved several other items there. She laughed when she found Paolo Santo. "I don't suppose that this will purify you out of the deal?"

He scoffed at the lightly colored and pungent smelling wood. "It takes a large amount of holy power to get rid of me. Not that I'm currently sensing any of that coming from you. You are but a witch. How do you think the crusades started?" He chuckled before giving a small wave. "Hello."

"Uh," she frowned. "I've never really had a consistent teacher, so I haven't learned about that in history class."

"You won't find that in any normal history book." He mentioned idly, looking around the room. "The Vatican was very careful not to mention us during those times." He explained, sauntering over, and inspecting the tools. "Odd torture equipment."

"No, I mean, I never learned about The Crusades. At all. And, that's not torture equipment. Those are tools to fix the car you just wrecked." She told him seriously. "Guess I'll have to look up how to fix that, too."

He sighed, and turned to face her. "Tell me where to look up the information, and I will learn how to fix it." He told her seriously. "It is my job to make your job easier, no matter how-" he surmised, looking at the curious hunk of machinery in the center of the room, "odd."

"How long has it been since you were, like, summoned, dude? Do you not know what a car or the internet is?" She asked, starting to get irritated.

He ignored the phrase she called him and thought aloud. "I believe the last time I was summoned I was near a place called Stalingrad." He smiled, enjoying the memory fondly. "The bloodshed was magnificent."

She shrugged, and led him back to her room. "Well, you're basically speaking gibberish to me, but I can show you my laptop before bed. I've got school tomorrow."

He followed her, not by choice, but with a purpose. "Simply show me how it works, and I will learn it." He told her seriously. "As for school, I will try to find a form that is more suited to your environment."

"You can do that?" She asked as she booted up an old laptop, typing in her password. "You read English, right?"

"I read all languages." He replied to her, watching her type in her password and quickly memorizing it. "And, as for my form, yes. I can take on any form you wish or whatever the situation calls for." He explained, turning his arm into an obsidian black, wickedly long, and razor-sharp blade.

"Woah, woah, buddy! Put that away! We don't use swords in this time." She exclaimed as she dodged out of the way of the weapon.

"Then, would this be more appropriate?" He asked confused, turning it instead into a demonic looking rifle, with bits of hellfire slowly streaming up and out of it.

She shook her head. "No. None of that. Weapons are illegal at schools. I'm not going to jail for this."

He let out a growl, and turned his arm back to normal. "Fine. I will find something that is 'legal'." He grumbled, rolling his eyes, and using air quotes.

Finally, the laptop was up and running, and she showed him the shortcut to the internet browser. She clicked on a little icon in the corner. "This is the internet. It's a massive place where data is stored with information on all kinds of stuff. This is a search engine. You just type in what you want to know, and it brings up the information. So, I can type in 'The Crusades', and it'll bring up articles for me to research. Just don't believe everything you see. People can really write anything they want on some sites."

"I am not an idiot." Zangrunath quipped back. He watched her intently as she showed him how to use the device, and, after a few minutes, he shrugged. "It seems simple enough. I will find out how to fix the 'car', and, then, a form that works for your school." He told her simply.

She yawned. "Alright. Good. Goodnight." She moved to lay down in her baggy oversized t-shirt and leggings without getting changed, and nearly jumped out of her skin when the fresh brand on her back touched the mattress.

He shook his head. "I don't understand what is so good about night."

She ignored his words, grunting in frustration, and rolled onto her stomach. She grumbled at the pain in her back before closing her eyes to rest. It took her a while to get to sleep. She wasn't used to the glow of her laptop screen while she slept, but, eventually, the exhaustion of using so much magic earlier in the evening and the following excitement caught up with her. Only then, did sleep take her.

He quietly began to type on the laptop, starting to research the things he needed to learn, and, when he was through with those tasks, what he had missed in the last century since he had been gone. After some quick clicks, he was able to learn that not much had changed short of much more impressive weapons and tactics. Clearly, there were demons helping still in this day and age. He smirked, glad that his kind were still running things. Once that was done, he had to pause in order to find out where she went to school. He couldn't wake her, so he went through her school bag, and found the school logo on a planner there. Using that information, he searched up images of what would be a 'new kid', and magically forged papers for his arrival tomorrow. Once that was done, he waited for his- master- to wake.

Thursday, January 9, 2020

At six in the morning, Ellyria was startled awake by the alarm on her phone. She turned it off, and started to get dressed in a dazed and groggy state. The skin of her back was sensitive, tugging and pulling every time she adjusted her bra. It still didn't feel right, but, in her hurry, she ignored it, pulling on a dark colored blouse, not that anybody would see it given the cold weather, before moving down the hall towards the bathroom. She started to do her hair and makeup, running a comb through her straight, black hair.

As she was leaning forward to work on her eyeliner, her shirt sagged at the collar, revealing something on her shoulder. She made a face, and pulled off her shirt to find a symbol burned into the entirety of her back. It was a modified version of what she'd drawn with salt the day before. She sighed, remembering the strange nightmare the ritual had given her before getting dressed again. She didn't have time for this. She moved back to do her lips, jumping when she noticed horns in her reflection, this time. "Okay, what the Hell?"

"I am always with you." Zangrunath whispered, appearing next to her, and leaning against the wall. "The reflection is just there to be a constant reminder of that." He smirked at the confused look he saw in the mirror.

She clutched her chest as she tried to calm down. "I'm still dreaming." She commented, pinching herself hard. "Okay. Not dreaming. This is real. Oh, I don't have time for this."

"This is very real." He told her as he pinched himself, causing her pain as well. "We are one, so be mindful of that." He told her seriously, looking on with the same serious expression.

She flinched at the sudden pain he caused her. "Shoot. I'm sorry."

He stepped back from her, and turned into a young man about her age with tanned skin, black hair and near black eyes. He was almost six feet tall and well built. "Will this form work for your school?" He asked her seriously.

She gasped just as he transformed before her, and her breath caught. Where a devil was moments before, now, there was a handsome boy. She reminded herself what he was, and looked away. His new form was just as tall as his true form, which was to say that he towered over her by more than half a foot. If she wanted to look at him eye-to-eye, she would have to stand on her tiptoes to do so. "Oh, great. I got changed with you around."

"Nothing I haven't seen before countless times." He replied flippantly, checking his form over a bit in the mirror before his eyes turned to hers. "You are not the first female to summon me." He looked his hands over carelessly. To him, this was just another job.

She sneered slightly, and looked at his face, which might as well have been a male model or movie star given the lack of diversity in the small town. "Does this contract thing have a privacy mode? What if I need alone time to cast or something?"

"I will be there." He told her simply, but his features were stern and serious. "It is also my job to protect you everywhere you go." He explained with no room for argument.

"So, nothing's sacred? Showers?" She asked, pointing to the tub in the room.

"I will be in the same room, if that helps somewhat." He sighed. He really hated explaining this to the caster every time he was summoned. "Again, nothing I haven't seen countless times before."

She looked down at herself, and sighed. "Great."

He looked at her seriously. "You did this to yourself. You cast the ritual based on an image, which was wrong, mind you, without knowing any of the consequences of what would happen. Deal with it." He grumbled.

"Okay, so, we feel each other's pain, and you are always around. Anything else I should know about this before it comes up?" She asked, crossing her arms across her chest.

"Once the deal is complete, your soul gets damned to Hell," he shrugged in clear annoyance, "but that will be a while."

"I- excuse me?" She gulped.

He facepalmed, and groaned before gesturing to the door. "You know absolutely nothing about this. Let us go to your room, so I can show you."

She was shaking as she left the bathroom, too preoccupied by the news that her soul was damned to notice her mother before they collided. When the dazed woman bumped her, Ellyria ran into the wall and jammed her shoulder a little bit, making her rub it in pain. The younger woman was just so slender by comparison that her mother could just throw her around.

The older woman's eyes looked glassy from drug use, and she didn't apologize for giving Ellyria a bump. She hadn't even felt it herself.

"Oh, Mom! You okay?" Ellyria watched her mother for a moment with a sigh.

"Uh, huh. Get to school." She replied mechanically as she went to the couch where she promptly passed out.

Ellyria put her fingers on her temples. "That's a problem for another day." She murmured, looking to her demon. Za- Zang-? What was his name again? "She can't see you?"

"Not if I don't want her to. That being said, she didn't see me." He told her honestly, looking at the older woman curiously. "Wasn't trying to hide." He whispered, trailing off for a moment. He looked back at Ellyria while pointing a finger at the girl's mother. "Is she okay?"

"You can call her Lynne. She's-" Ellyria frowned, finishing the short walk to her bedroom, and sitting down on the bed. "She hasn't been sober for a day since my father died. I'm not even sure what she's taking at this point."

"Do you want me to fix her?" He asked her seriously as a grin dominated his face, which made his now human features look sinister. "It would be rather simple."

"You, you can do that?" She asked, feeling hope start to form. It lightened her chest for the first time in a long time.

"Well, she might have a heart attack, but I promise she will never touch whatever she is on again." He smirked, as his mind began coming up with ways to torment the drug addicted woman.

"No. No, I can. I can fix her. I don't want her to get hurt." When he made it in, she conjured a little breeze to shut the door, glancing at the grimoire resting on the dresser beside her bed. She closed her eyes, and shook her head. "I can- I don't know."

Zangrunath sighed. "Fine. Suit yourself, but it won't last that way. She needs to have a reason." He shrugged, pointing at where Lynne would be behind the now closed door. "Magic will only delay the inevitable." He told her seriously, having seen things like this before back in Hell.

Ellyria sighed, and shook her head again. "Why am I not a good enough reason?" She asked rhetorically with a few tears in her eyes.

She took a deep breath, and a more determined look washed over her features. "You were going to tell me about this deal."

Not caring about her tears, he walked over to the laptop and quickly pulled up the image she used for the summoning before grabbing the grimoire and flipping through its pages. "That image, first of all, is clearly wrong." As he flipped through the grimoire, there were several blank pages and others with ritual seals, none of which matched the one on her back. He sighed, setting it down, and continued. "It is also a pale imitation of the real thing. I am surprised you summoned me at all. That being said, the ritual is used to gain large amounts of power or complete a goal. Bodies usually, but the outcome is the same." He explained to her, disappointment clear in his voice.

"The cost for the power, is the damnation of your soul to Hell to be used and tormented as the Dark Prince sees fit." He told her in a matter of fact manner with a little wave that made her realize how many times he'd gone over this before. "Until then, we are one and the same. Wherever you go, I go. I protect and do as you ask. Until the deal is fulfilled, of course."

She looked at the circle he showed her instead of looking at him. "How do I get out of this?"

He chuckled. "Either you die, in which case, I get tormented for an awfully long time or an act of god. He doesn't do much, so good luck with that one." he gave a small smirk, knowing that it was highly unlikely to happen.

She started to hyperventilate. "No. No. No. No." She recited on repeat before adding, "oh, fuck." Amidst the beginning of her oncoming panic attack, she looked at her clock, which, at least, distracted her from the feelings she'd been having for a moment, "we've gotta get out of here. What does a person do in this situation? Just embrace it and become a Dark Lady or what? Does that make the Hell thing worse? No, don't tell me. No, tell me. Argh!"

Zangrunath rolled his eyes, and let out a little sigh. "Some do embrace it. I've seen people become reckless when they do so. It ends badly when that happens." He sighed, shaking his head as he mentioned that. "Most already have a goal in mind when they summon me, so that makes it easier. As for Hell, some would much prefer to commit every sin and go down there a Lord versus committing one and being just a sinner. At the end of the day, it is your call. I am just a tool to be used at your disposal."

"This is too much." She stood up quickly, making her head spin. "Come on. I'll drive. Don't need to. It's barely a walk, but it's not like Mom will be using the minivan."

"I already know how to drive." He told her with a little chuckle. "The internet is rather remarkable." He smirked, remembering all the videos he'd watched last night.

She looked at him with a cautious look. "Whatever. You can drive. Let's really make this fever dream kick into full gear."

"Alright." He shrugged, following behind her, and out the door. He took the keys from her, got into the car, and started it, waiting for her to get ready as he adjusted the seats and mirrors for the short drive.

She grabbed her backpack, and tossed it into the back seat. She sat down and uselessly buckled up in the passenger seat. She closed her eyes. "Need directions or did you look that up, too?"

"Already taken care of." He smiled, backing the van out of the driveway, and driving them in the direction of her school. "Had to make sure I would blend in, so I did some research. We will need to stop by the front office to drop off the registration forms and whatnot, but that shouldn't be too troublesome." He explained, sounding bored of the whole thing.

"Look. I don't want to go either, but I'm not gonna have a truancy officer from the great State of Oklahoma going after my Mom because of it." She sighed, stressing the drawl and twang to her accent just a little bit for a moment. They passed a few other kids walking to school. "Besides, only a couple more months to go, and I'm free."

He gave her a curious look. "Free? Are you already under a different contract? If so, that would be fun to- negotiate." He grinned mischievously.

She waved a hand. "Just a human social contract. School goes until after we turn eighteen for most of us. I graduate in May."

He deflated a good bit after hearing that. "And, here I thought, it would be something interesting."

"Sorry to burst your bubble." She responded as her stomach rumbled. "Of course, I was so distracted by all this," she waved to all of him. "I forgot to eat."

He shook his head at her. "Humans. Always so frail and weak." He sighed, glancing at her as the car pulled to a stop at the corner just before the school parking lot. "Do you need to turn around to get something?"

She shook her head. "No time or money for that. I'll hit a vending machine later."

"Fine, but make sure you eat. It would look bad if my quarry were to die of starvation." He gave her an odd look, not knowing what a vending machine was before shrugging as he pulled into the parking lot across the street of the large, fenced off area that was the school. It wasn't a big school, but there were multiple prefabricated buildings.

"Humans are plenty sturdy. I can go days without food. It's just uncomfortable. I won't starve myself out of the contract. Besides, I'm sure you'll force feed me before that happens." She grumbled, grabbing her bag, and getting ready to walk to class. "Wait. Do I have to go with you?"

"At least, near the office." He told her as he parked the van, and got out. "Can't go very far from you."

She sighed. "Fine. Alright. Let's go." After she hopped out of the vehicle, she muttered to herself. "So much for ever having a boyfriend."

"Why is that?" He asked, hearing her words. "It hasn't stopped other casters before."

"Most guys tend to stay away from girls who have other guys hanging around them all the time." She told him. "Kinda puts off the wrong vibe."

He blinked at her a few times before he spoke. "I can still disappear, if need be." He told her plainly. "I don't care who you sleep with. It does not matter to me." He shrugged.

"First of all, don't say anything like that to me again." She warned him. "If I want to talk about that with you, I'll bring it up. Second, I don't even know why I'm worried about it. It's never going to happen anyway. I'm just the girl whose Dad died. That's all they know me for anymore."

"Did I touch a nerve there?" He shook his head, taking a step away from her, and continuing to follow her. He looked around as he did so. The curious eyes of students of all ages were turning their way, and he added with a growl, "forget about them. They are just cattle at the end of the day. Not worth more than the space they take up."

She growled back in somewhat intimidating fashion. "Some of these cattle, as you so aptly call them, are my friends. Thank you very much." She looked around, seeing some other teenagers milling about, walking towards their classes while the much younger students were led by teachers or playing in the playground sand nearby. She stopped at the door to the office, and pointed. "Go, and you're going to need to have the same schedule as me. So, your elective class is Home Ec."

Zangrunath looked around and saw just how much Ellyria stuck out here. The other kids all looked relatively the same. Blonde or brunette. Tall. Unextraordinary. But, his master looked different from the other ones of her age. She was shorter with black hair, and dressed differently. He shook his head, moved along to the next thing, and chose to think nothing of it. It wasn't his place to ask, nor did he really care. "I will be out in a minute."

He promised, waving her off, and entering the office with the sound of a heavy door closing behind him.

"Sure hope so." She snarked back, leaning against the wall as the first bell rang. She looked up to see other students passing by through the gates of the school. She pulled her coat closer against her as she looked at the dusting of snow on the ground. Adrenaline had kicked in during the ritual last night. She hadn't even noticed the cold.

She nodded and waved at a few kids who greeted her, but, for the most part, she was ignored, especially by the cheerleaders. One of them was Heather, and the slim blonde cheerleader turned up her nose at the sight of Ellyria on her way into the building. Although she was annoyed by the snubbing, she preferred it that way. Being ignored was a good thing for people like her, and ever since- She redirected that thought, and shook her head to clear away the memories. A few minutes passed, and the door opened with Principal Jones stepping out of the office with her demon in tow.

"Well, Mr. Grunath, it's nice to have you as part of our family." The older gentleman with greying hairs on the side of his head smiled, looking at Ellyria waiting beside the door. "Ah, Miss Grant, glad to see you are bringing our two families closer together." He greeted, placing a hand on both of their shoulders. Mr. Jones smiled, leading the way to their first class. "Well, let's get you to class, shall we?"

"That's how you pronounce your name? Zane Grew-nath?" Ellyria looked over to the fiend in disguise, muttering to Zangrunath under her breath. "Families closer? What?"

"Zang-ru-nath." He corrected her, as they walked. "Zane is the name I gave him to sound more human. I told him we were distant cousins on your father's side." He explained quietly. "The man was gullible enough to believe it." He explained, shaking his head.

"Wonderful." She sighed, looking at the appealing form he took one more time before focusing on the task at hand. She already knew where they were going, but she couldn't be caught looking at her cousin. "Zangrunath." She tested the name on her lips again. "Algebra is first." She added for his benefit.

He shrugged. "It won't bother me at all." He told her as they approached the class. "Math is relatively simple."

As they got to the class, the principal opened the door, and led them in. He briefly talked to the teacher before he left. The teacher, Mrs. Dorsett, looked at the two of them before she got the attention of the class. "Alright, class. We have a new student joining us today. His name is Zane Grunath. He is Ellyria's cousin, so let's treat him well, alright?" She smiled, getting a few claps, and letting Ellyria show them to their seats.

Ellyria blushed at the newfound attention, but sat down, and handed 'Zane' a spare notebook and pencil. "Sorry. I only have one calculator."

He took the paper and pencil before he began to do the calculations on the paper without issue. "It is nothing too difficult." He bragged, placing the pencil down, and staring out the window several minutes later when he was done. "Child's play."

"Well, fine, but I find math difficult. Okay?" She sighed as she tried to follow along with the teacher, doing the same calculations with a calculator that he'd blown through in minutes. "Please, be quiet."

"Alright." He shrugged, sitting back in his chair, and relaxing a bit as he idly watched around the classroom. He saw a few eyes dart his way from some of the other girls, and scoffed.

Ellyria could feel the eyes on her and Zangrunath, and she tried to ignore them as much as possible. After doing two or three problems and still feeling the eyes on them, she looked up to glare at the other girls, especially Heather. When they flinched away, she looked back down. "You look too good." She whispered to him.

"Too good?" He whispered back, almost sounding offended. "This is being modest." He grinned, gesturing to himself. "Had I actually tried, they would be unable to speak." He sighed, looking them over with a serious look. "All they care about is looks, they aren't worth it." He scoffed.

She scoffed. "There are better things."

Zangrunath turned to look at her. "And, what is it you think is better?" He asked her seriously.

She glanced at him as she finished the last question with five minutes to spare after finally catching on to the hang of the new material. "Well, you told me about it earlier, didn't you? Power."

He gave her a smirk. "Indeed. It all just depends on the power."

She pulled the chain from around her neck to show him a lightly pulsing quartz crystal attached to it. "My preferred method."

He shrugged. "That is one type." He told her. "There are many. My personal favorite is unbridled destruction. The truest form of power." He grinned with a small fire in his eyes.

She tried not to laugh at him. "Pathetic."

He let out a small growl, and looked at her directly "What?"

"Power." She took the stone back, and held it to her lips, whispering to it lightly.

Seconds afterwards, the teacher walked up to them, and smiled. "Since you're still new and learning the school, why don't you and your cousin leave a few minutes early?"

Ellyria smirked, eyeing Zangrunath as they quickly packed up, ignoring the stares of Heather as she gave a couple of glances their way while they grabbed their things. When they left the room, she finished the sentence. "Control. That's the power I prefer."

He smiled, and leaned against the wall. "Manipulation and coercion." He hummed, letting some air out. He was impressed. "I wasn't expecting that from you." He gave her a small smirk.

She looked at him for a minute before starting to walk to their next destination. "You never asked."

"I just wasn't expecting the demonstration." He commented, starting to follow her towards the next class.

They made it about halfway to their history class before the bell rang. "If we're going to be with each other for a while, then, you should get used to my magic. I use it to make life easier."

"Don't worry. I intend to, and, as I've said before, it is my job to make your life easier." He told her seriously as students began to walk to their next classes. "You shouldn't need to worry as much."

She grabbed her crystal again, and cast another spell, which had the other students starting to avoid them by a wide margin. "Sorry, but you're the majority of my worries at the moment. No offense."

"Give it time, and you will forget I am even here." He shrugged. "This is just part of the process." He explained, having been through this many times before. He eyed the few students who glanced their way. "Even if it is annoying." He sighed.

"Tell me about it. Just five more months, and, then, we never have to see this place again." She assured him as they made it to their next room. "Hey, Mr. Harrison."

"Ah. Ms. Grant, I see the rumor is true then." He smiled, looking at her, and, then, to Zangrunath. "This must be your cousin. Hello." He greeted, outstretching his hand for the young man.

"Hello, sir." Zangrunath replied, shaking the man's hand with a small sigh. He hated keeping up this ruse.

"Uh, yeah. We had some family move back into town, so here we are." She smiled. "We can sit anywhere, right?"

"Of course." He nodded, gesturing to the classroom. "And, don't worry, the principal already explained it to me, everything is already taken care of." He smiled back.

She found a seat at the back of the room, and looked to her new shadow. "Alright. What did you even say? Don't answer that." She shook her head. "I don't have any other notebooks for you. Sorry."

He chuckled at her. "I simply spoke the truth, and asked him to let the teachers know in advance." He smirked. "Like I said, he is very gullible." He chuckled a bit more before looking at the board. "Oh, I am not worried about history. I helped write it." He smirked a toothy grin at her.

"Are you worried about any of my classes? I have Home economics fourth period." She murmured.

"How do you think some of the best chefs got their skills? Let me tell you this, it wasn't sheer luck." He whispered to her.

"Really, now?" She asked. "So, like, selling your soul is actually a thing?"

"Of course, it is." He nodded. "It is one of the easier ways to get a soul. One gift or special ability, for the cost of their soul? Done." He explained with a wave. "Sure. Why not?"

She thought that over for a minute. "Can you see which people have done that?"

"Of course." He replied quickly. "It's like looking at an empty glass. It might be a fancy glass, but empty nonetheless."

Ellyria frowned, thinking about that. "So, instead of looking like me," she gestured to all five foot three and one hundred ten pounds of her. "I look, darker? Like something's missing?"

Zangrunath shook his head. "Not yet. Our deal has yet to be fulfilled." He told her with a sigh. "Selling your soul is easy; you instantly get the power you want. This ritual is different. There are two halves to it. I need to make sure you get what you want, and you need to make sure I am doing everything to help you get it. It is a two-way street. Only when both parts are fulfilled does your soul get taken." He explained for her.

She thought it over. "So, once I get what I want, you go away, and my soul is damned? Is that basically it?"

"Yup." He nodded idly, flipping and spinning a pencil in his fingers. "It still has to be worth the price of your soul, which given the ritual, needs to be fairly good. Thus, killing hundreds, usually."

"I don't know what I want." She whispered as the bell rang again, and other kids started to take their seats. "Hell, I haven't even gotten acceptance letters to college or anything. How will I know that whatever I ask for adds up?"

"Hell, if I know." He told her with a shrug. "I have seen people do it for a plethora of reasons. Murder, revenge, money, leadership. Even had one guy who wanted to experience everything life had to offer." He explained listing off several different things. "In the end, you will feel it in your soul what you want your goal to be, and it is my job to help you get that." He sighed, idly sketching a map of the Balkans.

Mr. Harrison started class, but she was too distracted by the conversation to care. "I just want things to be easy for a while." She sighed.

He sighed. "Then, I guess this will be a long one." He stretched a bit, and looked at her paper. "So long as it doesn't take a century I don't mind."

"It's actually gonna be interesting to see what you agree with, with what he's teaching."

"I bet the details will not be nearly as vivid as what I know, and it will be very general in comparison to what actually happened." He sighed briefly looking at a textbook. "Well, at least, Caesar got what he wanted."

She looked at him so quickly her neck popped. "Caesar?"

"Yes, that Caesar." He nodded. "Et tu brute?" He spoke in perfect Latin. "He asked for his name to go down in history and to never be forgotten. Now, you are learning about him." He smirked.

"Vini, vidi, vici." She hummed, looking up at the ceiling as she accurately pronounced the Latin 'v's with the 'w' sound.

"Not bad." He smirked. "Et ego quæ numquam oblivione delebitur." He quoted simply, and fluently, without skipping a beat.

She eyed him. "I only dabble, but I heard oblivion?"

"And I shall never be forgotten." He repeated in English. "Forgotten has many different definitions, including 'to be destroyed'."

"You're going to have to teach me Latin." She told him. "It's used in witchcraft, but I've really only been learning it case by case since it's a dead language and nobody speaks it."

"Well, that's what happens when empires burn." He shrugged before nodding at her. "That will be no problem. It is easy enough, and it is the basis for 'most' languages."

She let out a derisive laugh. "Caucasian languages."

"Yup." He nodded. "After that, it is just reverse researching."

Ellyria looked back up front only to be hit in the head by a piece of paper. It fell on the table in front of her, and she carefully started to unfurl it. When she did, she glared at Heather's blonde hair and pink, well, everything. Nobody was looking, so she burnt the paper with a little snap. "I hate this place." She muttered to herself.

"Do you want me to burn this place to the ground? I can use her as kindling." He lowly growled, looking at the waste of air that existed in the same room as him.

"No." She shook her head. "She's already peaked. I'll just watch her crash and burn once she leaves this place."

Zangrunath gave Ellyria a look, and, then, looked back to the girl in question. "Say the word, and I can expedite the process."

She shook her head again. "I'm already about this long game, so I don't know why you're trying to rush me now."

"She attacked you." He told her simply. "I let my guard down, and you got hit." He complained, still eyeing the girl with murderous eyes.

Ellyria rolled her eyes, and waved a hand so she could properly speak to the demon without others noticing. "Did you feel pain?" She didn't notice the girl behind her doing a quick double take.

"No." He told her simply. "It still happened."

"Look, she's a bitch, but she doesn't deserve to die for that. I'm perfectly content to watch and wait as her perfect little world burns around her in a couple of years." She told him seriously.

He looked at her, and sighed. "People have died for less." He grumbled, looking back at the blonde, and smirking. "No dying, right?" He asked seriously.

She shook her head. "No killing. No accidents. If you have to get back at her, have her get detention or something. I don't care."

A smile crossed his face, and he quickly looked around the room before vanishing. A moment later, he reappeared. "Done." He smirked, looking at Ellyria. "I can see why you were playing the waiting game. It was too easy."

"You're right. I don't have enemies for that reason." She looked back to the teacher, ready to watch the show. "I'd much rather watch their mistakes ruin them while I sit back and watch."

Zangrunath nodded, and, a few minutes later, the girl raised a hand to use the bathroom. Mr. Harrison let her go, but, when she stood up, her purse fell off the desk. Its contents toppled over onto the floor, sliding to the feet of their teacher was a lighter and a pack of cigarettes. "Heather!" Mr. Harrison yelled at her. She'd had the sense to turn beet red in embarrassment, now. "Principal's Office. Now!" He ordered, pointing to the door. She nodded, and made her way to the office, her face looking humiliated as she left.

"How was that?" Zangrunath asked Ellyria with a grin.

"That, I like." She smirked. "This is the beginning of a beautiful friendship."

He thought that over for a long moment. "I think I could get used to this." He smirked.

"Good. If we're stuck together, then, we're doing this my way, and, I'm not a big fan of blood." She winced.

"Then, they shall be manipulated as you see fit." He told her honestly. "I have to listen to you, after all."

"Only ninety some school days to go." She told him seriously as she sat back. "I'm dispelling the masking spell, now."

"So be it." He replied before he added in her head. "This will suffice for now."

She glanced over at him, and responded in her head. "Is this two-way?"

"We can talk like this, yes." He replied in kind.

She smirked before turning her attention to the lesson. Her eyes glanced at the time. Where had the hour gone? They only had five minutes left. "I've got English next." She told him mentally.

He chuckled back in her head. "Oh, I love language." He smiled, leaning back, and looking at her. "How you word a deal can literally destroy a person's life."

"Let me guess, contracts." She asked.

"Oh, yes." He smirked. "Where a comma can literally mean the difference between life and death."

"I read about a family whose deceased parents forgot to use the Oxford comma in order to split the inheritance equally three ways. They went to court, and the oldest, whose name was at the front of the list, won. Effectively, splitting the inheritance fifty, twenty-five, twenty-five." She commented.

"Exactly." He nodded. "It is so much fun!" He responded mentally. A wide smile appearing on his face.

She thought about it. "It's kind of fascinating, but it seems like a lot of work."

"It is," he agreed, "but the payoff can be wonderful. As that family would know all too well." He chuckled. "Needless to say, your class will be a cakewalk."

She thought about his words for a while, even getting up and packing her things when the bell rang. "I think I'd like something like that."

"Money?" He asked her curiously. "Or, the ability to use words as weapons?"

She tapped the crystal around her neck. "My words are already weapons if I want them to be, but you're right. I like the idea of that kind of power."

"That can be done." He smiled. "You are going to have a lot of homework." He chuckled at her as they walked.

"A lot more school." She deflated even more. "And, a lot of debt."

He shook his head. "Don't worry about trivial things like that. I will make sure it is taken care of." He told her, going over plans in his head.

She nodded as they started walking to the class. She didn't use the spell that kept others away this time, so, of course, the captain of the football team ran straight into her. She blushed. "Sorry, Corbin."

"No worries, Elly." Corbin smiled, winking at her. His short, brown hair was spiked up at the front a little bit with gel, and his muscular build was apparent, blocking the hallway from her view. He wore a well-worn letterman's jacket that smelled lightly of cologne. The scent reminded her of oranges.

Zangrunath watched from a few feet back, not doing anything, but keeping a careful eye on Corbin.

Ellyria stepped around the boy who was much taller than her, and, even, a little taller than Zangrunath's disguised form. She brushed off his letterman's jacket. "Uh, have a good day." She sighed as she started to walk away. "Every stinking time." She murmured.

"Running into him?" Zangrunath asked her curiously as he looked back at the athlete who was walking away.

"We used to be friends. Our conversations now are basically that." She shrugged.

"If you want to spend time with him, that can be arranged." He offered her.

She shrugged. "It doesn't matter. Had my shot. Screwed it up. It's not happening."

He looked at her, and, then, back to the young man. "You do know he likes you, right?" He asked her simply, sounding a bit confused.

"I know." She responded. "We were literally," She gestured, her fingers almost touching. "This far from being an item when Dad died. I got the phone call right before our lips touched."

Zangrunath groaned, and rolled his eyes. "And?" He asked her seriously. "You can still have that." He gestured to the boy. "Go get him."

She shook her head. "I accidentally used my powers during the call. Used a spell to wipe his memory. Hasn't been the same since."

He smacked his face so hard there was a resounding smack that could be heard before pulling his hand down. "Teenagers, I swear." He sighed. "It is always the same with you."

"Ouch!" She complained, feeling the smack.

He let out a sigh as he followed her again. "You wiped his memory. Okay. Good. Now, you have a clean slate. He still likes you. You can start over." He explained to her.

She looked at him as they stopped outside of English class. "I want to be better before that happens."

His shoulders sunk, and he sighed. "Fine. Whatever you want to do." He grumbled. "All work and no play for you. Got it." He muttered under his breath, shaking his head a bit.

"Have you seen my house?" She rounded on him, feeling defensive. "I take care of it. I do the chores. I buy the groceries, and make meals. I pay the bills. Obviously, since my mother's out of commission. I don't have time for that. I barely have time for you, and don't get me started on the casting. I have a grimoire to study."

He took a step back at her sudden onslaught of words. He listened to her carefully as she spoke, clearly this was a huge problem for her that needed to be fixed. He looked at her intently, and, when she was finished, he simply nodded. "Sorry." He quietly apologized. "I will make it easier on you. I promise." He told her honestly. "You have my word."

"I'm sorry." She sighed, walking into the room. "I'm not normal." She looked him over. "Obviously."

"Clearly." He nodded back. "It is alright. Everyone needs to vent."

"What I need is a day off, a ley line, and a clearing to blow up right and proper." She only half-suggested, knowing it wasn't going to happen. She had too many responsibilities to get to let loose like that.

He thought it over and gave a nod. "Alright, I will see what I can do." He promised, sitting down and starting to focus on something else entirely.

She raised an eyebrow, but, from his look, he wasn't all there. She turned her attention to class, but she wasn't really listening either. There was just too much going on to give Ms. Hoffmann's class the attention it deserved.

The class was almost over by the time Zangrunath began to look around the room. He took a breath, and shook his head before he looked to Ellyria. "You said that home economics is next. Correct?" He asked her suddenly.

"Yeah." She replied tiredly.

"And, what are you making in that class?" He asked back, looking at how tired she was.

"Not a clue. We're talking about yeast lately, so probably bread. But, the teacher didn't say."

"Do they allow for some variation?" He asked her with a raised eyebrow.

She shrugged. "To a point."

He nodded, and looked at the clock. "Then, be ready for some good food." He grinned at her.

"I expect good things, then." She smiled. "Home economics is my last class of the day, too."

He thought about that curiously. "Have school days shortened?"

"I overloaded my schedule in other years. I only need three credits this year, but the school requires four minimum. So, I took home economics." She shrugged.

"Good to know. It will look better on paper as well." He told her with a nod as the bell rang. "Let's get you some food." He smiled, gesturing for her to lead the way.

She showed him to a room, which was at the back of the lunchroom. "Ta da." She announced.

He looked around at the kitchen, and shrugged. "It will do." He replied as he made his way to the teacher. "What are we supposed to be making today?" He asked seriously.

Miss Nelson blinked a bit before she looked at the fiend in disguise. "Bread today." She told him simply.

"It should be more of a free day. It would encourage more diversity." He smirked, using a somewhat entrancing voice.

She nodded, in a bit of a daze, and looked over the class. "That is an excellent idea. Thank you, young man. I'd like to see what it is you can make since it is your first class with me."

He shrugged, and walked to the workstation next to Ellyria's, and began making food as the rest of the class filed in. When the bell rang, the teacher explained the assignment or lack thereof, and the group was dismissed to their work.

Ellyria wasn't feeling particularly creative, so she decided to just go through with making a simple loaf of bread. She separated the flour and dry ingredients and added warm water to the yeast. She didn't really have a plan, per se. Maybe just some sweet bread. Right now, she was more interested in what Zangrunath was doing. She almost couldn't take her eyes off him.

Zangrunath was hard at work, taking flour and eggs and kneading them together before taking the dough and stretching it out thin. He repeated the process several times before he cut it up. After a few moments, pasta was made. He started boiling some water, and got some tomatoes for a simple sauce. He chopped up the tomatoes, and put them into a pan with some tomato paste, adding a few herbs and spices for flavor. By the time the water was boiling, he had the sauce simmering. He put the pasta into the water, adding some salt, and, just a few short minutes later, he drained the pasta. Then, he quickly plated it all up. He took the finished plate, and placed it in front of Ellyria. "There. Enjoy." He told her with a small smile.

Ellyria's stomach growled loudly, and she blushed. Without any further hesitation, she took the plate, and started eating it. After a few bites, she paused. "Thank you." About halfway through her plate, she paused long enough to take her bread out of the oven to let it rest before returning to her meal. She saw the girls at the workstation beside them staring at her, and turned her head to look back. A sigh escaped her. Diane and Taylor were usually the closest she got to normal, but, from the looks of the stars in their eyes with Zane beside her, that looked less than promising at the moment.

"Do not mention it." He replied with a wave, going back, and cleaning up his area as he spoke to her. "You were hungry, and needed food. Clearly, you couldn't get a meal at the cafeteria, so I made you one." He explained.

"I could've waited, but I appreciate it." A minute later, the bell rang, and a smile took her face. "Let's get out of here."

He nodded. "Lead the way." He gestured, waiting for her to go. "You shouldn't have to go without food." He told her quietly.

"I honestly can't afford to go out, and we didn't have time to get snacks. It's fine." She shrugged.

He looked her over, and shook his head at her. "No, it isn't." He told her mentally. "You have the power to summon me. You shouldn't be living in squalor."

She glanced over at him with a pathetic expression that she simply couldn't cover up. "It's not squalor. Things are just- tight. I need Mom to go back to work. The life insurance isn't going to last forever."

"How long ago did your father pass away?" He asked her curiously, as they made their way to the parking lot.

"A little over a year." She responded. "He just didn't leave behind enough, unfortunately." She sighed, adding. "That, and my Mom's drug addiction has taken a big chunk of that."

"It seems to me like her problem is quickly becoming your problem the more you talk about it." He told her seriously as they approached the van.

She looked away from him. "I've been babysitting her for a year, so, yeah, it's my problem."

"Then, let me fix it." He offered seriously.

"I just- wish I was a good enough reason to be clean." She sighed, getting into the car.

He got into the car, and started the engine. He paused for a moment before he looked at her. "She will see the error of her ways." He told her quietly. "I just need you to say 'yes'."

"She won't die?" She asked seriously.

"She won't die." He repeated. "She will wake up. It might take a few days for her to feel normal, but she will be fixed." He told her honestly, not able to lie to her.

She looked out the window, leaning her head against the cool glass. Her eyes closed. "Why does this actually feel like a deal with the devil?"

"It isn't." He reassured her. "It is me doing my job to make your life easier."

She looked over at him. "I'm not selling her soul?"

"If she keeps it up, she will lose it before you ever have the chance to fix her." He told her honestly.

A few tears came from her eyes. "Yes. Do it."

He nodded, and backed the car out of the parking space, pulling out of the parking lot. "It will be done." He replied with a determined look in his eyes as they drove the short distance back to her house.

"Thank you." She whispered, wiping her face clean. "Sorry. Not very, 'witch with a demon contract' of me."

"Do not worry." His lips turned up into a small smile, giving her a quick glance. "People have cried for less."

"I guess so." She sighed. "Just get me home so that I can study that grimoire finally."

"Of course." He nodded at her, and he remained quiet as he drove her home.

She took a moment to settle down, and quickly thought of something in order to change the subject. "Do you get summoned less since the witchy thing isn't exactly a big thing anymore?"

"Yes," he sighed, "people are becoming less accustomed to the ways of magic, and, as such, summoning is occurring less often. To be fair, your weapons are becoming more like ours, so I think people are giving into their sins more often." He sighed again, and pulled into her driveway. "Either way, it is nice to see some people still using the old ways." He smiled at her. "Even if it is an accident."

"I'm sorry that I'm such a trash witch. By all rights, I shouldn't have been able to summon you. I guess, I just kind of- brute forced it." She grabbed her things, and started towards the door. "Oh, I forgot about the windows." She groaned.

He was about to reply to her previous statement, but saw the mess. He sighed and looked at her seriously. "I can fix it. I just need more space."

"What?" She asked.

"So far, I can only move about twenty feet away from you at most." He started explaining by looking at the gap between them. "I would need to be able to go around your entire house in order to fix it. It would just take time."

"It's fine. I can do it. It's just going to take more energy than I wanted to use." She told him seriously. "I already used a lot last night."

"That is fine. I expected as much, and you casting today didn't help." He told her simply. "This would just take some runes being engraved around the house, like a border for me to roam around in." He explained simply. "It should be in the book."

She opened the door, thinking about it as she walked in, finding her mother where they'd left her covered in her own sick. She looked away, and stepped down the hallway. "You draw the runes. I'll read the grimoire. I need to rest before I do much more right now."

He looked to her mother, and sighed. "I can't do that." He replied, hanging his head. "Only the caster can be the one to draw the runes. If I do that, bad things happen to me."

"Oh. Got it." She whispered as she closed the door to her bedroom. "I just need to recharge before I can do runes, then. I can probably draw from some of Dad's old stones."

"That is fine." He nodded. "Rest, for now. We can worry about it later."

She nodded, tossed her pack against the wall, and grabbed some items from a drawer. Incense, lighter, salt, and several rocks of different colors. Orange, purple, and green. She made a pattern on the ground before looking up. "Crud. Are salt circles a problem?"

"It isn't a problem." He told her, shaking his head, and sitting down outside of the circle. "Just do what you have to do."

She sat inside of the circle, and took off her shoes, tossing them outside of the circle. She lit the incense, and blew it out to let smolder. She held the rocks in her hands, and closed her eyes, starting to focus on regaining the energies she'd used the previous night.

As she sat and focused on getting her strength back, Zangrunath looked around the room. He wanted to get to know the young woman he was helping more. He knew she had issues at home, but he wanted to know about other pressing matters. He had a rough idea of what she had to put up with, but, after seeing the amount of bills on the dresser, he was starting to see just how bad it was. He glanced in the direction of Lynne in the living room through the closed bedroom door, and growled lowly. He disliked that woman. He was going to make sure that she realized what she had done wrong, and he was going to make sure she never went back to that lifestyle. He wanted to take a step out of the room but couldn't; he was bound to Ellyria. He sighed, and sat back down. The stronger she was, the stronger he would be. He could wait for now.

Ellyria could feel her father's magic still stored in the stones. She felt sadness as she started to draw it into her so she could selfishly use it, but he didn't need it anymore. After about an hour, the stones were drained, and she finally opened her eyes. When she looked up at Zangrunath, her eyes were rotating colors from blue to green to grey from her normal brown thanks to the influx of power. She took a breath. "I feel better."

He nodded at her. "Good." He stood up, and walked around some more. "Forgive me. I am not used to staying in one place for long."

"Sorry." She smiled sadly. "Let's get you a little more freedom. Shall we?"

"Don't be. I should be used to it by now." He replied, stepping to the side to let her lead the way. "By all means." He grinned at her.

Ellyria grabbed her father's book, and brought it out back with her. She opened the book, and found several of the pages on warding blank. Her stomach sank for a minute before she remembered something she'd seen her Dad do when he was first teaching her to cast. She moved her thumb to her lips before apologizing, "sorry," as she bit into the finger, and pressed her thumb to the page.

As the blood smeared over the magically bound pages, letters of red began to reveal themselves to her. She moved her finger over the page, but where she expected a trail of blood, there was nothing, just more letters and symbols. She pressed her finger for a few minutes, before Zangrunath gestured to her. "That should be enough." He assured her quietly. "Don't want to lose all that power you just got back."

She nodded. "It's just blood binding. The book does most of the work." She explained, though she stopped when he asked. "The runes shouldn't be too hard. Activating them-" She trailed off, making a face.

"It will be troublesome, yes." He nodded, finishing her thought. "Once you do it, though, you will have more space, and I can take care of the more menial things around here for you." He told her confidently.

She pulled a selenite wand, which looked more like a dagger, out of her pocket, and started to draw the runes around the property line, muttering incantations under her breath.

He silently followed her around from the back to the front yard, keeping an eye out for her in case of any odd passersby. He watched with some eagerness as she made the line of runes connect with itself. "Good job. Now, to activate it." He gave a sigh of relief, letting out a long breath as he did so.

She took a deep breath, and rubbed her hands together before pressing them against the first and last rune. She was grateful to still be barefoot now. She needed as much energy as she could get for this. She closed her eyes, and started to channel her energies into the runic border. She started to concentrate. This would take a while.

As the magic began to fill the runes, Zangrunath could feel his magically tethered distance from her begin to expand. He nodded with a smile at her. After this, she could rest well. She deserved it. While she slept, he would work, and do what he did best. He would make life easier for the one who summoned him. Until then, he would wait for her to finish. Then, his job could truly begin.

The young witch focused for several hours. She didn't notice when she'd done it or even that she was doing it, but she had tapped into the natural energies of the earth in order to boost her own stamina for a short amount of time. However, the magic was palpable for Zangrunath who had been around many witches before. There were stones on her person, but all were completely drained of energy before she'd even begun. After a while, Ellyria opened her eyes. The only way to tell time had passed was by the light of the sun. She looked west to see it setting, and felt lethargy hit her. "That was a lot."

"You did a good job." He smiled at her as he felt the last of the magic she used begin to fade from her. He walked up to her. "I can now move freely around your domain." He replied with a nod. "You go get some rest." He instructed, extending a hand, and helping her up off the ground. "I will clean up everything."

She nodded, standing up with his help, and heavy limbs. She took a breath, pretending to be stronger than she was as she dragged herself into the house, through the kitchen, and passed her mother on the couch. She got to her room after stumbling into a wall. She wobbled a bit across the carpeted floor before she fell onto her bed, and passed out.

Zangrunath followed her to her room out of habit, and, when she passed out on the bed, he gently tucked her in. He walked to her bedroom door, and quietly shut it behind him as he made his way to clean up the kitchen. He sighed at the mountains of dishes, assorted liquor bottles, and discarded food packaging, but, before he could begin cleaning, he was stopped when a noise came from the couch. He saw Lynne stumbling around. An evil smile took his face, and he quickly vanished into the shadows on the ground. He knew how to make his job easier.

As Ellyria's Mom staggered into the kitchen from her place on the couch, she grumbled incoherently, hearing a few noises. She shuffled in, and saw nothing. After glancing around one more time without actually seeing the room, she waved it off, and made her way to her bedroom. She wanted her fix. Her feet moved to the bedroom, and, somehow, the walk seemed to take longer than normal. Lynne looked down the hallway to her room, and saw that she had made no progress. She took a few more steps, and proceeded to go nowhere. There was a brief moment of clarity as something didn't feel right, but the drugs were outweighing the voice that was telling her to stop.

She started to move faster to try and get to the room, but, now, it seemed like the hallway was getting longer. She shook her head. She wasn't feeling good is all. She tried to keep moving, but the hallway was spinning around her. Her body was moving faster, nearly running, but her progress was still nonexistent. She fell to the ground, and started to shake. This was just a bad fix. She just needed a little help. "Elly! I need help!" She called out nervously, but her voice didn't reach her sleeping daughter. Tonight, it fell on deaf ears.

Lynne tried crawling now. Her eyes were growing wet as she attempted to move, but, still, she went nowhere. She called out again to Ellyria several times, each call getting more desperate, but, again, there was no response.

The hallway suddenly grew much closer as the woman was tossed into her bedroom. The lights were all off. She looked around nervously in the dark, unsure of where she was or how she got there. She crawled, trying to find her stash before she was pulled into the air by one of her legs. A terrified cry escaped her as she saw the form of a devil start to slowly take shape from the pressing shadows out of the ground. It held her carelessly by her ankle, as if she were just a plaything to it. She screamed, but a large hand stopped the scream from coming.

Zangrunath lifted her higher, her eyes meeting his, as his form towered over her. For a moment, he found it odd that the woman's features were so different from her daughter's up close, but the thought was fleeting. He grinned widely at her, magically revealing several rows of razor-sharp teeth. "You have a choice to make." He growled. His voice booming eerily in the room.

Her body was frozen in fear, but her lips moved, too afraid to remain silent. "W- wh- what?" She stammered. Her eyes were red and watery, and snot dripped from her nose.

"The drugs or your daughter." He threatened, giving her his ultimatum. He dropped her carelessly on the ground, not wanting to be any closer to the trash than necessary. "Or, the next time we meet, it will be the last time you see her smiling face." He grinned evilly, disappearing to Ellyria's room in a cloud of fire and smoke, and leaving Lynne to contemplate life and her decisions in the dark on the floor of her room.

Friday, January 10, 2020

Ellyria slept through the night and even her alarm. When her phone went off, she flicked a finger, and it turned off with a thought. She rolled over, and let rest take her again. When her eyes eventually opened, she looked at the clock on her nightstand, and panicked. "Oh, no." She bolted upright, and started to get dressed in a panic before she saw Zangrunath out of the corner of her eye. She paused, letting her shoulders slump. "You let me sleep in."

"You needed it." He replied honestly. "It was better than the night before."

"You're right." She sighed, sitting down. "I'll just call myself out sick."

"No need to." He smirked lightly. "I think your mother might have already taken care of that."

Ellyria's eyes went wide. "What?"

"Your mother already took care of that." He repeated slowly for her. "She heard the alarm go off, and decided to call the school, saying you needed a day off." He explained, sitting down in an orange bean bag chair, and relaxing.

Ellyria couldn't help as a few tears came. She looked up at him with grateful eyes, and whispered. "Thank you."

"It is fine." He smiled at her. "I simply gave her an ultimatum. You or the drugs." He shrugged. "She chose you."

A few more tears fell, and she swiped them away. "Mom." She murmured quietly.

He smiled a little more before he vanished from sight. There was a timid knock at the door and a voice called out. "Elly? Are you up? Can we talk?" Her mother asked with nervousness clear in her tone.

"Y- yeah. Give me a minute to get dressed." She called out, pulling on a pair of jeans and a band shirt. She met her Mom in the living room a couple of minutes later. "Hey."

"Uh, hey." Her Mom greeted with a tired looking smile. "I wanted to let you know that you can stay home today, if you want." She told Ellyria. "You've been working really hard lately, and I just wanted to- to let you get some rest." She whispered, starting to tear up. "I'm sorry for making you work so hard."

"Mom," Ellyria murmured as she pulled the older woman into a hug. Her mother's taller and heartier frame was a comfort even through the faint smell of alcohol and sickness, among other things. Still, but she looked so much better. She smiled despite herself. "T- thanks. You look good."

"Thank you." She murmured, wiping away a tear. She let out a small sigh, and took a small step back. "If you're hungry, I can make you some breakfast. If you want." She offered.

Ellyria shook her head. "It's okay. There's not much in there. Didn't have the chance to go grocery shopping." She sighed. "I think I'm actually going to take off and go get some fresh air, if you don't mind?"

She shook her head a little sadly, but put on a smile. "That's fine." She replied with a small sniff. "I need to do some cleaning around the place anyway." She gestured to the living room, and tried not to look upset. She turned, and took a few steps away before stopping. "I'm sorry, Elly. I never meant to do that. I just-" She started before getting cut off.

"Please, don't." Ellyria shook her head. "I just can't right now. I'm sorry."

Lynne took a deep shuddering breath, and nodded. "That's fine." She responded, shaking her head in disappointment with herself. "If you want to talk, I will be here." She offered in a motherly tone. With that, she went to the closet, grabbed a broom, and started to clean up.

Ellyria grabbed her purse, and the car keys. She was out of the front door in seconds, getting to the van. Zangrunath was already waiting in his disguise in the driver's seat. She handed him the keys. "Get me out of here."

"Of course." He nodded, starting the car, and leaving the house. He started to slowly drive around the neighborhood until she knew where she wanted to go.

Ellyria looked up at the roof of the car. "I want to break things."

"Large empty field?" He asked her simply.

"If you can find one with a ley line or energy vortex, even better." She nodded.

He smiled, and pulled out a piece of paper. "Already on it." He grinned. "We should be there in about thirty minutes." He turned the car onto Grand Avenue, and started making his way north to Highway 64D.

"Thanks." She mumbled.

"Like I said before. It is my job to make your life easier." He told her calmly.

"She just- I can't believe her. It was like nothing happened. I have piles of bills on my dresser, and she just offered to make breakfast like it wasn't a big deal." She growled.

"Those with an addiction will oftentimes try to go back to a state where they once found happiness before the drug abuse." He told her almost mechanically. "It is a coping mechanism."

She sighed. "I get it. I do, but that was hard." She took the anger she was feeling and pushed it into one of her crystals. She could feel it vibrating in her hand. She looked down at it. "You gonna bite me?" She asked it threateningly as if it might respond. She tapped the stone a couple times, letting out a little sigh as she tried to calm herself down. After a couple of minutes, she glanced out the window, watching the greenery pass by, and seeing a sign that read, 'Welcome to Arkansas'. "I can't even go to the game tonight since I got called out from school for who in the Hells knows what."

Zangrunath turned his head to look at her briefly as he drove. "Game?" He asked her curiously. "What game? Is it like a blood sport?"

Ellyria laughed at that. "Blood sports don't really exist anymore that I know of, at least. I'm sure basketball was a thing the last time you were around, right? Our high school has a home game tonight. It's, kind of, a big thing." She tried to explain, giving a little shrug. "Small town stuff."

He shrugged. "The last time I was around was to tip the sides of battle." He told her honestly. "I didn't care for any recreational sport. Let alone anything that involves throwing balls into baskets." He explained, shaking his head.

Ellyria sighed, and rolled her eyes a little bit. "I know. The ritual is meant to start and end wars. Blah, blah. I get it. I really messed up." She leaned her head on the window. "I kinda like watching them play sometimes. It gets pretty competitive, and it's- fun."

"Well, if you ever want to go, I can't stop you." He reminded her with a sigh. "I must make sure you are happy and pleased in every way." He commented idly. "You are my master, after all."

"Please, don't call me master." She looked at Zangrunath with a sour expression.

"As you wish." He glanced at her, and sighed again. He knew it would take time for this relationship to fully work, but this was a small start. "We will be there soon." He told her as the paved road became a long, narrow dirt road. "You can go blow the place up to your heart's content."

"It probably won't be nearly as impressive as the other witches you've seen in battle." She frowned. "Unless you've never seen what happens when we get access to the leys." She smirked. Her father had only ever taken her to a ley one time, and she'd barely gotten a feel for the magic there before they'd had to leave for some reason.

"I helped Merlin become the legend he is today." He smiled back. "I know what that is like. Don't worry about what I think. Just unleash Hell." He encouraged, pulling into a small, wooded clearing, and parking the van.

She shrugged, and opened the door, pulling her shoes and socks off. The feeling of the natural energy was strong all around them as she walked closer to the center of the field. Her eyes were closed, but she didn't need sight right now. Here, she could see without eyes, and didn't need minerals to aid her magic. The moment she connected with the ley line, a tremor shook the ground all around, and the wind kicked up. Her eyes opened, and they glowed blue as lightning struck down on her where she was standing. A barrier of the crackling energy surrounded the area, and an emotionally charged scream echoed in the air.

Zangrunath followed her, and could feel her power become palpable as she got closer. He was shocked when the display began to strike around him, and was floored by the barrier blocking entrance or exit of the clearing as well. He looked at the young girl, and was even more intrigued by her now than when he was summoned. She was stronger than she led herself to believe, much stronger. She was doing magic that only a handful of people in his long lifetime could do, and she was less than half their age.

Ellyria charged balls of lightning, and tossed them into the air, letting them explode into static when they were a good distance away. She cowled herself in the energy, and created a pillar of light and sound as thunder rolled. Out of the corner of her eye, she saw

Zangrunath, and smiled at his look. She made a rope of lightning, and pulled him to her as if the feat were nothing. "Not so weak now, huh?" She muttered in a voice that wasn't hers at the moment.

Zangrunath looked her over carefully, and nodded. "No, not at all." He replied quietly, pondering what would have happened if she had completed the ritual here instead of at her house. He turned to look away from her, and shuddered at the thought. What was she, and who was her father? He needed to know; this wasn't normal.

After about an hour, several trees nearby were scorched and felled. The pressing emotional weight in Ellyria's chest lifted. She took a deep breath, feeling calm, now. She closed off her connection to the ley. Her eyes turned back to their normal brown color, and her wild hair settled on her back. She ran her fingers through the black locks to calm them down and straighten them again. She sighed in content. "I feel much better."

Zangrunath nodded. "Good." He quietly assured her, looking at her, and letting out a sigh of relief. "Glad that I could be of assistance."

"Sorry you had to see that. I normally keep my cool better." She smiled. "Let's go eat. Shoot." A frown stole her features. "Let's go to my house to eat."

"It's fine. It was very- informative." He nodded back at her before holding up some cash. "This should be enough for you." He smirked, handing her the money.

"Where'd this come from?" She asked nervously. "Wait. Do you eat?"

"Your mother." He replied simply. "And, no. I do not eat, sleep, or drink unless I have to. Or, if I have nothing better to do, of course."

"Alright." She sighed as she took some of her uncharged stones, and started siphoning what she'd taken from the ley into them. "Bring me somewhere with waffles or something."

He nodded, and waited for her to walk to the car. "I will try." He told her honestly. "I did not prepare for that, but I will attempt to find you a place."

She started to walk towards the car, "There's a Waffle house in Fort Smith, nearby. I'll help you find it."

"Then, that is where we shall go." He nodded, watching her walk for a moment before he got into the car himself. "It was impressive to see that." He told her honestly. "Very few people can do that."

She looked at him, but shook her head. "Yeah. Right." She scoffed. "Thanks for the ego boost, though."

"I'm serious." He replied impassively. "I think I know how you managed to summon me with an imperfect seal. You are a trueborn witch."

"I'm not entirely sure what that last bit means." She told him. "Aren't we all the same?"

"No." He countered, shaking his head. "Most witches use ley lines and stones as tools to cast and summon things. That is true. A trueborn witch needs none of that. They can access the ley lines from anywhere." He explained, starting the car, and letting it idle for a moment. "Because, what I saw just now, was far beyond what a 'normal' witch could do at a ley line." He continued to elaborate.

"That's not normal?" She asked quietly.

"If that was normal, magic would still be practiced today." His tone matter of fact. "You combined several manipulations and principles at once. Things that would take decades to learn, were natural for you. Had you performed the summoning ritual here," he started, pointing to the ley line. "You could have summoned any demon you wanted. Maybe, even, The Dark Prince himself." He finished, shuddering at the incredulous thought.

Ellyria shuddered. "What does it matter, though? I still know nothing about any of this. What I do know is stolen knowledge from the internet and what I've been able to figure out on my own. I've got one grimoire that my Dad never even really told me existed, and I'll basically have to bleed myself dry to make all of the pages visible to me thanks to the blood binding."

Zangrunath paused, and stood still for a long moment. "You could rule the world, set fire to the sun, blow up the oceans." He explained in disbelief. "If that was from snippets, you being able to fully control all of your powers- You wouldn't need me to do that. You would be set on your own." He shivered, letting out a sigh.

"I don't want any of that." She shook her head.

"Good." He gave a stalwart nod, letting out a sigh of relief. "That would be Armageddon, if you did." He shuttered, putting the car into drive, and driving back towards town.

"I don't know what I'm doing, but I have this vision. I walk into the room. I'm successful. When I speak, people listen, and, if they don't, well, they always listen." She told him.

"That sounds like a goal." He smiled at her. "One that we can work with."

She nodded, moving her fist out for him to bump. "I'm in."

"In that case," he replied, moving to bump her fist. "We have a deal."

"Keep a nice window seat ready for me in Hell." She joked.

He laughed, and looked at her seriously. "I'm sure you will get the penthouse."

"I'm basically a demon in training. Aren't I?" She asked seriously.

"Not quite." He smiled at her. "Think unpaid intern." He joked.

"How do you like your coffee, sir?" She laughed as her stomach rumbled. "Ooh, coffee."

"Let's get you fed," he smirked, continuing to drive.

ARTICLE II

Thursday, February 13, 2020

The evening was cool, and Ellyria was lounging in the backyard reading her father's grimoire. It had been several weeks, and she still hadn't finished it. Some of the languages inside were old and unfamiliar. She knew that Zane could read them to her if she wanted, but it felt like cheating. So, she was making good use of the translation app on her phone, finding it fascinating to learn that she was looking at Greek and Latin. Of course, the arcane symbols and writings needed no explanation, but, the notes, those were just as important, if not more so. Each new entry seemed to only bring more questions than answers, especially the entry she was currently reading.

She was starting to shiver, and pulled her coat more tightly around her. She needed to go inside soon but being surrounded by nature was calming. Her phone buzzed in her pocket. She pulled it out, and glanced at it, opening her messaging app.

'Hey, girls, you going to the basketball game tomorrow night?' Diane asked the group chat.

'Of course! Wouldn't miss it.' Taylor chimed in moments later.

Ellyria paused for a long moment, staring at her phone, and thinking about her response. She wanted to go, but part of her knew that Zangrunath was annoyed by the crowd that would be at the event. Even she was aggravated by her friends hitting on him. A wave of frustration washed over her about the whole ordeal. She missed her friends. Taking a breath, she texted back, 'Not sure yet. Need to see how tomorrow goes.' She locked her phone, and pocketed it again, standing up to go back inside.

Maybe, she'd be feeling up to it tomorrow. Right now, she wasn't so hot on the idea.

She opened the back door, which led into the kitchen, and a waft of savory smell greeted her nostrils. The scent of well-seasoned meats and veggies present in the air. "That smells amazing." She commented as she closed the door behind her, leaving it unlocked. This town was so small that crime was basically non-existent. What was the point in locking the backdoor? She maneuvered past Zangrunath who was busy cooking, and sat down on a stool at the kitchen bar.

"You're welcome." The demon idly commented as he cooked, pulling a sizzling pan out of the oven. He started to plate things up for her.

She closed her eyes, and tried to relax for a moment as she waited. "Hey, Zane?" She asked.

"Yes?" He replied, placing the meal in front of her, and starting to clean up the kitchen.

"Are you able to read my grimoire?" She asked. "There's this-entry."

"It depends on what it is, but I can read most of it." He explained, appearing next to her in a puff of brimstone a moment later. "What is it?"

She looked up at him from her food. "I was worried the blood magic kept you from reading it, but, right here," she opened her book, and pointed at the section she was curious about. "I want a second set of eyes on this passage."

He leaned down, and looked over the page. He perused it quickly, turning to look at her. "It just explains how certain witches and warlocks are able to pass on traits to their young, and this section here," he replied, pointing to the words. "Explains how the reveal of magic is tied to puberty, more or less." Zangrunath shrugged.

"It mentions adulthood." She frowned at his summarization.

"By the time you turn eighteen, you should have complete control over your powers." He sighed, looking at her seriously. "It won't be a problem for you. You are already strong enough as it is." He stated, straightening up, and looking at the unlocked door. He walked over, and turned the lock on the deadbolt, hearing the click of the tumbler inside. Just because this place was so boring didn't mean he should be complacent about her safety. "You should only get stronger by the time your day comes around."

She shook her head a bit. "That, I'm not worried about. What I'm trying to get at is, you've been around enough people like me. That's not normal. It's normal to have control of your magic, but little of it when you're younger. This book just said that I have a lot of magic, but little control."

Zangrunath gave her a nod. "That is true. However, each person is different. You are a trueborn, so there are bound to be differences. The only real concern for you is blowing yourself up with pure magic, but that happens at much younger ages. You don't need to worry about that. Otherwise, it would've already happened. You have plenty of time to learn control. Even the other casters I met over the years still practiced control into their later years."

"It just seems odd based on what I've learned about other witches." She shrugged, going back to eating the delicious food.

He started to package up some leftovers, and put it into the fridge for later. "They didn't have the same potential as you, so, in my opinion, the rules are different for you."

"I guess this means, my Dad was just as strong as I am, if not more so." She sighed. "I wish I knew more."

"If he was, he certainly was trying to hide it, then." He told her simply. "He would have been able to get any job he wanted. Why he worked on cars, I will never know." He sighed, still needing to fix Ellyria's car but waiting on parts.

"That wasn't his job." She told him seriously. "Just a hobby or a cover up. I don't know."

"Then, what was his job?" He asked her curiously. "Because I am curious about him."

She stood up, pushing her mostly clean plate away, and stretching a bit. "He worked over at the power plant."

"Okay, but where did he work?" He asked, not caring too much about that.

"Just outside of town over in Arkansas. Baldor Electric, but they were bought out by some other guys recently. Can't remember the name." She sighed.

Zangrunath let out a sigh, and looked at her. "I will find out later." He muttered. "This man must have had a hell of a skeleton to stay- here." He commented, looking around the small home, and thinking about where they were. If he flew up ten feet, he could probably see the entire town.

"Hey! I live here." Ellyria complained, looking away from him towards the calendar that was hanging up on the wall nearby. It looked like her Mom was off work tomorrow night. Maybe, she should just go to the school game. Her eyes lingered on the date for a moment, and she groaned. "Ugh."

"Not by choice." He rebutted. "What's wrong?" He asked her, hearing the distress in her tone.

"Tomorrow is Valentine's Day. Expect pink glitter and flowers everywhere." She huffed.

Zangrunath let out a long drawn out sigh that bordered on a grumble. "I will manage."

"At least, we get a three-day weekend afterwards." Ellyria looked over at him. "That's nice."

He shrugged. "I guess. It doesn't matter to me. I am always doing something."

She nodded. "You do keep busy. I just do homework and magic."

"It is my job to make life easier for you." He repeated for the hundredth time. "No matter what it is."

"What about you, though? You don't get to enjoy your time here?" She asked.

"It depends on the job." He started. "If it is ending one's enemies, I find it very enjoyable." He smiled a big toothy grin at her. "But, all of this- stuff." He started, giving a sweeping wave around the kitchen. "I find it to be tiresome and pointless."

She frowned. "I'm sorry. Maybe, I can bring you some excitement?"

He shook his head at her. "It is not for me to be fulfilled; it is you who has to be fulfilled. My needs don't matter. You are what matters." He pointed to her.

She nodded. "Thank you. Doesn't make me feel any better about it." After a minute, she started towards her room. "Can I try something?"

"If that is what you want to do. Yes." He replied, following her to her room.

"I wouldn't do this unless it was a last resort, but the whole 'we are one' connection got me thinking-" She trailed off, sitting on the floor and offering her hands palm up.

"And, what is that?" He asked, sitting down across from her.

She had a little worried look about her. "I think we could share energy to make the other stronger."

He thought about that for a moment, and gently placed his hands on hers. "I don't know if that is possible, but I am curious to see if it can be done."

"Me too." She smirked, starting to concentrate on sharing her magic with Zangrunath. "Let me know if you feel yourself getting any stronger."

He closed his eyes and focused on feeling his power. He waited for a few minutes before he began to feel a small spike. "I think it is working." He informed her. He was shocked that she had come up with this; this was a first.

She peeked open an eye, and closed it again. "I want to see how much I can share."

"Just don't drain all of your magic." He told her seriously. "If you start to feel weak, draw it back into you."

"Oh, I won't hurt myself for this." She promised, continuing to concentrate on sharing her power.

"Good." He nodded as he felt his power steadily rising. He shifted slightly as the magic kept going. He wasn't used to this odd sensation.

Ellyria kept pushing magic towards Zangrunath for what felt like a long time before she physically started to feel weaker. She was getting used to purposefully tapping the leys from anywhere, but it was something she still needed practice doing. She still found herself using stones quite a bit, and noticed that the ones on her were no longer pulsing with the power she had stored in them. Maybe, she hadn't been tapping the leys after all. A frustrated sigh escaped her. She let the flow stop, and opened her eyes. She was surprised to see that his black eyes were now almost pulsing with darkness. A ring of blazing fire forming around his irises. "There." She whispered, pulling her hands away.

"Well, it certainly worked." He told her, feeling the spike in his power that was much stronger than what he was expecting.

"I doubt we'll ever need to do this, but I thought it was interesting." She smiled not startled in the least by his increased strength. It was her magic doing that. One of the first things that her father had taught her was not to be afraid of her magic, and, of all her lessons, that one had stuck with her.

"It will be a dark day if that happens." He told her seriously. He wanted to try the inverse out, but he decided against it, offering his hands again. "Okay, you can take it back, now."

She nodded, and smiled at him. "I guessed as much. I doubt people in Hell really lend power. And, you can keep that until you use it. I was trying to tap the leys, but it's just magic I had stored in the stones on me."

He looked at her oddly before he moved back slightly. "Good to know." He nodded, squeezing his hands into fists, and recoiling them from her. "And, no. In Hell, it is either yes or no. Not, I will gladly pay you Tuesday for a power increase today."

She looked at the clock, and sighed, taking the used gems out of her overloaded pockets. She placed them on the windowsill. "I forgot to cleanse these during the full moon on Sunday. Needed to use up the magic anyway." She commented conversationally while still internally frustrated by her failing.

He nodded, standing up, and watching her for a moment. He let out a small sigh. "Thank you." He grunted, almost forcing the word out of him. "I will go make my rounds." He disappeared in a puff of smoke before her eyes.

"Scaring Hell spawn by being nice since twenty-twenty." Ellyria sighed, laying down to get some rest.

As Ellyria slept, Zangrunath began to stalk around the perimeter of the house, using his shadowy form. He didn't want to worry her, but, the last few nights, there had been a few individuals who had been watching the house, either by walking past it or by parking the car in front of the house across the way. They hadn't gotten close. He almost hoped they did. He had been craving a kill since he started this job, and the idea was exciting him to no end. But, for the time being, he would sit and wait. If they came into the yard, he would strike with sweet, swift action.

Friday, February 14, 2020

Ellyria and Zangrunath survived two grueling periods. Math was annoying since Mrs. Dorsett received a delivery of flowers mid lesson, but Mr. Harrison's class was just laughable. Several students received balloons as gifts, and they were looking at maps. She didn't remember seeing a whole map. As they were walking to English, Ellyria realized she'd forgotten to cast the non-detection spell seconds before a body ran into her, and she toppled backwards only to be caught by a strong pair of arms. Her mind took a moment to process the situation. Zangrunath had caught her, but Corbin had bumped her. "We can't keep meeting like this." She joked.

Zane sighed, and stood her upright. "Ha-ha." He rolled his eyes, taking a step back, and begrudgingly picking up the bag of chocolate he had acquired over the day. "Stupid Valentine's Day." He grumbled.

Corbin smiled. "Yeah, it's nuts around here today. Sorry about that, Elly. I wasn't paying attention."

"It's fine." She blushed, looking down. "Uh, happy Valentine's."

"Yeah. Happy Valentine's." He waved back before striding off.

Ellyria sighed, continuing forward. "Of course, we run into each other. Literally. Today."

"You should go talk to him." Zangrunath sighed as another girl ran up to him and handed him another package of chocolate before running off. He growled at the gift, and threw it into the bag. "I. Hate. This. Day."

"I told you on day one. You're too attractive." She glowered as she watched Corbin walk away. She shook her head, and turned back towards their next class. "Come on. We'll be late."

"Lead the way." He sighed. "You should still talk to him." He suggested as they walked.

She looked over at him. "I don't want to have to erase his memories again. It's better this way."

"You shouldn't have to erase them." He reasoned. "He should be glad to have someone like yourself." He advised out loud before continuing in her mind. "Let alone a powerful witch."

"It's supposed to be a secret. Even my Mom didn't know about my Dad. She still doesn't even know about me." She responded mentally as they entered their class and the bell rang.

"Secret or not, you should still try to have more fun." He replied into her head. "I know you have had more free time. You should, at least, spend it doing something fun." He shrugged.

She sat down, and started getting her papers together, handing an essay forward for the teacher. "I'm fun." She argued. "I like to read, and I meditate every night."

"So, you sit or sit and do nothing." He countered as he passed his own papers forward. "I meant like dancing, drinking, or even sex." He sighed mentally. "Something actually fun."

"I don't dance. Not bad at it, but not a fan of dancing in public. Drinking, been there, done that. Sex," she shrugged.

"Ugh." He groaned. "You are one of those types." He groaned, making a face.

She made a face back. "Those types?" She asked in his head.

"The ones who save themselves. Trust me. There is no point. It doesn't matter if you save yourself or not if you still end up in the same place either way." He replied in her head.

She sighed in his head now. "The whole dead Dad thing blew every datable vibe I ever had last year, so it kinda never came up. Now, it's weird because you're going to be around."

"And?" He asked rhetorically. "Anything you do is nothing compared to what I have experienced already. It doesn't matter."

"It's hard to wrap my head around a demon being around when I lose my virginity. Okay?" She quipped.

"Then, don't think about it." He told her in response. "Just indulge yourself for once."

She tried to turn her attention away from him to listen to the teacher, but her mind was doing gymnastics. Should she? Or should she just leave it be? She tapped her toes, and, soon, her pencil followed, tapping a rhythm into the desk.

"Could you stop that?" Zangrunath asked her mentally. "It is starting to get annoying."

She stopped moving, and huffed. "Sorry." She half-heartedly apologized as her mind reeled. Was she boring? Should she try to have more fun? She had a brand on her back that was sending her to Hell one day. Was it all that bad for her to enjoy herself? She thought it over for a while, but she couldn't bring herself to do anything about it. Wouldn't she corrupt him? That wasn't good in her books. Maybe the devil's, but not hers. She sighed. "I can't send him to Hell just by spending time with me, right?"

He shook his head. "No. Anyone can go to Hell. It's their choices that make them go there." He told her. "If that was true, I would have sent thousands more down there already." He chuckled lightly.

She glanced from him, to the teacher before raising her hand. "May I please use the restroom?" She lied.

Ms. Hoffmann nodded, and went back to the lesson as Zangrunath quickly disappeared when no one was looking.

Ellyria rushed down the hall with her hall pass, stopping outside of a class she wasn't part of. She looked in the window, and saw him, pacing for a second as she tried to pep herself up. "I can do this. I can do this."

There was a small chuckle in her head as Zangrunath spoke to her. "If you can stare me down without flinching, you can talk to him." He reassured her.

"In front of a whole class, though." She sighed before opening the door and looking to the teacher. "Hi, uh, I'm sorry, Ms. Duncan. I just have something to deliver really quick."

Ms. Duncan gave Ellyria an odd look, looking at the clock, and sighing. "Go ahead."

Ellyria looked to Corbin, striding up to him as confidently as possible before planting a kiss right on his lips. "Sorry it's a year late." She mumbled to him. "Happy Valentine's."

Corbin kissed her back. He was speechless, for a moment, as the class went nuts, letting out whistles and catcalls. "Uh, that's fine." He replied, a smile pulling at his lips. "Thanks. Happy Valentine's day to you, too."

She smiled back, looking to the teacher with a huge blush. "Detention, right?" She asked, starting to leave without being told.

The teacher was stunned, but gave a dumbfounded nod. "Yes, after school."

Ellyria smirked as she rushed back to her classroom with Zangrunath in tow. "There. Happy?" She asked mentally.

"Very much so." He smiled in her head. "The show was delightful."

"Thanks." She blushed, looking away from him in embarrassment.

"I like this version of you. So much more in charge." He told her honestly. "That is the type of person I like to see with these deals. Those who know what they want."

She nodded. "I'll try to be better. I'd hate to bore you."

"It won't matter if you bore me or not, so long as you get what you want." He explained to her. "That is all I care about."

"I want him to meet me in detention." She winked over at him, feeling bold.

"Don't worry. I have a feeling that will happen." He smirked back.

She raised an eyebrow, looking around the room. "Really? I see no grand distractions in here."

He chuckled. "I am almost offended that you doubt me sometimes." He gave a mocking sigh. "I have my ways."

"I believe it." She smiled as the bell rang. "Where did that hour go?"

"Out the door with that kiss." He chuckled.

She grabbed her things, and Zangrunath's bag of chocolate. "You're not going to eat any of this diabetes inducing goodness, are you?"

"Help yourself." He offered with a gesture. "I was just going to burn the lot when we arrived back at the house."

"I'll pick out the stuff I like before you perform the ritual." She chuckled.

"Don't worry. It will be quick." He told her simply, glad the day was almost over.

She looked around at all the pink and merriment, and didn't feel so bad anymore. "Never thought I'd be one of those saccharine bastards."

He shrugged at that. "I hear it is better to be alone with someone than to be alone by yourself." He quoted idly. "I don't care either way."

She hummed a little. "Alone with someone. I kinda like the sounds of that." She thought for a moment. "I'm alone with you a lot, though."

"I am bound to you. There isn't a choice here." He looked at her seriously. "That is your choice." He pointed at the person coming their way. "Enjoy." He grinned, moving out of the way for Corbin to meet her.

"Uh, hi." She smiled, forgetting her earlier courage. "Sorry if I made your teacher angry."

He shook his head at her. "Don't be." He dismissed the apology, smiling at her. "The look on her face was priceless. Thank you for that."

She blushed as she looked up at him. "You're welcome. It was totally worth my first detention."

He chuckled at her words. "Then, I will see you there. She gave me detention too." He made a flippant waving gesture.

"Wait, don't you have a game tonight, though?" She asked him anxiously.

"Yeah, but don't worry about it. It's a home game. I won't be late." He smiled, kissing her cheek. "See you later," he murmured, walking off towards his next class.

She smiled, and walked into home economics, seeing Miss Nelson waiting patiently for the class to find their places. "Alright. I don't know what I was worried about."

"Doubt is a fear people need to kill like a dying animal." Zangrunath told her mentally. "It makes people weak." They got to their workstation, and took seats on the stools there, waiting for instructions. As they did, at the station just to their left, Diane and Taylor were looking between each other, and giggling merrily. A moment later, each of them broke away from their places, walking over with huge blushes, and giving Zane heart shaped pink and red boxes of assorted chocolates.

Ellyria grumbled, watching the ladies walk back to their places. It was starting to get annoying, being ignored by her friends in favor of the demon. Part of her didn't want to be home with her Mom tonight, but, suddenly, a bigger part of her didn't want to go to the basketball game either. She sighed in frustration, "we'll have to come back later for detention. Might not have thought that one through."

Zangrunath tossed the packages of candy into his ever-growing bag with a poorly hidden growl, and waved her off. "Ooh, you have to spend more time out of the house with the guy you like. However will you survive?" He teased.

"Well, there'll be more fun things later." She laughed, missing all the teacher's instructions. "What are we making?"

"Boiled eggs." He told her as he grabbed a pot and eggs. "As easy as it gets."

She nodded. "Which way? Soft, medium, or hard?"

"All of the above." He explained, filling the pot with water, and putting it on the stove. "It isn't hard."

She nodded. "I know it's not, but I normally just do it with magic out of laziness."

"Laziness is the reason why deals were made in the first place." He chuckled. "People didn't want to do the work."

She put her pot on the stove and turned up the heat. "Hell, I know how to do it, and I don't want to."

"Exactly." He snapped his fingers. "Why deals still keep getting made."

She added a little more heat to the pan with magic. "Well, now, I feel super lazy. I have, like, the big deal."

"Arguably the biggest." He agreed with a nod, thinking it over. "Not my first choice doing all of this, but it is what it is."

"So, do you, like, choose to be here? Or, is it by force?" She asked. "I get we're bound, but what about before I did the summoning?"

Once the summoning was complete, I was forced to remain by your side." He explained to her. "Before that, it was just mindless work. Torturing, hard labor, maiming. Paperwork, mostly." He shrugged, as if what he just described was commonplace before starting to take his eggs out of the water.

She looked at her eggs, which she hadn't put in the water and the time. "Shoot." She muttered, popping them into the pot, and focusing on one of them to heat it more.

He sighed, and moved her to the side. "Relax." He directed her as he picked up two more eggs. "That is your hard boiled." He explained, pointing to the egg into the pot, and then the two in his hand. "Medium, and soft." He told her as he placed them into the water a few minutes apart. "Then, you just take them out at the same time."

"Thanks." She sighed, following his instructions, and pulling the eggs out when the time came. "Let's get the Hell out of here."

He waved a hand for her to move. "I follow you."

She nodded, and started to walk. "Let's go burn you some Valentine's."

"Yes, please." He enthused, his eyes smoldering like fiery embers. "Destruction is fun."

"You need to spend time in the clearing?" She asked him seriously.

"You want to be able to go back to that clearing?" He asked her back just as seriously.

She nodded. "Yes."

"Then, no. I don't need to go there." He told her honestly.

"You really need to kill things. Don't you?" She sighed as she tossed her things in the van.

"Needs and wants don't matter to me." He told her with a grumble. "I have to follow you and your orders."

She frowned. "I'm sorry."

He stopped, and looked at her seriously. "Why are you sorry for a demon?" He asked her seriously. "There is no need for any of that. I am already damned."

She shrugged. "All you do is work for me, and I don't even have anything that really brings you joy going on. I'm sorry."

"Don't be. I am a tool to be used as you see fit. You say; I do." He reminded her while getting into the van. "That is what happened when you summoned me. You made it this way."

She nodded, and looked out the window. She didn't have the energy to argue at the moment. "Let's just get home to do homework. I want my weekend free."

"Alright." He agreed, starting the car, and making their way to her house.

She got out of the car, and slumped into the couch where she started to spread out her work. She could hear her Mom getting ready for work, but she ignored her for now. She just needed to get this done.

Lynne was going to say something, but saw how hard Ellyria was working. She let out a small sigh, finished getting ready, and made her way to the door. She stopped there, and turned back around. "I'm off to work. I'll see you later, Elly." She called before she left the house.

"Night!" Ellyria waved as she finished up the last of her calculus. She looked at her English work and history, and groaned, grabbing herself some tea and a snack. She dragged herself back to the table, and looked at the ceiling. "When did homework become soul sucking?" She asked herself.

There was a moment of silence before a voice rang out. "If it was soul sucking, I would have changed professions." Zangrunath joked.

She looked around for him, and laid down on the couch when she didn't see him. "I have the house to myself, right?"

"Of course." His voice rang out again.

She muttered. "Let's break all my stigmas today. Stay outside, please." She moved a hand down the front of her body nervously, and did her best to just concentrate on feeling good for a little while. She relaxed as she temporarily forgot about schoolwork, demons, and family problems.

"As you wish." He replied, continuing his patrol of the yard. Invisible as a shadow, he stalked the runic border she'd created. He could tell she was nervous, that much was evident. He honestly didn't care. To him, she was in charge. What she said, goes. So, he would make sure she could, at least, relax. He chuckled a bit to himself. It had taken her longer than he expected, but she got there. He continued to stay outside as she had ordered, and would wait until she gave the okay to come back inside.

Ellyria cleaned up, and went back to her homework. Once the grammar homework from English class was done, she mumbled, "You can come back in, if you want. Thanks."

"Like I said before, you say, I do." He told her mentally with a chuckle as he continued his vigil.

She finished the rest of her homework, and looked at the time. "We should probably start walking back, since Mom has the van."

He appeared next to her, and nodded. "I should have the parts to fix the car soon. Just waiting on parts to get here from China." He sighed. "Stupid shipping."

"It's alright. They're dying of the plague right now. We can forgive them." She laughed, pulling on her shoes.

"Still it's no exception for poor protocols." He complained, making a face. "There was, at least, some customer service during the black plague. How times have changed." He explained, going to get the door for her.

Ellyria sighed as she locked the front door, and rolled her eyes when he couldn't see. She was growing used to Zangrunath's tangents regarding times long since passed. It was kind of fascinating to listen to. Fascinating and annoying. She redirected her thoughts. When he got like this, she had learned over the past month that it was best not to engage. She should just move on to the next topic. "I'm just glad to finally get my hands on my old birthday gift." She responded with a shrug.

"Birthday gift?" He asked her curiously. "What do you mean?"

"My Dad bought the Grand Prix for my seventeenth birthday, but never got the chance to finish fixing it." She told him as they walked.

He nodded in understanding. "Well, if all goes well, it should be up and running in a week." He told her as they walked.

She smiled. "Thanks. I'm glad that it won't just sit and collect dust anymore."

"It will run smoothly when I am done." He told her honestly. "Like a Hellish war machine."

"Sometimes, I wonder if what you say is true or crafted to make me wonder if it's true." She laughed.

"I literally cannot lie to you." He deadpanned. "Do as you like with that information."

She nodded. "I guess, I didn't realize that."

"It is one of the many reasons why people make deals with us. We don't need to lie for people to ruin their own lives. Most times, they do that themselves." He chuckled darkly.

"Been there. Done that. Didn't even get a t-shirt." She laughed.

He laughed at that. "I wish we sold t-shirts. So much more profit."

"In true devilish fashion, monetizing the afterlife." She shook her head. "I would wear it. 'I sold my soul, and all I got was this lousy t-shirt'."

"You can get them on the internet." He told her. "They go for, like, thirty bucks."

"I'll pass, actually. I'm getting way more than a t-shirt. Fast, friendly service. Solid five out of seven." She giggled.

"Who uses that sort of scale?" He asked her seriously. "Why not go to either five or ten? Why seven!?" He asked, sounding annoyed.

She doubled over in laughter. "I would literally have to explain ten years of the internet to make you understand that."

He shook his head at her. "I will never understand the youth, other than basic urges." He sighed, and waited for her to continue walking.

She handed him her cell phone, and clicked on a folder. "I can't take this into detention with me, but here are my meme apps. You can look. They're pretty funny."

He swiped at the screen for a few moments. "Why is this frog on a unicycle?" He asked her, confused. "That makes no sense."

"Why isn't he?" She shrugged. "It's funny."

He shook his head again, and swiped a few more times before he laughed. "Hah! That boy died."

She facepalmed. "You're gonna love confession bear, confession tiger, and probably insanity wolf."

He raised an eyebrow, and typed in the latter. He smirked several times, and laughed at a few others. "These are funny." He told her honestly.

"I will want my phone back eventually, but you can get to those sites on my laptop too." She told him as they arrived at the school.

He nodded at her. "Just say the word, and I will give it back." He promised with a small frown before he smirked at the screen again, looking more at the phone than anything around them or where they were going for a moment.

The pair navigated around groups of students in the mad rush to get into the car line for pick up or, for the high schoolers, to their own cars in the parking lot. Both were too distracted by all the hustle and bustle about them to notice a pair of eyes fixed on Ellyria. A frustrated growl was drowned out by the happy sounds of students, and, as they drew closer, the owner of that voice and those eyes, whirled around in a blur of pink and yellow movement.

They had their own business to attend to for the time being. There was a basketball game tonight.

They stopped at the doors to the detention room. Of course, she would somehow manage to turn a demon on to memes. "Enjoy." She smirked as she walked into the sparsely decorated classroom, and took a seat. She didn't see Corbin yet, but school did just let out. At a desk nearby, a boy whistled at her. She blushed. Word really did get around fast in this place.

A few minutes went by, and, eventually, Corbin arrived. He looked around, finding Ellyria, and sitting down next to her. "Hey." He greeted with a smile.

"Hey." She smiled back, winking once. "Thanks for getting detention for me."

"Don't thank me, that was all you." He chuckled at her. "Thanks, this is nice. Sitting next to a pretty lady on Valentine's Day."

She blushed, reaching out to take his hand. "It was overdue. Kept talking myself out of it."

He smiled back at her, squeezing her hand lightly. "I'm glad you did it. I was starting to think that I had missed out on you."

Ellyria opened her mouth to speak just before the teacher in charge of detention dropped a heavy book on his desk. They both jumped, and started to pay attention, responding when their names were called. "Alright. Time starts now. Sit down. Shut up." The teacher announced, looking at the clock, and sitting down.

Ellyria rolled her eyes. This guy was new this year, and she was glad she didn't have him as a teacher. She looked back at Corbin, and winked again. She took a breath, and cast the non-detection spell for what felt like the billionth time. She looked at him with a smirk. "Detention with me is a lot more like having a chat." She told him.

Corbin jumped as she spoke, looking at the teacher, and, then, to her. "I'm not sure how you're doing that, but I like it." He smirked back at her. "This is way better than just sitting down, doing nothing."

She smiled. "As long as you can keep a secret, you might get to see more."

He looked her over curiously. "I can keep a secret." A mischievous grin replacing his earlier smirk.

She eyed him back, but waggled a finger, snapping them instead. A flame suddenly appeared above her thumb like there was an invisible lighter there. "What do you think?"

"Holy shit." He gaped, looking at the flame in awe. He stared at it for several long moments before he replied to her. "That is awesome. How did you do that?" He asked her, suddenly even more curious about this girl.

"Magic." Her tone serious, but her expression playful. "Can't give away all my secrets."

He looked into her eyes for a long moment. He nodded, and kissed her. "That's okay with me." He told her as he pulled away. "I don't mind waiting to find out more about you."

She shifted in her seat a little. "I think I'd like to show you more one day." She snuffed out the fire, and sat back. "But, for now, tell me. What's changed for our mighty varsity quarterback since I had one unbelievably bad day?"

He watched the flame die out before he made a face at her words. "I'm sorry about your Dad. I wanted to say something sooner, but it seemed like you needed space." He told her honestly before he doubled back to answer her question. "In all honesty, not much. Another year older, and a whole lot more training." He let out a small sigh.

"It's the same for me, honestly." She sighed. "Except more metaphysical than physical."

"Well, at least, we were kept busy right?" He joked. "It's better to do something rather than nothing."

"It's better to do nothing with someone than alone." She countered, using Zane's words from earlier.

He smiled at her. "It is. Just wish I had someone to spend that time with over the last year." He told her simply. "You were the first person that I was even interested in to make an attempt at me. Let alone, such an impressive display." He chuckled.

"I'm sorry." She offered an apologetic smile. "I was so wrapped up in my own head, I didn't consider your feelings." She paused, looking up at him sadly. "I'm not going to lie. I really messed up back then."

He shook his head at her. "No, you didn't." He told her honestly. "Your Dad died. You had every right to do that. Don't apologize, I'm the one who should be sorry for not coming forward sooner." He smiled sadly at her. "Then, I wouldn't have to fight off the advances of Heather the mythical bitch."

She laughed, and waved a hand. "She'll get what's coming to her. That being said," she reached a hand up to his forehead. "May I?"

He leaned his head down so she could get to it a bit easier. "By all means."

"It was only about two minutes, but it wasn't right. I'm sorry." She told him as she touched his temple, and focused on giving him the memory of their near kiss and her fiery magical breakdown during the subsequent phone call. "I thought I was keeping the secret. I was just being selfish."

He shook his head a bit as the magic washed over him. He blinked a few times, and a tear ran down his face. He pulled her in for a tight hug. "I'm sorry you thought you needed to hide that from me." He soothed, patting her back. "I didn't know I was there for so much of that." He told her. When he pulled away, he looked into her eyes. "And, I'm sorry you missed out on this." He apologized, kissing her on the lips, and lingering there for several seconds.

She leaned into the kiss, and, when she pulled away, she wiped away a little tear. "You're taking this way better than I expected."

She blushed. "Thank you. Can we actually go out on that date sometime?"

"Of course, we can." He smiled at her. "Just name a time and place. As for all of this." He gestured to the room. "This town is weird, and you are, too. It makes way more sense if magic is involved, and, honestly, I like that."

"Well, I'll be damned. Zane was right." She laughed, squeezing his hand. "Don't tell him I said that."

"I won't." Corbin laughed in return, squeezing her hand in kind. "But, I have to ask. What was he right about?"

"That you wouldn't mind the magic bit. To just show you." She told him.

"No, not at all. I find it rather attractive, honestly. That type of power." He smiled at her.

She smirked. "Oh, you haven't seen anything."

"Well, I can't wait to see more." He smirked back.

She looked up at the clock. "Five minutes to go." She hummed, sliding out of her chair, and boldly sitting in his lap. "I think that I can distract you." She murmured before kissing him soundly as her fingers tangled in his short hair.

"Pretty sure you're doing a good enough job at it, now." He smiled into the kiss. His hands held her against him, and they rubbed lightly up and down her back.

She sighed into him, letting her tongue flick out to taste him. She felt the stone on her neck grow warm, and she looked down at it. She pulled it away from herself, and handed it to him. "The magicky juju says that this is yours, now."

He looked down at the stone, and gently took it from her. He inspected it for a moment, smiling back at her. "Thank you. It looks just like you. Beautiful." He flirted, stealing another kiss.

She kissed him, nudging his shoulder playfully. "You already have me. You don't have to charm me."

He smiled at her. "I can't help it, if it's true." He told her as he looked into her eyes.

She suddenly realized that she was still in his lap. She blushed. "How's this weekend for you?"

He watched as she blushed prettily, and chuckled. "That works for me."

"Tomorrow. Breakfast. The Denny's on Rogers." She told him. "I don't need a big Valentine's to do, even though I kind of instigated it."

He gave her a peck on the lips. "That's fine by me. I would much rather it be a simple date than a big fancy one." He told her in earnest. "And, I like that you did this. You made it way easier to figure out my plans."

She smiled, moving to her seat, and dropping the spell just in time for the teacher to look at the clock. "Alright, get out of here." He announced.

Ellyria stood, and winked at Corbin. "Best detention ever."

"I would take a hundred detentions, if you were with me." He winked back.

She stood up. "I guess that I'll see you tomorrow."

He smiled at her. "I will see you then." He promised, standing up as well. "See you at the gate tomorrow?"

"Tomorrow's Saturday." She cocked her head to the side as they walked out of the classroom, feeling the winter cold as they stepped outside, despite her coat.

He nodded, and gave a nervous chuckle as he followed beside her. "Well, I would pick you up, but I don't know where you live."

She held out her hand. "Phone, please."

Zangrunath arrived a moment later, and placed the phone in her hand before disappearing out of sight.

She raised an eyebrow, but looked at her phone anyway. She had meant to take Corbin's phone. "Did your number change?"

He shook his head. "No, it's still the same one."

She quickly texted him her address. "Mine isn't hard to find." She pointed at the street nearby. "Go down Grace. I'm right on fifth. It's the one with bricks, and a fenced off yard."

He smiled at her. "I will pick you around three, then?"

"For breakfast?" She laughed.

"Well, it is Denny's. They serve breakfast all the time." He laughed in return.

"As long as you don't mind me actually eating beforehand. I get hangry." She smiled.

"That works for me." He smiled back, squeezing her hand lightly. "I'll see you then."

She leaned in, and gave him a soft kiss. "Have a good night."

"You, too." He smiled, returning the kiss in kind.

She let go of Corbin's hand, and started heading down the street towards her house. She could feel Zangrunath there, but didn't say anything right away. She half expected gloating.

Zangrunath waited until they were well out of sight of the school, and double checked that no one was around before he appeared next to her. "What can I say except you're welcome?" He singsonged.

She sighed in defeat. "You're right. I should've done that ages ago."

"And, now, you finally have that date you have been wanting." He gestured back towards the school. "If you just follow through, good things happen." He smiled at her.

"Thanks." She hummed. "And, now, I need to figure out what the right amount of magic to show him without scaring him away is."

"Just don't bring him to the ley lines, yet. He might actually have a heart attack if you did that." He surmised before shrugging. "You will figure it out, either way."

She shook her head. "I could easily kill him at the ley lines. Not happening."

"You could, if you wanted to, but I don't think you will." He told her seriously. "Just ease him into it, and you will be fine." He suggested, looking ahead for a moment before he turned back to her. "Might not want to mention me for a while either."

"No offense, but Hell no." She told him. "Not happening."

"None taken." He replied, waving it off. "I don't blame you. Most people get weirded out when they find out that the person they are seeing has an actual demon bound to them."

She laughed. "I can't imagine why." She sighed. "Next goal, get laid. Maybe, wait a couple dates."

"With how you jumped on him back there, I give it one." He chuckled. "It won't be long."

"Uh, how do I explain the massive brand on my back?" She asked seriously.

"You do know only you can see that right?" He asked her seriously.

"What?!" She shrieked. "I thought it was visible. I've been avoiding my comfortable shirts."

"It is only visible to those who are familiar with magic enough to know what it means or someone who has made a deal." He explained seriously. "To everyone else, it's just a bare back."

She sighed. "I should've known. I'm an idiot."

"No, you just haven't read everything yet." He told her in response. "You need to finish that book."

"Yeah, I'm pretty sure that your ritual isn't in there. It seems like the darker stuff is in the older sections. I think there's more on those weird, blank pages that I can't see for some reason." She groaned.

"Well, an Annihilation ritual isn't normally used to contact dead relatives. It is used to start and end wars." He explained. "I am an agent of chaos and destruction, and can do a lot more than what I am currently doing." He reminded her with a small sigh.

She smirked. "Hey, agent of chaos?"

He sighed, and looked at her. "What is it?"

"Let's cross the bridge, and go get nachos." She teased.

He let out another, longer sigh. "Fine, lead the way."

"I'll buy." She offered as she walked him to Taco Bell. Her mind still worried about other things. Her date, and the mysteries of her father to name a few, but, for now, she'd be content with picking on her demon.

ARTICLE III

Thursday, March 5, 2020

Ellyria was laying on top of Corbin on her couch. The lights were out, but they could see fine by the light of a few crystals. He rubbed her butt again, and she giggled, moving his hand back up, and kissing him long and languidly. "We're supposed to be doing homework, mister."

He chuckled as she said that, giving her another kiss. "Says the one who started this in the first place." He teased, eyeing her playfully. "I was content with actually doing homework."

She eyed him back for a minute. "I. Gave you. A kiss." She enunciated as she poked his chest. "And, you dragged me here."

"A kiss that involved tongue." He smiled at her.

"What can I say? You are wonderfully distracting." She sighed, looking up into his eyes. "Sorry I'm a tease."

"No, you're not. Don't lie to me." He chuckled softly before he gave her a loving kiss that quickly became more. He took his time and was careful not to do anything she didn't like, and made sure that her first time was loving and memorable. When they were finished, he turned to her. "That was magical." He kissed her cheek.

"Thank you, Corbin. That was amazing." She smiled, getting up, and pulling on her clothes. She saw him grab his shirt, and she stopped him for a minute, touching the stone on his necklace. She closed her eyes, putting some more magic into it. "Sorry. I don't know why the magic wants me to do this. My grimoire doesn't say anything about it."

"You are welcome." He smiled down at her, and gave her a kiss on the forehead. "I trust your judgement. I know you wouldn't hurt me." He reassured her, placing a hand on her cheek.

"Not on purpose." She told him honestly. "I just wish I knew more about it. That used to be my primary stone."

"You will be fine." He told her, placing his head on hers to look her in the eyes. "You are an amazing person, and I hope that I am there to see you shine when the time comes." He smiled, stealing another kiss from her.

She smiled up at him, enjoying the closeness. "You will be." She held him for a minute before asking. "What college are you going to, and does it have a law school?"

"I was thinking about Ohio State. It's out of town, but it will get me pretty far thanks to football." He smiled. "What about you? Where are you planning on going?"

"I put in for a bunch of places, actually. Some closer, but most of them further away. East and west coast places. I think my Mom might've sabotaged it, though. I haven't gotten a letter, good or bad, from any of them. Not even Harvard." She sighed, walking towards the door. "Thought I'd, at least, get a rejection from them, by now."

He held her for a moment. "No matter where you go, you will do great." He smiled at her. "You are way smarter than me, so I know you will be fine." He complimented as he started to follow her.

"I've got a lot more school to go, actually." She looked at him. "I want to study contract law. You?"

"Well, I would like to go into the NFL, but, in case that doesn't work out, I was thinking about cars. A job at a raceway." He told her with a smile. "I like fast cars." He admitted.

She laughed. "I know. I've been in yours. Shelby's beautiful."

"She's a good girl. I still have a few things to tweak, but she is almost done." He chuckled.

"We can take her to the party next week, right?" She asked. "My Grand Prix's still out of commission. All of the parts are in China, of course."

"I'm sorry." He apologized in earnest. "Yeah, we can take her. That's not a problem."

She smiled. "Thanks. Oh, hey. My birthday's the Tuesday after spring break. Do you want to do something? Sneak in at midnight? Dinner?" She winked.

He smiled back, and gave her a wink in kind. "How about all of the above?" He offered.

She smirked. "I just want to do something other than school that day. All of the above works."

"We will." He smiled, giving her a small kiss. "I will make sure it is a birthday to remember." He promised, grabbing his few remaining items.

She looked at the time. "Aw, I guess there's always tomorrow."

He glanced at her, and nodded. "Hopefully, we can actually get homework done tomorrow." He chuckled.

"Yeah," she frowned. "There's always tomorrow." She pulled him in for a kiss. "I'll see you then."

He smiled as he kissed her back. "See you then." He gave her a hug, and waved as he left.

Ellyria fell onto the couch, and threw her arm over her eyes. She rested for a minute. "Hey, Z?" She asked, getting a bit experimental with his name.

Zangrunath appeared next to her, not caring what she called him. "Yes?" He smirked.

"Do you know why my stone wants to be around Corbin? Why I have to charge it?" She asked. "I really need to figure out how to reveal those blank pages."

He thought it over for a moment. "There is probably a connection between you two that the crystals are picking up on." He told her with an odd face. "To be honest with you, I have no clue. I just get summoned and kill people normally. This is all new for me." He told her truthfully.

She nodded. "We need to look up that other ritual. Articulation, you called it."

"Yes." He sighed. "It allows you to talk to anyone you want in the afterlife." He told her. "It would have saved so much trouble if it had been done in the first place."

She sighed. "Look, you're getting a soul out of it, so does it really matter?"

"Well, kinda." He replied, using some of the slang that he was starting to pick up from her school and the internet. He considered her words, and looked at her properly now. "The Articulation Ritual doesn't require a soul. It just has limits on how often you can talk to the same person. This one, however." He pointed between the two of them. "Does."

"Look, I've learned my lesson. I screwed up. Nothing I can do about it besides accept it at this point, so, since the Articulation Ritual is not in my current grimoire, what do you suggest doing to look it up? Obviously, my failed attempt last time should not be repeated." She replied a bit curtly.

He let out a low growl, but shook his head. He went into the living room to get some paper from the printer. "You will be happy to know that I know the ritual circle." He told her, sketching the glyphs and wards on the paper in perfect clarity.

"You just said that in a way that tells me that there's a specific time I can talk to him." She sighed, thinking for a minute. It was a little odd how well she had gotten to know him so quickly, but, then again, they were in rather close quarters. After thinking over her options, she finally guessed. "Samhain?"

"Yup, when the spirit world and this one are at their closest point." He explained, standing up and handing her the paper. "Also, I just know the glyphs, I can't actually cast it. That is on you."

"I expected to cast it on my own." She frowned. "Just not that I had to wait seven months for Halloween."

"Why do you think they call it the day of the dead in Mexico?" He asked her rhetorically. "That is how they actually talk to their dead relatives."

She nodded. "I might actually need a ley line for that one. Don't want to accidentally cut it short."

"You will have until sunrise, so you should be fine." He replied waving her concerns off before going to get dinner started. "The ley will just be a bonus."

"Either way, I like being near the leys. It's win-win." She smiled, following him to the kitchen. "Thanks for not interrupting earlier."

"I might be a demon, but I am not an idiot." He told her as he began to cook. "You would have killed me if I interrupted. Doubly so if it was with him." He waved the spatula a little as he spoke.

She thought about it as she rested an elbow on the counter. "I don't think I'm really capable of killing outside of life and death, to be honest. But, I would've ordered you to do something you wouldn't enjoy."

"You could order me to kill myself." He told her honestly, making a face as he did so. "Just, please, don't. It takes a while for us to re-form if we die during a contract, and the process is extremely painful."

She hopped up onto the counter, and looked at him with a mirthful look that promised pain. "Oh, no. That would be too easy for you."

He stopped in the middle of cooking, and looked up at her. "What could you possibly do to torture me? Because I have seen and done it all." He inquired.

"I would take you to the mall, find a nice spot at the food court right outside of Abercrombie and Fitch, and tell you to join the models. And, of course, you wouldn't be able to kill the women that fawned over you." She smirked.

"That would be annoying, yes." He told her as he began cooking again. "But, not torture."

She shrugged. "All I have going for me at the moment is psychological torture. If I hurt you, I hurt me."

"Yes, I know. Thankfully, it won't kill you. It is really only there to let you know that something is wrong." He rationalized, stirring the meat he was cooking.

"And, vice versa, I'm sure." Ellyria smiled.

He nodded. "Yes, it also has the added benefit of making you harder to kill. I take a good portion of the damage in order to make sure you stay alive."

"Really?" She asked. "So, I could, like, cut myself, and- huh. That's interesting."

He pointed the spatula at her quickly. "Self-harm negates it. If you kill yourself before the deal is finished, your soul instantly gets taken." He firmly told her. "In case someone tries pulling a fast one." He warned, shaking his head. "But, you could jump off the roof and survive, yes."

She nodded, a little taken aback. "Well, I wasn't going to actually do it. I'm not the type to do that." She thought for a minute. "So, if for instance, I'm a movie character running away from something, and I have to jump to avoid being caught?" She let her question hang in the air.

"It would hurt like hell," he told her seriously, "but you would survive."

Ellyria thought about that. "Let's hope that never happens." She shivered.

"Let's hope." He sighed before he remembered something. "You will also heal faster, so keep that in mind, as well." He informed her, plating up her food, and putting another plate in the microwave. "Here you go. Enjoy." He gave her a small smile as he handed her the food.

"Thank you." She told him, looking at her mother's meal, which he had just stored in the microwave. "And, thanks, for her. She thinks it's me cooking."

He waved it off, and leaned against the counter. "You would have been annoyed had I not done that. I am here to help you however I can, is all."

She sighed, taking a bite of her meal. "I'm trying not to be angry at her, still. You're fine."

"You have every right to be mad at her. She nearly ruined your life." He told her matter-of-factly. "Consider yourself lucky for summoning me when you had the chance."

She chewed for a bit only speaking once she had swallowed her bite. "I think she might've tossed all of my college acceptances."

He let out a sigh, and looked at her seriously. "Would you like me to see if you got any responses?"

"If I got accepted by Ohio State, that would be great. It's where Corbin's going." She responded. "How do you even check?"

"I know people." He smirked. "Also, in this day and age, it isn't that difficult to cross reference documents emailed or mailed." He shrugged. "Worst case, I make some phone calls."

"I would appreciate knowing one way or the other." She thought about it for a while. "If I didn't get in there, I definitely didn't get into any of the elite schools." Her words trailing off with a wanting sigh.

He thought it over for a moment. "Your grades are high, right?" He asked her, trying to think of her odds of getting into different places with what he had learned of modern-day college acceptances in the past few months.

"Except for a blip from the second semester last year, which I explained in my introduction letter." She told him, hoping he understood the subtext of why she had bad grades last year without having to explain it. "I know that the Ivy League schools were a long shot, but I could use the ego boost of knowing I got in."

"You should be fine, but, worst case scenario, I can pull some strings." He told her with a smirk, stretching lightly. "I will look into that for you, and let you know by the end of the week." He promised with a nod.

"Thanks. I hate to have strings pulled for me versus my own merit, but, damn it all to Hell, I want it." She told him firmly.

"My pleasure." He smiled at her.

She smiled as she finished her meal, loading her dishes in the dishwasher, and walking towards her room. "I'm going to meditate and head to bed."

"Then, have a good night." He gave her a nod. "I will go check the yard for pests." He chuckled lightly before disappearing.

She sat up against her headboard, looking at the calendar briefly. Tomorrow was a full moon. She'd need to be up late for charging her stones, then. She knew that Zane had told her she didn't require such things, but nobody was around to teach her how to do that. Shaking her head to clear it, she closed her eyes, and started to focus, practice would make perfect soon enough. Though, she was still none the wiser to the very real pest control problem out front.

As Zangrunath began to patrol the yard, he saw another figure of similar build to the previous pests he had dealt with in the last few weeks. He didn't care about them, at first. But, recently, they had become more aggressive at trying to get to the house. One had almost made it to the back door before Zangrunath removed him permanently. He made sure not to leave any trace of the body, not that anyone would ever find it, but it never hurt to be too careful. So, as this new figure moved around the fence, looking in, the demon in waiting was eager to see what this new toy would do.

The man was carefully looking around the yard, he knew this was the right house. The Grant residence was well known around his neck of the woods, and he was tasked to make sure that there weren't any issues with the young Grant girl. He was a little worried. One of his associates had disappeared after looking into the house. He let out a sigh. What could this girl do to make him worry? He was a magic user with a few decades under his belt, and she was barely eighteen yet. Knowing this, he stepped into the yard, and made his way towards the back door.

Zangrunath smiled evilly as he watched the man step into his own demise. When the man was nearly touching the doorknob, he struck. He covered the man's mouth, and put his arm through the man's chest, holding his heart in his hand before tossing the body to the side. Zangrunath smiled and ate the heart with a chuckle, turning to the now cooling body. He closed his eyes, and let his body become shadow. The dead body on the ground absorbed into the demon's inky black form, and, after about a minute, there wasn't anything left. Zangrunath let out a belch, and disappeared again to continue his patrol. He wouldn't worry Ellyria about this, he knew she wouldn't want to hear it anyway. Besides, he was doing his job. Keeping her safe.

Friday, March 13, 2020

Ellyria was starting to get ready for the party later that night when her cell phone rang. She looked at the caller identification, and stared at the number for a second. It looked vaguely familiar. She couldn't put her finger on why, though. She swiped the green button, and put the phone to her ear. "Hello?" She asked.

A female voice that she recognized from announcements at school talked back in an urgent tone. "Hello, this is a recorded message from Moffett Public School. Effective immediately, all onsite school programming has been cancelled for the week beginning Monday, March twenty-third, twenty-twenty. The school gates will remain unlocked until four p.m. today. Please collect all books necessary to continue classwork in a remote learning setting. In order to make arrangements to pick up books, please dial-"

Ellyria hung up her phone, and called out around the house, "Zane!"

A moment later, Zangrunath appeared in a puff of brimstone beside her. "Yes?"

"Do we have all of our books? There was just a call from the school." She informed him, gesturing towards her phone.

He thought about that for a moment. "No, but, between the two of us, we have all of them. Somebody was complaining that her history book was too heavy in her bag, and left it in her locker."

She thought about his words for a moment. She did remember that. "You're right. I guess that's a benefit of being in the same classes." She smiled, opening her lips to ask him another question when she saw a video call coming in from Taylor. "Oh, boy." She commented, accepting the call.

As soon as the video connected, both Taylor and Diane were side by side, looking into the phone. They were at one of their lockers clearly still on campus as students passed by in the background. They squealed with excitement. "No school!" Taylor enthused, flipping her muddy brown hair behind a shoulder.

"Yeah, I just heard." Elly responded, hitting the button on the volume down a couple of times. "I've got everything that I need, so, don't worry about me."

"Alright." Diane chimed in from beside Taylor, putting a book into her backpack. "We were just calling in to check on ya'll. Glad you're good to go. You going to Todd's tonight?"

Ellyria nodded, realizing a second later that they weren't paying close enough attention to see it. "Uh huh. You guys just interrupted me getting ready."

Taylor gave Diane a little, playful smack. "See? I told you she was fine."

"Oh, please!" Diane chimed in, looking like she was about to start an argument.

"Play nice, ladies. We'll chat later tonight." She halfheartedly promised, hitting the end button on the call, and rolling her eyes. She looked over to Zane. "I have no idea how I put up with them before you came into the picture."

Zane shrugged a little, not caring for the women either way. "Hell, if I know. They are annoying." He told her honestly, having no reason no lie to her.

She sat down on her bed before she finally remembered her question from before she got the phone call. "Do I need to worry about this corona thing? It sounds like it's getting pretty serious if they're shutting down school without explanation." She asked, starting to look a little nervous.

The demon shrugged. "Probably not. I take the brunt of things for you, so, even if you get it, it will be mild." He told her, having been watching the health situation with avid interest over the past several weeks. "Even then, I have dealt with the bubonic plague, and my previous master turned out fine, this should be nothing for you." He assured her.

Ellyria sighed, and the tension in her shoulders eased slightly. "Okay. Good, and thanks."

"You're welcome." He nodded as her phone made a noise to inform her that she had messages.

Ellyria grabbed her phone, seeing Zane disappear seconds later. She saw a text from Corbin, and smiled, 'Two weeks of no school!' He enthused.

She smiled, and giggled. 'I know. I just found out, too. See you soon.' She tossed her phone onto the bed, and ran off to the bathroom to get ready again.

A few hours later, Ellyria took Corbin's hand as he helped her out of his classic sixty-nine Shelby. She smiled at him, stealing a kiss as they walked down the crowded street towards Todd's house party. The night was dark, and, from the looks of some of the other people they saw walking around, the drinks were already flowing.

"Todd's a real gentleman, sacrificing his house for us." She giggled.

Corbin laughed at that. "Oh, the most gentlemanly man you ever met. I heard through the grapevine that he is turning his jacuzzi into a punch bowl." He teased. "A real go getter."

She made a face. "I hope you're joking. That's disgusting." She commented as they rang the doorbell.

A moment passed, and a familiar face answered. "Well, hello, you two." Zangrunath smiled in his disguised form. "Welcome to the party." He told them simply, moving to the side, and letting them into the house.

"Hey, Zane." Ellyria greeted, seeing an actual punch bowl. She let out the little breath she'd been holding. There were a bunch of other kids grinding and dancing to the music, and she looked to Corbin. "If you get me drunk enough, I might be convinced to dance in public."

Corbin nodded amiably to Zangrunath before he looked to Ellyria. "Is that a request or a statement?" He asked her seriously. "Because I'm interested."

She winked, moving into the crowd to go say hello to her friends. "Well, I'm not here for the calming atmosphere."

Corbin smiled at her, and gave her a small kiss on the cheek. "Alright, I will be back in a minute with a drink." He promised, looking at Zangrunath. "Watch her for me, will ya?" He asked, turning, and leaving the two of them.

"He always does." She commented, speaking loudly among the loud electronic dance music that was blaring. "Right, cuz?" She joked.

"With my life." He answered back in a serious manner before replying in her head. "I hope you don't mind if I cause a little chaos here tonight. This is just too good an opportunity to pass up." He smiled, seeing two young men headbutting each other once before one blacked out.

"Just no maiming or killing, please." She responded mentally. "I can deal with the rest."

"Of course." Zangrunath assured her with a nod. "Also, you will need much more than whatever he is getting you to get drunk." He told her, flippantly gesturing in the direction of Corbin. "I will try to drink some as well, so you can get your 'dance'." He chuckled.

She chuckled. "Thanks for the innuendo, I guess. I fully intend on drinking myself silly, so noted about the quantity."

"Don't worry. I will make sure you don't get too bad." He promised, stealing someone's drink and downing it in an instant, completely ignoring their complaint. "You just enjoy yourself." He instructed, sauntering off, and joining a small group to have his fun.

Ellyria turned to see Corbin holding a red cup filled with a mystery drink. She smiled, clinking glasses anticlimactically, "Bottoms up."

"Cheers." Corbin toasted, taking a drink from his cup. "It should be good, I don't know what you like, so I just started with the punch. I know there is vodka in there, so I figured it was a safe bet."

She quickly chugged the drink, and kissed him. "This is a good start." She told him, angling them towards where Taylor and Diane were making a video on one of their phones. Elly smiled widely, and pulled Corbin over into the camera. "Hey, girls."

Diane hugged her. "Two-week vacation!" She enthused.

Taylor stole the next hug. "You two are so cute. Let's do shots together." She giggled, skipping off to the kitchen to grab some plastic shot glasses. She returned a moment later with four, filled with a golden colored liquid inside. "Tequila makes your clothes fall off!" She announced, bobbing to the music as she handed out the glasses. She clinked hers with everybody else's.

"Thirty-six more days to freedom!" Diane chimed in.

Ellyria laughed at that. "But who's counting?!"

Corbin laughed, and took the shot with the others. He took Ellyria's cup, and leaned into her ear. "I'm going to go say hi to the guys on the team really quick while I get you a refill."

She nodded. "Okay, thanks!" She smiled, bobbing her head to the music as she talked with the ladies for a moment while she waited.

Back behind her Zane was mesmerizing some teenagers with the hypnotic stare he could use, and they were falling for his tricks hook, line, and sinker. The embarrassing bets and antics were marvelous. He was enjoying the chaos all while keeping a vigilant eye trained on Ellyria. He saw Corbin step away for a moment, and a protective growl rumbled in his chest. He shook his head. At least, he was there to keep an eye on her.

As soon as Corbin was away from Ellyria, the clacking of heels could be heard from nearby, and, moments later, Heather was in front of her. She flipped her hair out of her face, and crossed her arms. "How did you do it? What sort of spell did you cast on him?"

Ellyria scowled at Heather, and glanced over to see that Diane was now recording the conversation. Part of her was defensive of Heather's reference to magic, but she chose to ignore it. She was just jealous, was all. "What are you on about? We wanted to date for a long time."

Heather scoffed. "Whatever. Just leave him alone. He was supposed to be my boyfriend. Not yours. The captain of the football team and the head cheerleader are, like, supposed to be a thing."

Ellyria's eyes met Zane's as he stepped behind Heather and grabbed her shoulder. "More like a big-headed cheerleader. Get out of here. Nobody wants to deal with your crap right now. This is a celebration."

Zane's hand gripped Heather's shoulder tightly. "I'll show you out."

Ellyria crossed her arms, seeing Corbin walking up next. "Thanks, Zane. I doubt the trash will take itself out."

"You dirty little-" Heather started as Zane's other hand covered her mouth. He picked Heather up as she kicked and screamed like her weight was nothing, and deposited her outside, locking the door behind her.

Corbin handed Ellyria her cup, and lifted his among the somewhat startled crowd. "To an extra-long spring break!"

"Woo!" The crowd howled, everyone taking drinks of their own cups, and going back to dancing.

Elly downed her punch, and looked into Corbin's eyes. That little encounter had put an edge on her good time. "Is there any Fireball?"

He was a little taken aback by her chugging the drink, but smiled at her. "I think there is." He responded, grabbing her hand. "It's this way." He started leading her to the kitchen.

She followed him, and found the kitchen to be slightly tamer than the drinking games and dancing in the living room. She grabbed two more plastic shot glasses, waving a hand to make them freeze a bit. "I like it cold."

He chuckled. "That's fine." He opened the bottle, and poured two shots for the two of them, handing her one. "Enjoy."

She lifted her glass, and downed the liquid. Her head started to get a little buzz finally, but she still had a ways to go. "I'm still feeling good. Might drink you under the table tonight." Then, she leaned into his ear. "Might screw you under it too."

He smirked as she mentioned that. "I wasn't planning on drinking that much. One of us has to drive." He chuckled before whispering back to her. "And, it would be my pleasure." He winked, taking another shot.

She took the shot with him. "In your car?" She asked with an excited little shiver.

"If you want to." He shrugged, eyeing her wantonly. "I will leave that up to you."

She smirked, filling up her shot glass again. "I would suggest on top of it, but I don't want to mess with the body. The interior's a little more durable."

He smiled widely, and leaned into her ear again. "I wouldn't mind doing some body work, if it meant doing you." He whispered.

She fanned herself a bit. "Good thing I know some good places to park. That was hot."

"I have my moments." He smiled, taking a sip of a drink.

She took her shot, and looked at him. "I'm trying really hard not to tell you to bring me a place that will instigate drunk casting."

"I wouldn't do that to you." He told her honestly. "I don't want your secret to be known."

"No, no, it's remote, but I wouldn't be able to not tap the magic there like this." She smirked. "My hair doesn't even stay down like normal there. It just floats."

"You can go super Saiyan?" He asked her seriously. "Because that is cool." He smiled at her.

She held up two fingers. "I think the eye color changes at SSJ two."

He smiled at her. "Okay, that I do want to see." He told her honestly. "It would be incredibly sexy to see you with that much power."

She kissed him a little more sloppily than she meant to. "I think that I'd like to show you."

He looked at the party, and took her hand. "Then, let's get out of here." He suggested, grabbing one last drink for her. "I want to ravish you with that power in you."

"Fuck me." She muttered quietly to him as they snaked their way between bodies.

"I fully intend to." He whispered back to her as he led her to the car quickly.

When she sat down and buckled up, the world spun. "Oh, now, I'm feeling it."

"You okay?" He asked her as he started the car. "I want to make sure you're okay. You did drink a lot."

"Oh, this," She pointed between them, "is happening. Just finally feeling it now. We're halfway there, so follow this road north for another ten minutes until you get to Dora. Then, you'll take a left at a dirt road."

He smiled at her, and gave her a kiss. "We will be there soon enough." He assured her, taking off to the field in question.

"So, did you sell your soul for this car or what? I have got to know." She asked curiously.

He chuckled, and shook his head. "No, this car belonged to my grandpa, and he wanted me to have it so long as I fixed it up, of course." He smiled at her. "Several years and a lot of flipped burgers later, I got her to run."

"So totally worth it." She told him. "She's beautiful."

"Yeah, she is nice." He agreed, rubbing the steering wheel a bit before putting a hand on her leg and rubbing it instead. "But, I think you're better." He smiled at her.

She closed her eyes. "Mmm. Thank you. You're not so bad yourself. Better than magic."

He smiled at her, and massaged her leg a bit more before he saw the turn coming up. He slowed the car down as they made their way onto the dirt road. "And, it looks like we are close."

"You'll know when to stop." She told him as she kicked off her heels. "Big open field."

He continued to drive, and, in a few short minutes, he found the field in question. He pulled the car into the center of the field, and turned the car off, getting out to help her out of the car. "We're here." He smiled at her.

She took his hand before placing her first foot down. It made a little tremor throughout the clearing as it touched, and her hair started to drift up. Her other foot touched, and her eyes glowed as the air settled all around. The wind stopped for a second. She looked at him, and smiled.

He looked at her in awe for almost a minute before he remembered to breathe. He held her hand, and looked her over admiring the changes. "You look amazing." He complimented, giving her a small twirl.

She spun, and almost tipped over. "Thank you. This is- disorienting with the alcohol."

"Sorry." He apologized as he held her for a moment to stabilize her. He moved her to the front of the car, and gave her a soft kiss. He could feel electricity. "Woah."

She pulled away, and showed him her hand, and five fingers glowing with the current he'd felt. "Sorry. I won't hurt you."

He nodded, and gently lifted her onto the hood of the car. "It's alright. Like I said before, I trust you." He reassured her, giving her a much longer kiss now.

"I love you, Corbin." She murmured as things got heated. Random magic started to appear throughout the clearing, and lit up the night sky with the brightness of day as lightning crackled all around them.

Amidst the magic and the heat of the moment, Corbin looked at Ellyria with a newfound light in his eyes, and whispered to her. "I love you."

They'd both forgotten condoms, so they both took care of each other in other ways tonight. When they were both finished, Ellyria's head spun thanks to the alcohol. "Can we head back? The night is way too bright here." She half-heartedly complained as the magic still lingered in the sky.

He looked around, and nodded. "Yeah, let's get you home. You are going to be tired tomorrow." He teased, helping her get dressed.

During dressing, she nearly fell several times. "Thank you." She mumbled as he helped her into the car.

"You are very welcome." Corbin responded while buckling her up and giving her another kiss. "I'm glad you had fun."

She leaned back in the seat, and held his hand as he drove. She drifted in and out of consciousness for the drive, but she remembered whispering, "I love you," more than once. With her eyes closed, she felt rather than saw her hand get kissed several times.

Corbin cherished the peaceful moments together on the drive as he carefully navigated her home. He was a little surprised to see Zane already there waiting for them. "Oh, hey man. Didn't expect you here so soon. Thought you'd still be at the party."

"It kind of died off after you left." Zane shrugged, lying smoothly. He easily hefted the exhausted and intoxicated witch out of Corbin's eyes, and gave him his entrancing smile. "I've got this. Do have a good night." His voice, soothing and calm.

Corbin nodded, looking a little dazed, and gave Ellyria a quick kiss, leaving her there with her cousin to take care of her. "Goodnight." He muttered seconds before his car door closed with a thunk.

Zangrunath took her inside to rest, and laid her down in her bed. He pulled her blanket partially over her, and watched for a moment in order to reassure himself that she was well. Once he had determined that she was healthy and comfortable, he merged into shadow in order to patrol the yard once again.

Ellyria rolled over in bed, pulling her comforter high over her shoulders. She dozed peacefully, once again, despite Zangrunath's favorite pests in the yard that night.

Zangrunath stalked carefully around the two men to make sure that they didn't spot him as they entered the yard. He knew he could take care of them, the only question he had was why were they so determined to keep coming back? You would think people disappearing would make people want to avoid the unfortunate location, but, no, apparently, with this group, it only made it worse.

He let out a small sigh, and quickly took care of them. Once again, making sure that their bodies would never be found. He let out a mirthful chuckle. He could feel his strength growing slightly, and it wasn't just from Ellyria. He could move farther from her and move faster back to her. He knew it would only get better from here, and that she would get stronger, too. He looked up in her direction from outside, and chuckled. She was different from the other people who had summoned him. She was stronger, and, also, younger. He was going to make sure she would get her dream.

Monday, March 23, 2020

Ellyria whiled away the hours of Spring Break at home. The news was starting to call the stay at home orders from the states around the country quarantine or isolation. She was beginning to get stir crazy. She really did feel isolated at her small home with nobody but Zane and her Mom for company. She rolled over on her bed, and grabbed her phone. It didn't take her much thought to open her texting app, and to choose Corbin. 'I've never missed school more than at this moment.'

She saw that he had quickly seen her message, and noticed that he was responding, eagerly awaiting his reply. A small giggle escaped a second before his response came. 'I get your meaning. Don't worry, though. I'll still see you tonight, birthday girl.'

'Don't you tempt me with a good time.' She texted back. 'I can't wait to see you. I've missed you.'

'Soon.' Corbin responded quickly. 'Maybe, I'll get that word trademarked. Might be funny.'

'You goof.' She responded, sending him a gif of a girl throwing wadded up paper at someone. 'I'll see you later, then.'

He sent a winking emoji, and some hearts. 'Later.'

Ellyria lightly tossed her phone to the side on her bed, and rolled over to stare at the ceiling. What in the world was she supposed to do while she anxiously waited for her Mom to leave for work, and Corbin to get here? She was running out of good ideas at the moment. "Zane?" She asked the empty room, knowing he would somehow magically hear.

The demon poofed into existence at her feet, and sat down on the bed. "Yes?"

"I'm curious. Do you think eighteen is going to be anything different from seventeen for me? I'm a little anxious about it." She told him honestly.

"Probably not much." He told her. "It's just another year."

She nodded a couple times. "You got Mom onto the overnight shift for tonight, right? I don't want her to be home while Corbin's over."

"Stop worrying about that. You already know the answer." He smiled, and held up two fingers. "She is working a double. She won't be home until noon tomorrow."

She winced. "Oof, you're evil, but thank you." She tapped one of her toes a few times. "Are we there yet? I just need it to be tomorrow already."

"Flattery will get you far. " He smiled. "It will be tomorrow soon enough."

She grabbed her pillow, and smothered her face with it. "I'll just meditate after I get some lunch in me. Should kill some time." She mumbled into the fabric.

"Alright, is there anything you want for lunch?" He asked her.

"Not really." She shrugged.

"Then, I will just make you something simple." He promised, standing up from his place to get started.

She nodded awkwardly with the pillow still over her face. "Thanks. Sorry I'm so out of it. The idea of going to bed one day and waking up an adult the next is weird. It's- it's," she pondered her word choice for a second, "daunting."

"You are making it into a bigger deal than it is, you know." He told her seriously. "It will be like any other day of the week."

"I know." She sighed. "It just feels important. Thanks for putting up with me, right now."

He nodded with a small, impatient sigh. "It's fine. I don't really have much of a choice in the matter.

She let out a sigh of frustration in return. It was becoming fewer and farther in between, but, today, his presence was just too much for her. "I'll take that lunch, now. Thanks." She told him by way of a dismissal.

Zane's eyes blazed with fire, but he nodded, leaving the room to make her some food. "Very well."

She waited until he was gone, and sat up, grabbing her phone. She jumped a second later when the phone started ringing. She looked at the number, and it looked familiar. So, she answered it. "Hello?" She replied.

"Hello, this is a recorded message from Moffett Public School. Effective Monday, March thirtieth, twenty-twenty, all classes will resume using online modality. All before and after school programming is cancelled until further notice. Should you need technology in order to accommodate remote learning, it can be checked out via drive thru pick up beginning-" Ellyria groaned, and hung up.

"It just keeps getting better." She grumbled, hopping out of bed, and starting to stomp down the hall in order to inform Zane. She stopped in her tracks when she saw her mother down the hallway, getting ready for work already. "Hey, Mom. You okay?"

"Yes, dear. It's just going to be a long shift at the diner." She smiled tiredly, yawning with a cup of coffee in her hands. "Happy early birthday." She hugged Ellyria. "I'll take you out to dinner Friday night. Okay?"

"Yeah, I'd like that. Thanks." Ellyria smiled. "I'm sure you got a call, too. We're doing online school for a bit."

Lynne nodded, taking another sip of her beverage. "Yeah, the robocall woke me up."

Ellyria frowned. "I'm sorry. Anyway, I haven't eaten lunch, so I'm gonna grab a bite."

"Enjoy." She smiled, walking into the bathroom to get cleaned up.

When she could hear her Mom's shower running, Ellyria finally made it into the living room. She sniffed the air, and hummed in appreciation. "That smells great, thank you."

When Ellyria arrived at the table, Zangrunath placed a plate of pasta in front of her with a meat sauce. "Here you go. Eat up." He simply stated, turning and cleaning up the few dishes.

She smiled, and started to eat with gusto. "Mmm. I didn't realize how hungry I was."

"Instead of eating on time, you took more time just to talk to your boy toy." He told her seriously. "Of course, you would be hungry."

She sighed at his words, but didn't say anything as she continued to eat. Eventually, when the plate was clean, she spoke again. "Whatever, Zangrunath." She closed her eyes, and rubbed her temples. "Sorry. I'm just in a mood today. Ugh!" She growled impressively, storming away towards her room as several items nearby all repelled away from her.

He sighed, and quickly cleaned up the few items. He disappeared just before Lynne came out to the kitchen to get some food.

Ellyria swiped several items off her dresser. Salt, stones, Palo Santo, and moved it into the garage. The room was still almost identical to how her father had left it. She sensed old magic here, but it had all been used up since then. She made a meticulous circle, lit the Palo Santo, and sat down in the center of it. She dove deeply into meditation in order to try calming down from whatever was bothering her right now. It would all be better tomorrow. Resting always helped.

Zangrunath waited for Ellyria's mother to leave before reappearing in the kitchen. He had several things to do today, but he started making a cake for her. He didn't want to, but, with how much she had said it in her sleep the last few nights, he might as well take it as an order. He did have to rummage through an old diary while she was sleeping to find out what her favorite was, but it wasn't difficult to find. By tomorrow, she would, hopefully, feel better about all this nonsense.

Unconsciously, Ellyria started to levitate in the middle of the circle she'd created. Her legs remained crossed, and her hands gently resting together, forming a little circle. Her deep breaths were steady and restful. Around the room, the lights started to lightly flicker on and off, but she didn't notice it.

There was a small double take from Zangrunath as the lights flickered. He quickly checked around the house, checking quietly on Ellyria last. He was shocked by the sheer amount of magic she was getting, given that they were nowhere near a ley line. He wanted to get her attention to let her know what she was doing, but decided against it. She was already pissed off at him. He didn't want to cause further problems, so he disappeared back into the kitchen to finish off her cake.

Over the course of the next several hours, Ellyria's hair started to stand up like it would around the leys, and her body became wrapped in a cloak of pure magic that moved like fluid around her. The stones she'd worked into the circle lifted off the ground, and started moving in perfectly timed circles around her. The longer she remained in her trance, the more magic she seemed to gather, and the stranger things started to get.

Zangrunath left her to meditate for quite some time before he started to notice oddities. He just started doing his rounds outside when he saw the sprinkler flowing upward. He stopped, and looked at the house. He quickly teleported via shadow into the kitchen, and saw that things were floating on the ceiling. All the clocks' hands were spinning backwards. He quickly started on his way to the garage before he felt gravity start to shift and force him into the wall. He let out a growl, and shifted into his true demonic form. With the power boost, he made it to Ellyria quickly, grabbing her. "Ellyria! You need to stop!" He told her firmly as he struggled to stand next to her.

As the runes scribed around the house began to glow white hot, Ellyria heard something at the back of her consciousness. It almost didn't feel real. She ignored it, focusing. She was so close to something. Something important.

Zangrunath watched as she continued to meditate, and he could see cracks starting to form into the concrete of the garage. "Oh, Hell." He growled, looking at the witch in front of him, and sighing as he turned his arm into a sharp blade. "Sorry, but it is either this or not having a home." He told her, though he doubted that she heard, stabbing himself deeply in the stomach, and yelling in pain as he did so.

Ellyria's eyes shot open, and she reeled around at the intruder. A hand thrust out, pushing the body against a wall before she realized who it was. She breathed through pain as her eyes flickered between different colors. "You idiot." She growled in a voice that had three different timbres. "Leave me be."

He shook his head, and stood up through the pain. He looked back to see the cracks in the wall spreading. "If you don't stop, you will destroy the house!" He yelled at her as another swell of gravity made him shudder where he stood.

She looked at him with the eyes that weren't quite hers, and sneered. "I'll remake it." She closed her eyes, and the magic swelled again as the cracks in the wall and ground repaired themselves.

Zangrunath growled at the reply, and angrily stood up straight despite his injury. "Fine. Then, I will make you." He grabbed his arm by the shoulder, and his muscles swelled violently. There was a sickening crack as he tore his own arm from his shoulder, spraying thick, black blood on the ground. "Ah!" He howled in pain.

She looked up at the ceiling, screaming in agony as her body fell to the ground. A pulse of magic burst out, making all car alarms in the neighborhood start blaring. All the lights in the room suddenly turned white hot, and shattered into nothingness. She sobbed on the ground, gripping her arm as if her own had been removed.

His breathing was heavy as he dealt with the pain. He took his arm, and placed it back on his shoulder. He held it there as it began to slowly stitch itself back together. He looked at her with poorly hidden fury alight in his eyes. "You will be fine." He growled, turning to go deal with the mess she had just made.

"Why?!" She screamed at him, not remembering the events from seconds before.

He reeled around, and yelled back at her. "You almost destroyed the house!" He seethed. "You were changing the gravity like it was clay!" He yelled, getting closer to her. "You were going to break the very fundamentals of the universe had I not stopped you! So, shut the hell up, and let me go clean up the shit storm you just unleashed." He demanded, disappearing from her sight.

Ellyria rolled over, and dragged herself to her bedroom where everything was misplaced. She dropped onto her bed, passing out. Her breathing was incredibly shallow. Not even a trace of energy was left in her or the house now.

Zangrunath growled, and cursed himself as he looked around at the destruction. The house was a mess, and her boy toy was going to be here soon. He knew he could do it, but it was a waste of energy in his opinion. He yelled as he felt the magic begin forcing him to do the job. Stupid contracts. He cleaned for well over an hour before he got to the remains of her cake. He tossed it out, and he wasn't going to make another one. It was just another day of the week, after all.

Tuesday, March 24, 2020

Corbin parked in the driveway, and walked up to the front door of Ellyria's house. He noticed that the water from the sprinkler was in odd places, but shrugged it off. It was probably broken. When he reached the door, he turned the knob to let himself in, but it was locked. "Huh." He knocked, waiting for her to answer.

Zangrunath growled when he heard the knock at the door. He knew that Ellyria was still out cold, and would probably be that way for quite some time. Now, he had to deal with this. He sighed, and shifted into his human appearance, answering the door with his best smile. "Hey, you."

Corbin raised his eyebrows when he saw Zane answer. "Hey." He greeted, standing there with hands in his pockets. "Elly invited me over."

Zangrunath nodded, and turned to the side to let him in. "Yeah, I know." He grumbled, shutting the door behind him as he entered. "She is in her room sleeping, now, but I won't stop you. Just be warned, there was a power surge earlier, and it kind of left her feeling tired." He explained vaguely and only half-truthfully.

Corbin started to head to the hall before he stopped. Something about Zane's words had just clicked in his mind. "Power surge. You know? Is she okay?"

"She is just tuckered out is all." Zane responded as he went around cleaning. "And, I am just the lucky one cleaning up after it." He sighed.

"Thanks, man." Corbin nodded, heading into her room, and finding Ellyria sleeping. It was dark in the room with only the flashing light of a recently restarted alarm clock to see by. She was splayed across the whole bed. There weren't even snores to tell him she was alive. He got close to the bed, and shook her lightly. "Hey, Elly? You okay?"

Like when she was meditating earlier, she didn't move or speak, and simply continued to rest. The reasons were completely different this time. Before, she was desperate to find out what she was chasing during her meditations. Now, she was simply mentally and physically exhausted. She needed this sleep.

Corbin looked at Ellyria worriedly. He moved her so that she was under her blankets. He watched her sleep for a long moment before he got up to go talk with Zangrunath. "Is she going to be alright?" He asked seriously.

Zangrunath nodded as he swept part of the kitchen. "Yup, she just needs sleep." He explained without making eye contact with him.

"What happened?" Corbin asked. "She seemed fine yesterday."

"A power surge happened." Zangrunath sighed at the man. "It set off every car alarm in the neighborhood, and blew out about twenty bulbs around the house that I still need to fix." He sighed again, shaking his head a bit. "People react differently to power fluctuations."

"Want me to run and get you bulbs from the store?" Corbin offered, looking towards Ellyria's room again.

Zangrunath paused for a moment, and nodded as he continued to clean. "Yeah, that would be helpful."

"I'll be right back, then. Anything else you need?" He asked, pulling his keys from his pocket.

"If you pick her up a chocolate cake, she will appreciate it." Zangrunath told him. He didn't really want to bake another cake.

"Will do." Corbin nodded, heading out the door. There were a couple people walking by the house that seemed a little overdressed for midnight. Hell, taking a walk at this time of night was strange, but it was a small town. People were always weird here. He hopped into his car, and drove off on the errand, heading across the bridge into Fort Smith.

Zangrunath followed Corbin to the door to close it behind him. He hesitated when he saw the people walking towards the house, giving pause to look them over. Something about them seemed familiar.

Zane was just about to close the door when one of the strangers called out to him. "Excuse me? Is this the Grant Residence?"

Zangrunath nodded in curiosity. He would let this play out just to see what they wanted. "Yes. May I ask what you need at this hour?"

"We need to talk to Miss Grant about some disturbances in the last few weeks." He told Zangrunath as the two stepped closer to the door.

"I'm sorry, but she is at work. Working a double tonight, I'm afraid. She won't be back until tomorrow." Zangrunath smiled at the men before starting to shut the door, but one of the men stopped him by catching it.

"We don't mean her." The second man demanded expressionlessly, pulling a gun out of his pocket.

Zangrunath's face went from a smile to a more serious one in an instant. "I see, and why is that?" He asked the man that was standing in front of him.

"Like I said, we have questions about some disturbances." He pressed. The man holding the door next to him, also drawing a gun. "Now, step aside."

Zangrunath noticed demonic and occult runes etched into the weapons, glowing lightly with powerful magic. Of course, these men had weaponry that could effectively hurt him versus the annoyance of a normal gun. He nodded to the men, feigning compliance, and stepped to the side as he mentally called to Ellyria. "You need to get under your bed, and cover your ears. Be ready for some pain. I'm sorry in advance." As he finished, he shut the door behind the men, quickly shifting into his true form. He turned his arm into a blade again, and stabbed one of the men in the side.

Reacting quickly to the disturbing change in circumstances, the other man turned, and fired his gun at the demon in front of him. Some of the bullets whizzed by the being in his initial panic, but his training kicked in quickly. The bullets started to hit, but several of them ricocheted off Zangrunath's tough muscles. He had never seen this before. Not with these weapons. He carefully aimed one last shot at a soft looking spot in the demon's toned stomach, smiling in satisfaction when he saw it rend flesh. That was too hard for an average demon. "What on God's green earth are you!?"

"Your worst nightmare." Zangrunath growled as he reached out. He grabbed the gun, and bent the barrel with a sickening screech of tortured metal. He threw the gun to the side, and tore the assailant he'd just stabbed into two separate halves. A smirk gracing his features as a shower of blood rained down, tossing the body to the side before walking towards the remaining man.

The now unarmed man fell to his knees, and began to crawl back as the creature approached him. "Please don't hurt me!" He begged as his body shook with adrenaline and fear.

"I won't." Zangrunath smiled menacingly, lifting him up, and holding his form like a rag doll in front of his face. "Not yet anyways. Tell me who you work for." He growled as his eyes alighted with fiery rage.

The man's face grew impossibly pale in an instant, and he began to sob. "Section seven of the Vatican. We were trying to find out what was causing a disturbance with the ley lines, and, when our men went missing around here, we figured this place must be the cause." He shook, making quick, jerking movements as he tried futilely to get away.

"And, what were you going to do with Ellyria?" He asked, starting to get angrier, now.

"We were going to take her out. Just like her father." He cried as he realized his moments were numbered.

Zangrunath let out a demonic yell, and tore the man asunder. Once again, blood and viscera rained down around him. He seethed for several minutes, taking quick short breaths that did not calm him down. Finally, he took care of the bodies and the mess he just made as he always did. When the deed was done, he went to go check on Ellyria. "Are you alright?" It was his job to make sure that she was okay, after all.

Ellyria shook and sobbed from under her bed, curled up into a ball, and holding the place where Zangrunath had been shot. "Why?" She murmured over and over, trying to understand.

"We have a problem." He told her seriously. "And, a big one, at that." He informed her, sitting down on the bed, and leaving room for her to climb out from under it. "The Vatican knows about you." He added, pinching the bridge of his nose.

Pain lanced through him as he heard a crack coming from under the bed where she accidentally bashed it. "What?!" She clambered out from her hiding place.

He let out a growl, and shook the pain off. "You were messing around with the ley lines too much, and, now, the Vatican wants to make sure that doesn't happen ever again." He sighed, trying to figure out how to put this to a quick end.

"But, I- I wasn't tapping the leys today." She argued. She was still trying to figure out how to reliably do that, so she didn't think that she had, even unconsciously.

He let out a moan of frustration. "What is the last thing you remember from earlier?" He asked her seriously.

"Meditating, and, then, I woke up in pain." She told him honestly.

"While you were meditating, you conjured up enough energy to simulate a ley line." He told her simply. "You almost destroyed the house." He pointed out. "So, between that and having drunken escapades at the ley line nearby, I think they have a good reason to be a little ticked off." He finished with a growl.

"Why does it matter?" She asked quietly as the sounds of a car pulling up could be heard.

Zangrunath's focus went to the car, but he stayed in the room with Ellyria. "Because, if today was anything to go by, I can agree with them." He told her seriously. "If someone were to fully control the ley lines, they would basically be a god, and you do know how much the Vatican hates false gods, don't you?" He asked rhetorically.

She made a face. "I'm not a god."

"You almost were today." He quipped back. "Had I not stopped you."

"What are you talking about?! I was just meditating. Nothing was different." She yelled.

"I ripped off my arm to stop you!" He yelled back at her. "How did you not feel that!?"

"I remember that!" She fumed. "What happened?"

Out in the living room, they heard a voice. "Woah! Elly? Zane? Everything alright?"

"Then, there's this guy." Zangrunath groaned as he heard Corbin's voice. He sighed, and called out. "We are fine."

"Hey!" Ellyria called out, starting to go down the hall to meet him.

Corbin placed the few items down, and went to hug Ellyria. "Are you okay? What happened here?" He asked, looking around the house at the mess, recoiling back in horror as he saw Zangrunath in his true form for the first time. "What the fuck!?"

Zangrunath looked down at himself, and sighed. "And, today just keeps getting better!" He growled.

Ellyria sighed, looking at the scene all around her. Blood and gore. Demon on one side, boyfriend on the other. "Oh, hell."

Corbin mustered up as much courage as he could, and moved in front of Ellyria. "Stay back!" He called out to the demon, his body shaking as he did so.

"Corbin, Corbin." She grabbed at his shoulders to pull him away. "It's fine. That's Zane."

Zangrunath changed into his human visage, and sighed, starting to clean up the mess. He muttered several curses in demonic under his breath.

Corbin looked at the now human Zangrunath, and turned to Ellyria with a mix of emotions on his face. "What in the world is going on?" He asked her nervously, looking pale as he spoke.

"Zane protects me. I summoned him, so he does what I say." She replied simply. "I was- we were attacked."

Corbin shook his head at her. "What? Why!?" He asked a little loudly. "Why did you summon a demon? Why does he look like that? Who attacked you? And, why is there blood everywhere?" He asked quickly, barely stopping to breathe.

"Oh, for fucks sake." Zangrunath groaned, turning to look at the man. "The blood is from the guys who attacked us. I killed them, so I am cleaning it up." He sighed, going back to doing just that. "Talk to her about the rest." He replied bluntly, waving to Ellyria.

She looked up at Corbin with tears in her eyes. "I summoned him on accident, and we're kinda stuck together now. I was attacked by, and, I can't believe I'm saying this, the Vatican. I'm too strong apparently. I'm sorry you have to see all this." She sat down on the couch and started to cry.

Corbin looked from Ellyria to Zangrunath before shaking his head. He sat down on the couch as well, and put his head in his hands. "What the hell is going on?" He groaned.

Zangrunath sighed, and looked at the pair on the couch. "I am just as confused myself," he agreed, stopping his cleaning temporarily. "This has never happened before or, at least, not to me directly. So, as an expert on Hell, I have no clue."

Corbin looked up at Zangrunath, and shook his head. "Why did she summon you?" He asked him directly instead of Ellyria.

"I was trying," she wiped her eyes as her words hung in the air, "to talk to my Dad."

Corbin sighed, and looked at her before putting an arm around her. "I'm sorry." He apologized, letting out another sigh. "I didn't know."

"There is a lot you don't know about all of this." Zangrunath told him, "and you are going to need to take some notes on what we need to catch you up on."

Corbin looked at him with a mix of emotions. He looked at Ellyria, and rubbed her shoulder. "Fine, where do we start?" He asked the demon seriously.

Zangrunath raised an eyebrow at him, and chuckled. "Here I was expecting you to run out the door." He sounded impressed as he spoke. "First of all, she and I are one." He started. "We are bound together, so good luck trying to get rid of me." He finished with a smirk.

"Yeah, I can't undo the magic, so we're stuck with each other." Ellyria added quietly.

"But, he's not always around." Corbin replied to her. "We have been alone together." He told her simply.

"He's got his own magic." She told him. "Last he told me, we couldn't be more than twenty feet apart except for at the house."

"It is closer to fifty feet now, but, yeah, I am always nearby." Zangrunath added, smirking at Corbin as he did so.

"Wait. That would mean, in the field, you were there?" He asked morbidly.

"Yes sir, mister-didn't-bring-a-condom." Zangrunath laughed at the man. "Going to have performance issues next time around?" He chuckled.

Ellyria looked up at Zangrunath. "Oh, be nice. It's bad enough you can feel it."

"He can what!?" Corbin exclaimed.

"Don't worry buddy, I have had better." Zangrunath shrugged, going back to his cleaning, smirking and whistling a tune as he did so.

She sighed. "He's teasing you. He doesn't care. He's been around for a bunch of other witches like me, so this isn't sacred to him or whatever."

Corbin sighed deeply. "So, every time we had sex, he felt it?" He asked her seriously.

"And, any time I stub my toe or bump my head, and I feel everything he feels back." She rubbed her stomach again. "Can you get the bullet out or do you need help?"

Zangrunath growled lightly. "I can get it out, but it is going to hurt." He told her honestly.

"Let me, then." She sighed.

"Let you what?" Corbin asked her curiously.

"Let me remove the bullet." She offered, picking up the TV remote with her magic to emphasize her point. "At least, if it's me, fingers aren't going into orifices."

Zangrunath sighed, and nodded, walking over to her. "Please, just make it quick." He asked her seriously.

She nodded, and moved to grab a pillow, which she bit down onto before concentrating to find the object, ripping it out of him in seconds. She screamed into the fabric. Her hands pressing the place on her stomach where the object had come out of Zane. The remains of the bullet clattered down to the ground, making a small metallic thunking noise.

Zangrunath grunted in pain as she pulled the bullet from him. He could feel his body starting to heal quickly now. "Thank you." He told her honestly.

Corbin watched in shock as his girlfriend pulled a bullet out of a demon, and, somehow, she was the one screaming. He sidled up next to her, and held her, looking at her stomach. He was seeing no blood, looking up to Zangrunath in awe. "Holy shit."

"Far from it." Zangrunath told him. "They don't make these kinds of deals up there." He sighed, going back to his cleaning.

Ellyria panted, holding onto Corbin. "Try not to get shot anymore, okay?"

"I will certainly try." Zangrunath told her with a nod. "But, it might be hard." He replied with a small frown.

Corbin looked to Zangrunath. "Deal?" He dragged out.

Zangrunath sighed as he cleaned. "I am sure that you have heard about people making deals to gain power, fame, and money. Right?" He asked him. "Same thing here. Just a lot more complicated steps involved."

Ellyria looked at the panicked look in Corbin's eyes. "I accepted the terms and conditions without reading."

Corbin looked to Ellyria. "I don't want to lose you to him." He pointed at Zangrunath.

"Corbin," she frowned, not knowing what words to use to help him, "I'm sorry." She finished lamely.

Zangrunath looked at the two of them, and sighed. "If it makes you feel any better, one, I don't take her soul. Secondly, it will be a while before this is complete, and c, only when she gets her dream come true, does she lose her soul." He explained to the two of them, smirking when he saw both of them get aggravated by the way he'd bulleted his list.

"Yeah, I was under the impression that I finish living after the contract is up." She agreed, ignoring Zane's idiosyncrasies for what felt like the millionth time.

Zangrunath shrugged. "It differs from person to person, but, when the contract is complete, I go away, and you live out your life for some unknown amount of time before you pass on." He explained to her. "It more so depends on how much use you serve the big guy."

"Ugh!" She groaned. "Stop. I don't want to think about it."

"Smart move." Zangrunath told her honestly.

Corbin shook his head as he processed what he'd just heard. He let out a long, drawn out sigh. After a moment, he took Ellyria's hand. "I just want to be there when you accomplish your dream." He told her. "And, as much time after that as I can."

She kissed him, and some of her tears met his lips. "Thank you." She whispered. "I love you." Ellyria leaned into him, eyes closing. "I'm so tired." She slurred in her exhaustion. "Must've used a lot of magic earlier."

"I love you, too." Corbin smiled back at her, and held her close to him. "Get some rest." He told Ellyria, lifting her up, and bringing her to her bedroom.

Zangrunath sighed, and continued to clean. "No, I got this, you two go relax." He mumbled under his breath.

Once Ellyria was comfortably in bed and tucked in, Corbin came back out. "Where do you need the light bulbs?"

Zangrunath glanced at him, and pointed in the direction of the garage. "In there. She vaporized them all." He grumbled. "Also, in the hallway, too."

"Wow." Corbin commented, taking the boxes of bulbs, and turning on the flashlight on his cell phone before heading into the garage.

"You should be lucky that you weren't here." Zangrunath told him conversationally. "Doubt you would have lasted long."

After a minute, Corbin came back. "So, it was more than the stuff she did in that clearing?" He asked, starting to work on the bulbs in the hall.

Zangrunath stopped, and thought it over. Then, he looked at Corbin seriously. "She did that, plus being able to take me on in my actual form." He sighed, getting the last of the blood cleaned up. "She also messed with gravity, and undid damage. Still trying to figure that out." He shook his head, and shrugged, looking baffled.

Corbin popped his head around the corner to look at Zangrunath properly. "Is that last bit not a normal magicky thing? I only know the one witch."

"It can be done with magic, yes," Zangrunath told him seriously, "but it didn't feel like normal magic. She wasn't repairing the damage. She was undoing it." He told the human. "Like, rewinding time." He explained. "Be warned, Corn cob, she is a strong one." He moved to go and fix a few broken pieces of glass.

He made a face, but didn't comment. He looked around the place, and just started to help clean, placing Ellyria's cake on the counter while he was at it.

Zangrunath looked at the cake and paused, looking at Corbin with a curious look. "You really do like her, don't you?" He asked, already knowing the answer.

"We kind of grew up together. I just took a long time to realize it." He smiled.

Zangrunath made a face. "Well, whatever you do, don't hurt her. Because, if she asks me to, I won't hesitate to turn you into a fine mist." He smiled at him.

Corbin nodded, but his eyes looked wide like saucers. "Noted." He glanced around the place. "Looks good. I'm gonna hit the sack. Work is going to suck tomorrow night."

"You should call off." Zangrunath told him seriously. "I'm not letting her go anywhere tomorrow. She will need the rest. I don't want you going off and telling everyone what I actually am. Even if it is accidental."

Corbin looked at him, and sighed, he was too tired to deal with this right now. "Fine. I will stay here tomorrow. Better?"

"Yes." Zangrunath responded before he waved the boy off, and went back to his deep cleaning.

Corbin turned, and made his way down the hall to Ellyria's room. He laid down next to her, closing his eyes. Sleep found him quickly as he snuggled up to Ellyria.

ARTICLE IV

Monday, March 30, 2020

Ellyria stepped forward in line. She made sure to keep people six feet in front of and behind her. She rolled her eyes. Social distancing was stupid. At least, she didn't have to wear a mask. The line moved again, and she shuffled forward. This was a poorly planned nightmare. She just wanted to have normal high school. Her classes earlier today had been laughable. Teachers and students not knowing how to use simple, labeled buttons or figure out echoing microphones and speakers. Now, she was picking up supplies for her home economics class that she probably already had at home. She didn't even think that it would matter if she tried to use it. "Congrats on the easy A for the rest of the year." She snarked mentally to Zane.

A smiled appeared back in her head. "Same to you, it will give me so much more time to plan ahead for things." He told her honestly. He gave a small grumble. "And, it will be far better to not be around these- idiots." He commented as a boy couldn't stay away from a group of girls.

She smirked to herself. "You didn't have to go to school with them when they were younger and stupider. Count yourself lucky."

"I have seen people literally walk headfirst into their deaths when it could have been easily avoidable by simply taking a moment and looking." He sighed deeply. "At least, I don't have that issue with you."

"I'm not an idiot." She replied, stepping forward, and sighing. Seriously, how long did it take to hand people a bag of stuff? "I wonder how Corbin's classes went." She paused, remembering he had a full schedule, "are going." She corrected.

Zane gave a mental shrug. "Not really important, but he is probably doing well." He commented idly. "He seems fairly smart, so I take it he is almost done for the day." He surmised.

She nodded, and sighed somewhat impatiently. "Sorry. It's just been, like, a week since I've seen him. Thanks, pandemic."

"I get it. You are in the 'young love' phase of your relationship." He told her with a small chuckle. "You just want to ride him." He told her in an uncaring, yet teasing, voice.

"I mean, yes, but no." She replied as honestly as she could. "Seeing him every day is normal. I miss normal."

He shrugged in her head. "I am used to random and spontaneous events, so I can't exactly say that normal is what I prefer." He told her honestly. "But, if it helps you, I will try to keep things as normal as possible."

She gave a stiff nod, knowing that she was supposed to be alone in public. "I know that I've gotten the Vatican on our backs and we're in weird COVID times, but, yeah, as best you can, would be nice."

Zane gave her a mental nod. "I have done a pretty good job so far, if I do say so myself." He told her with a chuckle. "I will continue doing my best to keep it that way."

"Thank you." She murmured as she got to the front of the line. She smiled, seeing that Mr. Harrison was the lucky winner of distribution duty. "Can I please get mine and Zane's things? Please, and thank you."

Mr. Harrison nodded, and smiled behind his mask. It was visible in the crinkles near his eyes. "Of course." He told her, turning to get the things she and Zane needed in order to do their schoolwork. "Where is Zane? I was expecting to see him here today. He is normally very punctual." He commented as he started to fill the bags.

Ellyria stiffened for a second, and thought quickly. She hadn't planned to answer that question. "He's actually around here somewhere, but he disappeared to talk to someone." She chuckled, being as honest as she could.

"Well, I hope to see him soon, then." He chuckled, handing her the bags. "Have a good rest of your day, and be sure to mask up!" He told her seriously, going to the next student, and starting to get them situated.

"Of course." She sighed, slouching a bit as she walked away, carrying the bags. "I don't want to wear a mask." She complained to Zane.

"You don't have to, but I understand the annoyance." He assured her mentally. "If need be, I can always-" He suddenly stopped as he felt a tug come from the back of Ellyria's head. "Fucking kill someone." He mentally growled, seeing Heather with a lock of her hair.

Ellyria turned around to see Heather, and sneered. "You know, the thing about cat fights is, normally, you know you're in one."

Heather gave a small smirk, taking a step back as she did so. "Oh, don't mind me. I'm just getting a memento." She told her with a little wave.

Ellyria watched Heather step back, and kept watching for a second. This was just getting weird. "This isn't, like, grade school, right? I'm not going to find out that the girl that tugs my hair has a huge crush on me?"

Heather made a face at her, and scoffed. "Please, I wouldn't be caught dead with someone the likes of you." She gave a grand flip of her hair, and walked away, pocketing the lock of hair. A victorious smirk gracing her features as she did so.

Ellyria sighed. "Thank G-" She paused. "Meh. Not going there, so, I guess, thank Lucifer." She giggled to herself at that one. She turned around, starting to walk off towards home again.

Zangrunath watched Heather walk off, and commented into Ellyria's head. "Please, just say the word, and I will end her bloodline." He told her in a half serious tone, clearly fed up with that woman.

"How about you just keep her a respectable pandemic distance away from me?" She countered. "I don't like this ordering you around stuff." She added.

"So be it." He told her with a half-sigh. "I will make sure we never have to go near her again." He commented simply, focusing more on where they were going now.

She nodded. "Thank you." She told him as she walked with her bags past a van with tinted windows that was much too nice for the area she lived in. She gulped, and ignored the urge to walk faster. "Let's just get home." She sighed, seeing her house getting close.

He nodded, and kept a vigilant eye around them. "Don't worry. I will keep you safe." He assured her. "Even if these Vatican bastards have no idea how to be stealthy." He chuckled as they walked.

She took a deep breath. "Have I mentioned that this has been the scariest month of my life?"

"Relax." He told her in a calming tone. "There is nothing they can do to you. They will have to get through me first, and I am an extremely hard person to kill." He said, trying to reassure her.

"Okay." She murmured, getting to the front door silently after a few more seconds, and unlocking it. She quickly stepped inside, and locked it, slouching up against one of the walls. "I hate this." She groaned.

Zane appeared next to her a moment later, and looked down at her. "Relax, you will be fine." He told her, picking up the bags, and bringing them to be put away. "They can't do anything to you. They have nothing to go on. You will be fine."

She nodded weakly, and sighed. "Doesn't make knowing that they have guns and having felt a gunshot wound recently any better, though."

A small sigh escaped his lips. "Just go do your schoolwork, and think of Corbin or something." He told her simply, getting fed up with the train of thought she was stuck on.

She took a deep breath, and let it out as a growl. Sometimes, he really knew how to piss her off. She pulled her phone out of her pocket and dialed Corbin. She needed a distraction.

Friday, April 10, 2020

Ellyria and Corbin stole a kiss from each other as they walked out of his house from dinner. She smiled over at him as he got into the Shelby in the driver's seat. "Thanks for that. Your Dad is hilarious, and your Mom is super sweet. Who knew Good Friday dinner could be so fun for someone like me?"

Corbin smiled as he started the car. "Yeah, they're pretty awesome. I'm glad you had fun. Was kinda worried there for a minute." He chuckled.

"Worried?" She asked, thinking about that for a second. "Oh, Corb, I'm not worried about the Dad thing."

"Not that." He chuckled. "The whole religious part. You know, with demon boy being around all the time. I was afraid that you might catch on fire or something."

She laughed at that, nudging him a bit. "Oh, come on. It's not like any of the things we know about demons from books and whatever have been true. He passes through salt lines."

"And, he can go into churches as well?" He asked her curiously. "I would have thought differently on that." He hummed to himself.

"Hey, Zane?" She asked the air. "Can you go to church?"

"No." Zangrunath's voice called out. "Only the Dark Prince himself can do that."

She thought about that. "What if I give you magic?"

There was a moment of quietness before he spoke again. "I'm not sure. If you did, it would need to be a lot. Even then, it might only be temporary." He told her as honestly as he could guess at.

"It's fine. I don't really intend to go. Mostly just curious." She looked over at Corbin. "There you go. No churches, but family meals are fine."

"Good to know." He smiled at her, placing a hand on her leg as he drove.

Ellyria smiled, looking at him as they drove through the stop sign on Grand. Her eyes went wide, and she screamed seconds before it happened. "Corbin!" Her hands moved up to reach him in order to uselessly protect him, but she was knocked back a second later as the world started to spin. A loud boom that sounded and smelled like gunfire rang out. Glass shattered all around them, and the world went dark.

The first few moments after the crash, there was an eerie silence. The now destroyed sixty-nine Shelby moved seemingly of its own accord as the shadow of the car began to take the shape of a wounded demon. Zangrunath seethed in anger before looking to Ellyria. She was alive. Corbin was not. He turned his focus to the cause of the collision, seeing a large semi-truck idling there with a partially crunched front end. He yelled a war cry, and charged at the vehicle, cutting into the front of it. He tore into the engine block in order to get to the driver.

A demonic hand tore through the dashboard, and Zangrunath pulled himself out to lay his eyes on who he was killing. In the driver's seat, he saw a young man who was shaking in fear. What really got his attention, though, was the demon that was controlling him. All the telltale signs there as he noticed the somewhat dazed and lethargic look that went along with each of his movements. Zangrunath felt his rage grow to new heights, swiftly killed the man in his rage. Before it could get away, he grabbed the demon by his neck. He squeezed his throat, hearing the satisfying sound of cracking. He watched with glee as the demon's face changed color. Finally, he made a wrenching motion, and removed the other demon's head from his shoulders.

Zangrunath seethed, destroying the truck before he went to help Ellyria. He took the door off the car, and gently picked her up. A pair of leathery, batlike wings that he normally kept hidden sprouted from his back, and he flew her home as fast as possible.

The cool night air made Ellyria stir, and she groaned in pain before her eyes opened. She coughed, and gripped her side. Her head was pounding. She let out a little sob. Her whole body ached. She searched out with her magic, so that she didn't have to move. She spoke into Zangrunath's head. "What happened?" Even her mental voice sounded like it had been through Hell.

"There was a crash." He told her simply, as they flew back to the house.

"What?" She asked.

"A truck hit the side of the car." He told her. He was still aggravated by the night's events. "Another demon attacked us. I think it was the Vatican." He growled as he landed in the backyard, bringing her inside.

She opened her eyes, and looked up at him. There were already tears in her eyes. Memories were starting to come back to her. "Corbin." She muttered brokenly.

He brought her to her room, and laid her down gently. "He didn't make it." He informed her quietly. "I'm sorry."

She curled into a ball, and started to cry in earnest. "No. No. Please, no."

He looked away. "I'm sorry. There was nothing I could do."

She grabbed onto his hand, and pulled him close, holding the demon for comfort without realizing what she was doing. She cried hard for a long time as she unconsciously started to channel magic into Zangrunath. "Please," she begged, not knowing what she was asking for at the moment.

He put his arm around her, and rubbed her shoulder as he felt her magic go into him. His wounds were healing faster now. "I cannot lie to you." He told her. "He is gone. I'm sorry."

She didn't hesitate. The situation all but making the decision easy for her. "Kill them," she whispered the order, "whoever did this." Feeling exhaustion beginning to pull her under, she closed her eyes, and cried herself to sleep.

"With pleasure." He responded with a growl, giving a nod. As he left the room, he stepped into the garage, and drew a circle. Inside of that, he drew an incredibly intricate series of sigils. He had to make sure that this trip would be fast. Ellyria would be alone, but he needed to learn about the summoner of that demon. This was personal, so he was going to pull every string he could before he got to rend their bones into flour. He stood in the center of the circle, and muttered the incantation. He was going to Hell.

As a small spark lit the circle, flames quickly engulfing Zangrunath just before he disappeared. He instantaneously appeared in front of a black, iron gate. Parts of it were red hot, and spikes of varying sizes protruded from the structure. At seemingly random intervals, skulls adorned it like trophies. He marched through with a purpose, but there were several other demons guarding the gates, looking at him curiously.

One of the demons looked nervous, given the anger and stature of Zangrunath in their ranks. He called out, giving the other demon pause. "Aren't you on a contract, right now?"

"I'm here on business." Zangrunath quipped back, making the group of demons nod, and move out of his way. Before him stood the impossibly large city of Hell. He spread his wings, and flew towards the center, passing over millions of tortured souls that all desperately wanted to end their eternal suffering.

He made his way to a tall structure, and headed inside. He marched up to the main desk, and slammed his hands on the table. "I was attacked by a welp of a demon! I want to know whose existence I am ending."

The room went silent, and a demon with a cloth covering blind eyes walked out of the back room. Hundreds of piercings covered his body, bearing chains and keys. "Explain." He stated calmly.

Zangrunath sighed, which sounded more like a growl, and leveled a gaze at the Keeper of Contracts. At least, with him involved, he was dealing with the highest-ranking demon here. "I was summoned to the mortal plane under an Annihilation Ritual. As per the bylaws of the demon code, no demon under me can interfere." He told the demon seriously. "The witch that summoned me is now gravely injured, and the insolent welp that attacked me is dead, for the time being until he can re-form." He explained. "I want to know who just broke the code."

The Keeper of Contracts looked blindly through Zangrunath, judging him, and trying to determine if there were any fallacies in his story. Once he was certain that Zangrunath's words were true, he waved him to the back. "Follow me." The clinking of keys against each other the only sounds between them at the moment.

The Keeper of Contracts led him into an office-like room and, then, through a set of doors opened into stairs that lead them down. They walked for several minutes as the heat around them increased, and hot spots of magma glowed in the walls, bearing the only light here. The staircase opened into a massive room full of various types of parchment and scrolls. They walked through hundreds of aisles of contracts, ranging from simple cash deals to exchanges of leadership and power. Finally, they stood before a set of blood red doors. The Keeper of Contracts opened them with a key attached to one of the many piercings on his body the chain it was attached to seeming to elongate and bend the distance at will.

Inside of this room, there were much fewer contracts, and even fewer shelves. On the opposite end of this room, there were three contracts, glowing red, and hanging up on the wall. The Keeper walked up to the middle one, and pointed to it. "This is your contract." He told Zangrunath seriously, pointing to the contract just to the right of it. "This is the contract of the one that attacked you. The caster wants your witch dead by any means necessary. This, of course, extends to you, by proxy." He explained. "The Annihilation Ritual is the only way to counter the Demon Code." He finished.

Zangrunath was about to speak before the Keeper spoke again. "However, there is no way for this contract to come to fruition."

"How so?" Zangrunath asked simply, looking curious as to what he just heard.

"The witch that made this deal was much weaker than your witch, and you are far stronger than the unlucky one that was summoned." The Keeper of Contracts smirked. "That renders this one's contract null and void." He told Zangrunath seriously. "Their contract cannot be completed, and we do not make deals that cannot be upheld." He turned to the wall, and took the contract in question down, placing it into Zangrunath's hands. "Get your information. Then, leave. Put that back when you are done." The Keeper ordered, leaving him alone in the room.

Zangrunath smiled widely, and let out a menacing laugh. He quickly looked over the contract, and found something rather odd. There was no mention of the Vatican. A puzzled look graced his features before he began to get angry. The name on the contract was for a witch named Heather.

It took all Zangrunath's control to not tear the contract in half where he stood. Instead, motes of fire escaped his nostrils, and he did as he was told. He put it back, and left the room, nodding to the Keeper of Contracts. Just before Zangrunath's feet met the bottom most steps of the stairs back up to the surface to make his way out of the building, the Keeper spoke to him. "Raise Hell."

"Of course." Zangrunath smiled back. He quickly made his way back to the gate, and, in an instant, found himself back in Ellyria's garage. He looked around at the room, seeing an aged wall clock. A few hours had passed. He growled, going back inside to check on Ellyria. He needed to make that sure she was safe. He was going to make sure that she was never hurt again.

Unaware of Zangrunath's sudden departure, Ellyria slept for as long as she could before the adrenaline in her system wore off, and she woke up in agony. She let out a little cry of pain, rolling out of bed to grab ibuprofen from the medicine cabinet. With shaking hands, she took out four pills, and swallowed them dry before she finally worked up the courage to look in the mirror. She instantly frowned. Her forehead was covered in blood, and there was clearly a bump on the back of her head, which explained the throbbing pain there and the ringing of her ears. There were scrapes on her face where the glass had gotten her, and she had a bruise running from the top of her right shoulder across her body from the seatbelt. All her muscles ached, and it hurt to move or stand upright. She grumbled as she shuffled back to her bedroom.

Zangrunath saw Ellyria still in her damaged state. He made a face, and took a step towards her. "I need you to tell me something." He asked her, sounding a bit hesitant to speak. "I need to know where Heather lives." He told her quickly, still under her previous order.

She thought about it for a minute. "The nice part of town across the highway, like, three houses down from Todd. Her parents are loaded."

"Good." He replied simply. "I found out who did this. It was her."

"What? Why? How?" She replied, sitting down heavily against the headboard. "She's not like me. I would know. I could sense it."

"You're right, but she isn't like you. She is weaker." He explained in a firm tone. "I don't know why she did it, but she wants us dead. In doing so, she used the Annihilation Ritual to see it through." He explained for her. "I will make sure she dies. Mark my words."

Ellyria nodded sadly. "What do you need from me?" She asked, ready to get up and out of bed, if need be.

"Nothing." He told her, moving closer to sit her back down into the bed. "You just rest. I will end her and burn her house down for good measure."

"I need to go with you, don't I?" She asked. "Fifty feet and whatnot?"

"Only if I don't have an order." He informed her with a smirk. "If I am ordered to go somewhere or to do something, I can do it with almost no restrictions."

She nodded, wiping away a tear. Of course, now, he informs her that she could have ordered him away at any time. "Uh, would you mind grabbing me a pint while you're out? I need to drown my sorrows with Ben and Jerry's."

He chuckled, and gave her a nod. "What flavor?"

"Chunky monkey." She replied.

"It will be done." He bowed. He straightened up, and turned around. "I will be back in an hour, at most. If anything happens, just let me know. I will be back in an instant." He told her as he made his way to the door.

She nodded. "Oh, and Zane?"

He turned to look at her. "Yes?"

"Bring me her severed head." She glowered.

Zangrunath let out an evil smile. "I will." He chuckled, disappearing before her eyes. He quickly became a shadow, and dashed towards Heather's house. It didn't take him long to find the structure he suspected. It took longer to double check that he had the correct location than it took to get there. He turned into his human form, and knocked at the door, smiling as he waited for somebody to answer.

A Hispanic woman in a maid's uniform answered. In a heavy accent, she greeted in English, "yes?"

Zangrunath smiled at the woman, and made an educated guess, seamlessly replying in her native language. "Good evening, ma'am. Is Heather home?" He asked with an enchanting smile.

The woman nodded, and smiled, letting Zangrunath into the foyer as she walked out of the room to fetch Heather. He heard her speaking from down the hall. "There is cute boy to see you." She informed the young lady in her heavy accent.

Zangrunath chuckled as he heard that. Perhaps Ellyria was right about his disguise. It might have stuck out a bit too much. However, it wouldn't matter in a few short moments. He waited for Heather to show her face, calmly biding his time until it was time for action. A few minutes later, he smiled widely at the blonde when he saw her arrive. "Hello, Heather. We need to talk." He menaced.

Heather stopped walking when she saw him, taking a step back into the hallway. "You." She muttered coolly.

"Me indeed." He chuckled, starting to stalk towards her. "I have a few questions to ask you."

He saw her reach into a pouch in her comfortable looking cargo pants, and light something with magic. "Stay away from me." She warned, thinking that the herb was strong enough to fend off a demon like Zangrunath.

He saw the sage starting to smolder, and almost wanted to sigh. Instead, he decided to have some fun with her. He recoiled in mock horror, looking her dead in the eyes. "What are you going to do to me?" He asked, pretending to be afraid of her.

"Purify you." She replied fiercely, sending the smoke his way with the wave of her hand. She summoned a tiny orb of pure magic, and tossed it at him. It struck, and lit up the room with bright light. She smirked, satisfied by a job well done. That was almost too easy. Maybe, she didn't need to summon that demon after all.

When the light faded, Zangrunath was gone from her view, and he was nowhere to be seen.

Heather flung hair over her shoulder, and turned around to go back to her room. "Good riddance." She sniffed. "Those things are so weak. Useless demons."

There was a moment of quiet before the whole house boomed with Zangrunath's voice. His voice coming from everywhere and nowhere at once. "You are pathetic."

Heather jumped, spinning all around, trying to find the enemy, but there was none to be seen. "What the? Mom!" She screamed in a panic.

"Oh, she won't be able to help you." Zangrunath's voice called out with an evil chuckle. "No one will be able to save you from what you have just unleashed upon yourself. Not even that pathetic excuse for a demon you summoned." He growled. "Where is he? I want to tear his head off again." His laughter making the walls shake.

She gulped. "H- he hasn't come back yet."

"Figures." He sighed. That was somewhat disappointing. "Then, I guess I better just get started with you." He chuckled, appearing behind her in his true demonic form.

Seeing the large demon, Heather screamed, making a break for the door.

As the girl turned to run, Zangrunath spotted a familiar stone glowing on a chain around her neck. It was the one that Ellyria had given to Corbin. He quickly appeared in front of Heather, making sure that there was plenty of smoke and brimstone. He smirked as she sputtered and coughed when she gasped it in. His fingers grasped the stone from around her neck, and yanked the necklace off with some force. His smile widening when he grabbed the pathetic waste of oxygen in front of him by the throat, lifting her up off the ground. "Why did you do it?" He demanded.

"I don't know!" She lied.

He threw her back into the wall several feet behind her, and stepped closer. "Bullshit! You performed that ritual knowing full well what the outcome would be. Now, tell me why!" He raged at her. His eyes glowing fiery red.

"He was supposed to be mine. I'm the strong one. The pretty one, and she took him from me. Always talking about me behind my back, playing pranks on me. Getting me in trouble!" She began with a stutter, and finished with fervor.

"No, he wasn't." Zangrunath reasoned as he got closer to her with every measured, torturous step. "You are weak. You merely conjured a peon while Ellyria summoned me, a general in Hell's armies." He smirked, spreading his arms and wings wide. "And, everyone talks about you, Corbin included. You were never going to be what he wanted. In the end, you won't even be remembered. You are and have always been a pathetic waste of space."

"He's better off dead than with her, and I hope she rots in Hell after summoning you." Heather spat, getting her last jabs in while she could. She could do nothing against this demon. She knew it was the end.

He growled, and grabbed her arm, ripping it from her shoulder in an instant, and throwing it whimsically to the side. "You will not talk about her like that!" He demanded. "He made her happy, and she won't rot. She will rule!" He yelled loudly at her before he grabbed her head and wrenched it from her shoulders.

A few minutes later, Zangrunath flew away from the burning remains of Heather's house. He managed to grab a few items that he thought Ellyria might like, and, now, he headed to the store to get her the ice cream she wanted. After his orders were through, he appeared before Ellyria, and handed her the treat. "It is done."

She took the small carton. "Can I please get a spoon? I don't think I can move at the moment."

He waved a hand, and a spoon appeared in his hand. "Here you go." He offered, handing the utensil to her.

She opened the container, and started to practically inhale the dessert. She hummed a bit, leaning back, and resting her head on the wall. She paused her eating for a moment. "Sorry. Can I get an ice pack too? My whole body aches."

"Just rest." He told her, quickly disappearing and reappearing with an ice pack. "Even with faster healing, it will still take time to fully recover." He told her truthfully.

"Thanks." She patted the bed next to her. "Would you mind staying close? I kind of don't want to be alone, right now."

Zangrunath nodded, and sat down beside her as she'd asked. "I can do that."

She took another bite of ice cream. "Did you actually bring me a skull?" She asked.

"I did," he nodded, "but I figured you would want to wait a bit before you saw it." He told her honestly.

"You're right." She nodded. "Kinda want to feel better before I deal with that."

He reached behind him, and took out the stone he'd gotten off Heather. "I think this might help. It might not be much, but it is something." He handed her the quartz stone.

She gave him a bitter smile, and took the quartz necklace as fresh tears streaked her face. "Yeah. It helps." She clutched it to her chest. "It wasn't enough to protect him." She let out another sniffle. "Why am I never enough, Zane?"

He shook his head, and lifted her chin. "No, you are far stronger than you know." He told her honestly. "You summoned me, and that in itself is a feat very few have been able to do." He assured her, looking into her eyes. "You are the strongest witch I have ever met, and I will make sure that nothing bad happens to you ever again."

She leaned against him, and sniffed. "Thank you. I needed that." After a minute, she sighed. "Can you do me a favor?"

"Of course. All you have to do is ask." He told her honestly.

"When the- the police are done with the Shelby, I want it." She sighed.

"I will do that." He promised with a nod. "Do you want me to fix it up as well?" He asked her.

She shook her head a little. "I'll do it."

"Alright." He agreed with her. "I will get it as soon as I can."

Her lip quivered a bit. "One more thing." Her voice broke.

He raised an eyebrow. "Yes?" He asked curiously.

"He went to the good place. Right?" She cried, voice breaking even though her words came out as a whisper.

He held her closely, and rubbed her back. "More than likely." He told her as best he could, not entirely sure. "He was a good guy, so he certainly didn't go below." He sighed, telling her the truth. "I am sorry."

"Good." She whispered, taking a big bite of ice cream.

He went quiet for a few minutes before he remembered one of the things he got from Heather's house. "I did manage to get this. She won't be needing it anymore." He handed her a small grimoire, which was bound using modern bookbinding techniques. Her own was much, much older.

She looked down at the book, and opened it, flipping through the pages. "It's not even bound in blood." She paused a minute. "Not that I'm complaining."

"She was weak," Zangrunath commented, "so that doesn't surprise me. That book will serve far more use in your hands."

"There's already some things I haven't read before." She commented, flipping through randomly. She looked up at the demon, and smiled. "Thank you."

"It was no problem." He assured her, smiling back. "Will there be anything else you need?" He asked, standing up.

"Just the usual. Maybe keep Mom from coming in here? I don't want her to worry." She groaned, moving the ice pack to a different spot.

"Will do." He nodded, moving to the door. "Now, if you will excuse me. I have to deal with police reports, and such." He sighed, leaving Ellyria alone for the time being.

Ellyria finished her ice cream, and laid down. Tomorrow would be better. Rest always made things better, she reassured herself.

As she rested, Zangrunath waited for the police to arrive. He knew they would, there were going to be some serious questions needing answers. All of which he couldn't answer honestly. So, Zangrunath decided to tell them a simple, yet effective, lie. Corbin had already dropped Ellyria off, and was heading home when the accident occurred. He would only have to use a small bit of magic to make the effect work, and, if they asked to speak to Ellyria, he would deal with that the same way. He would just make sure she got the uninterrupted rest she needed.

ARTICLE V

Monday, April 13, 2020

When Monday morning came, Ellyria looked normal, but her body still ached. She didn't want to go to school, even virtually, but appearances were important. So, she pulled on a baggy shirt, and a pair of pajama pants. It was all she could summon the energy to get dressed in, and walked to the kitchen to get some coffee, searching the cupboards frantically for a bag when she found none left in the container on the counter. She groaned. "Can we get coffee? I feel like death warmed over."

"Of course." Zangrunath nodded, gently placing a hand on her back, and leading her out the door. They locked up, and hopped in the Grand Prix.

"Sorry I'm so needy, but I need you to run interference today. I really don't want to talk to anybody." She sighed.

"That is fine. Just mute yourself. It'll be easy." He replied.

She nodded. "Thank you, Zangrunath. Sorry, I forgot your title. General Zangrunath."

He gave her a look, and shook his head. "In Hell, I am a general. Here, I am your servant. There is no need to apologize."

She shook her head. "You're not a servant. I haven't been pulling my weight. Thank you for helping make things easy for a while."

"On paper, I am one." He told her in response. "And, the only reason you were hurt in the first place was because I failed to protect you." He apologized with a low growl. "I should have done better."

She shook her head slightly. "You're a general on leave from his army. That's all. And, we both screwed up. There were signs written on the walls, but we missed it."

He gave a slight nod, but remained quiet for a while, turning into the drive thru of the coffee shop. "What would you like?" He asked her as they waited in line.

"Get me a grande black eye in a venti cup with half and half and raw sugar." She told him. "Oh, and you might as well get a pound of their house blend ground."

"I have questions. What is a black eye? And, why did you say large, and twenty?" He asked her seriously.

She smirked. "A black eye is two shots of espresso in drip coffee. Their cup sizes are short, tall, grande, venti, and trenta."

"They need to go take Latin. Half of those are sizes, and the other half are numbers." He sighed, shaking his head. "I don't like this place." He muttered as he arrived at the speaker and placed her order.

"I know that. You know that. Half of America- not so much." She shrugged, pulling out a couple bills for him to pay with.

He took the money, and gave it to the lady to pay for the coffee. He took the change and handed it back to Ellyria before he handed her the drink. "Here you go." He said, offering the cup to her. He waited just another moment for the bag of coffee, handing that to Ellyria as well.

She took the cup and drank deeply. "Oh, yes." She whispered, sighing with relief as she gripped the bag of coffee like it was a lifeline.

He gave her a small smile before he started to drive them back home. "Good, hopefully that should help you."

"Thank you. You're my hero." She murmured.

Zangrunath scoffed at the comment. "If I am a hero, the villain must be worse than the Dark Prince himself."

"Whoever is pulling the strings in the Vatican is on my list." She told him bluntly.

He gave her a nod. "I hope it is just locally. Because, if this goes overseas, we will have a big problem." He told her truthfully.

She looked at him wearily. "What are we in for?"

"If it is locally, we should be able to deal with it. Might just need to get to the right person to end all of this." He told her before letting out a sigh. "If it is the full power of the Vatican, you will need to draw much more power from the ley lines in order for me to fight them off." He told her honestly.

"Great." She sighed, taking another sip of coffee.

"I know. I don't want that either. I intend to make sure you don't get hurt ever again." He told her as he pulled into the driveway.

She looked at him, and took his hand, squeezing it. "Thank you."

He looked down at her hand and, then, to her. "Don't worry about it. It is my job." He assured her with a small smirk.

She shook her head. "I highly doubt that any of your other comrades would take such good care of me. It's personal for you."

He gave her a nod. "Of all the contracts I have ever been a part of, none of my summoners have ever died. You were the closest one to breaking that record by a considerable margin. Yeah, it is personal." He agreed, getting out of the car and getting the door for her.

She took his hand, and groaned as she stood. "I just have to fake it for a little while." She pumped herself up.

"You will make it through the day." He reassured her.

"Thanks." She stood up straight, and several bones cracked. "Let's. Do. The thing."

He nodded and followed behind her, keeping a careful eye out for any possible threats.

As they made the short trip from the driveway to the front door, she could feel the stares of the Vatican spies on her back. Despite Zane's proximity, it made her feel slightly terrified even to be at her own home. She wanted to cast the non-detection spell to make them stop looking, but knew that she couldn't. She muttered a few curses under her breath.

"Just ignore them." He told her simply, letting them back into the house.

She held her head up as best she could and stepped inside. "If I need to ignore them, you need to relax, at least, a little."

Zangrunath continued to look around for a moment longer before he tried to relax. "It will be hard." He told her with a sigh. "Heather got part of your hair while I was supposed to be protecting you." He worried aloud.

Ellyria placed down the package of coffee, and walked into her bedroom with the coffee cup. She sat down in her bed, opened her laptop, and logged into her classroom. "I know." She told him in his head. "At least, we should be fine during school hours."

He looked around the room and, then, out the window. "More than likely. It would be too high profile for them to do that." He replied in her head. He sighed, and reluctantly sat down beside Ellyria to keep up appearances with the school.

Mrs. Dorsett's camera turned on, and everybody was muted a second later as she called the class to attention. After a quick head count, she started speaking. "Good morning, everybody." She told them quietly. "I'm sure some of you heard the news over the weekend. Principal Jones has called a special online assembly for you kids to reflect and heal during this tough time."

Ellyria's eyes went somewhat wide, and she sniffed once, looking like she was about to tear up. She clicked the button to turn off the camera, and ran out of her room towards the bathroom. The sound of a slamming door echoing around the house a moment later.

Zangrunath sighed, and followed Ellyria into the bathroom. "Are you all right?" He asked as she wretched into the toilet.

"Physically." She grumbled in response, laying her back against the wall. "I hate this. I'm so close. This online thing is useless. I don't want to go anymore."

He gave her a nod. "I will see what I can do."

"Please don't take that as an order. I know we've got to pretend like everything is normal." She sighed.

"If you don't want to attend today, just say the word." He told her honestly. "It won't be difficult to do. I think people would understand."

"Why do the people I love keep dying?" She whispered.

He let out a sigh. "I don't know, but I can make sure that no more die while I am still around." He responded, offering her the idea.

She sniffed. "As long as you stay around, I'll be okay."

"I will stay until I help make your dream come true." He told her, offering his hand to help pick her up.

She stood up, and pulled him into a hug. "I'm sorry. It's just-" She trailed off.

He held her for a moment before pulling away slightly. "You will be fine. You are strong."

She took a breath, and paused. She looked down to her quartz necklace, and gripped it for a minute as it lightly pulsed an odd color in her hand. Her eyes closed, and, when they reopened, she looked better. "Woah."

"What happened?" He asked her, a little confused.

She moved around, feeling her muscles. "I remembered the new way to fix things from my birthday."

He blinked at her for a moment before he spoke. "And, how did you do that? Did you rewind time?" He asked, half joking, half serious.

"It's not time. It's," she stopped speaking, "no wonder they want me dead, Zane."

"What is it?" He asked her seriously.

She looked up at him, and her eyes were full of fear as she told him mentally. "Matter."

"You can rewind matter." He replied in her head, holding the bridge of his nose. "Fuck." He groaned.

She shook her head. "I think that I can rebuild it. Like, you could give me lead, and..."

"You could turn it into gold." He finished in disbelief. "Breaking the fundamental laws of the universe."

"I don't think it's a subsection of the Vatican." She mumbled.

"No, it's not." He sighed before letting out a growl. "You need to keep your powers on the quiet side for a while." He warned her. "We need to lay low."

She nodded. "If my Dad could do this-"

"He would have been a target, too." He replied to her. "How did he die again?" He asked her seriously now.

"A car accident." She responded bluntly.

"And, did they ever get the person who did it?" He asked, trying to make sure it wasn't as big as he thought it might be.

She shook her head. "It was a hit and run. They never found the other person. The car was stolen."

Zangrunath sighed deeply, nodding as he did so. "Of course, it was."

"Is there any way to talk to him outside of the Articulation Ritual on Samhain?" She asked.

"We go to the ley line, and do it there." He told her, shaking his head as he suggested that. "Given your power, it should be simple, but," he trailed off.

"It turns on a beacon of, 'come get me I'm powerful but busy'." She surmised.

"Yup." He immediately responded, popping the 'p'.

She thought for a minute, pacing back and forth in the small bathroom. "Is there an untraceable way out of town?"

He gave her a look, and nodded. "Yes, but it involves me possessing you in order to do it."

She nodded. "Find us a ley line a safe distance away, and we'll do it."

"Alright, we just need to get through the day. " He agreed, gesturing back to her room and laptop. "I can do a search when we're done."

"How do you search, typically?" She asked.

"It is like a sixth sense." He explained to her. "I assume it is how you feel it. I can see it, but not in the same way you would call 'seeing'."

"Oh, good. I thought you were going to say we were looking it up on the internet. That's traceable." She sighed, walking out of the bathroom like someone marching to war. She thought for a minute. "What's possession like?"

"It is like having your body worked like a puppet, with you having no say in what happens once it starts." He told her simply.

She gulped, but nodded. "You can- use my magic?"

"Yes." He nodded. "But, not with the same proficiency you can. It would be like wearing weights for me. I would have difficulty using it. It is mostly used for getting into places and tricking people."

Ellyria sat down on her bed, and saw that Mrs. Dorsett's online classroom was empty of all but her, now. She sighed, and looked at the chat where she found a small note.

'Here is the link to the assembly for when you are ready. Take all the time you need.' The teacher had written.

She took a deep breath, and clicked on the link. It took her computer a moment to think before she was placed in the waiting room for the meeting. When she was loaded into the virtual assembly, she felt as if hundreds of eyes were on her, and she swiftly turned her camera off. She listened to what Principal Jones was saying about Heather as best she could, hoping that she'd missed whatever was said about Corbin. She turned down the volume on her computer in an attempt to ignore it, and it worked for, at least, a few minutes until an idea struck her.

One of her hands reached out and picked up a random stone from her side table. She held it in front of herself for a minute, thinking hard on it before letting go. Her mouth popped open when it was left floating there.

"How did you do that?" Zane asked her in a serious, but morbidly curious tone.

"You said that I was controlling gravity when I was out of it that night. I wasn't controlling gravity. I was just manipulating the density of different things, which made it look and feel like gravity." She explained as best she could.

"Please don't do that too much." He asked her seriously. "Like I said, we need to lay low for the time being. At least, until we get answers."

She nodded, but replied silently. "Take us wherever you think is best to do the ritual. Far away is fine. I don't care so long as we can find out what we need to know."

"Will do." He concurred silently with a nod. "It won't be hard."

She tried to turn her attention to Principal Jones speaking again, but, the moment she heard Corbin's name, she looked to Zangrunath. "I can't do this."

He nodded, and closed the meeting app. "I will let someone know." He told her, grabbing her cell phone to make a phone call.

Ellyria closed the laptop, and climbed out of bed. She paced in the hallway for a second, catching a glimpse of her Mom making lunch in the kitchen. She walked over, and stole a long hug from her, sniffling a bit. "I love you." She murmured quietly.

"I love you, too." Her mother murmured, pulling away, and gently swiping some hair out of her daughter's face. She smiled. "Sometimes, you just look so much like your father."

"Thanks, Mom." Ellyria blushed. She gave a lock of her Mom's blonde hair a playful flip. "Yeah, I got more of him than I did you." She giggled.

Lynne paused for a long moment before smiling. "Yes, you did." She turned back around to finish making her sandwich.

Elly grabbed a bag of cookies from the pantry, and went back to her room. As she opened the door, she saw Zane already hanging up. She gave him a grateful smile, but it didn't reach her eyes.

"Okay, I talked to the Vice Principal, and she said she would let you take the rest of the week off, if need be. And so on and so forth." He informed with a sigh, putting a hand on her back and leading her to sit down on the bed.

"Thank you for taking care of me." She whispered.

"It's fine. Mental health is just as important as physical health." He explained with a sigh.

Ellyria nodded. "Let's get out of here."

"Yes." He agreed. "As soon as I locate the ley line, we can head off. It will just take me a while."

She nodded. "Alright. You do that. I'll keep watch, I guess."

He nodded. "If you need me, just let me know." He offered, heading into the garage. He closed the door behind him, and turned off the lights. He sat down, and closed his eyes in a similar manner to how Ellyria would meditate.

"Yep." She responded, popping the 'p' anticlimactically as she looked around the otherwise empty room. She found everything to be in order except for a small snag on the blanket she was sitting on. Her fingers automatically started to pick at it, making the thread come even looser. She huffed, and took her fingers away for a moment before an idea struck her. She had seen her father do something similar once. Well, sort of. She concentrated hard on what she wanted, looking at the other neat and tidy threads to help her keep her focus. A single fingertip gently pressed against the place; the simple touch leaving a small tingle behind. A moment later, she pulled her hand back, and saw a perfect blanket. No snag. Not even the tiniest indication that there had been a repair. She looked up at the ceiling, and murmured. "Is this why you died, Daddy?" She looked back down, and stood up with a groan, starting to tidy up. It was about time she started helping Zangrunath out.

Zangrunath let out a small breath before he began to feel the magic around him. He wasn't meditating, per se, but it was similar. He waited for several long minutes before he began to 'see' the small traces of the ley lines that went around the world. He could start to make out the one they had used recently in the distance, and knew that it would be stupid to go back there. So, he moved on quickly, and kept looking. He spent the better half of two hours searching before he found the one he thought they would have the best luck with. He opened his eyes, and made his way back out to Ellyria. "Okay, I found one."

She was cleaning the windows when he came out. She wrapped up what she was doing, and nodded. "Perfect timing. You just missed Mom leaving." She put the cleaner, and rag down on the coffee table, dusting off her hands on her leggings. "Alright. I'm ready."

"The ley line is quite a distance away. Almost all the way across the state, so it will take over an hour to get there." He sighed lightly.

She nodded. "Don't do anything I wouldn't do?" She asked in response.

He gave her a nod, and looked her over. "Okay, I need you to open your mouth."

She made a face. "Okay. That sounds invasive and semi-disgusting." She commented before opening her mouth widely.

He let out a sigh. "It is." He told her honestly, turning his body into mist, and forcing it into her body, trying to take over control of her being. Her body shook, and coughed as she instinctively tried to fight off the feeling of the mist entering her lungs. After several agonizing minutes, her body finally calmed down, straightening up mechanically at Zangrunath's beck and call. The demon was under control. "Good." He told her mentally. "It worked."

"It could've not worked?!" She responded a little louder than she meant to.

He winced in her body as her voice rang out. "There was a small chance, had you fought it off. It might have not worked." he told her seriously.

"Now, you're going to tell me there's permanent side effects of being possessed." She murmured into his head.

He shook her head. "Nothing worse than what you have already dealt with." He shrugged. "The ritual is much worse in the long run. Pain and all that."

She nodded mentally, but her head didn't move. "Weird. Let's go. Please."

"Let's." He agreed, moving to the back door. "This is why it was better for this to happen." He turned her body into a mist, and quickly moved out under the door, heading in a northwesterly direction. He was pleased to find that, during the time it had taken for him to find the ley line, the sun started to set. Doing the ritual under the cover of darkness would be best, and given them an easier get away, if need be.

If she could be clinging to somebody as mist, she would be. "Okay. Okay. I don't like that, but I can deal."

"Good." He replied. "Because, right now, until we get there, you don't have much of a say in the matter." He told her matter-of-factly.

"I know." She murmured back. "I trust you."

He didn't reply, but he sent the feeling of a nod. He moved as fast as he could in the form to get to the ley line as soon as possible.

After a while, Ellyria relaxed, if she could do so like this, and, with nothing else to do, she started to think. She groaned a couple of times quietly to herself as her mind whirled with questions and potential answers.

"What is it?" He asked worriedly.

"Thinking about talking with my Dad. Sorry." She did the incorporeal equivalent of looking away.

He let out a sigh. "It's fine. I was worried you discovered some crazy new power."

She shook her head. "You don't understand. It's all the same, singular power. Just different applications." She closed her eyes tightly. "Stop thinking, Elly."

"You will be fine." He told her as he flew. "Just focus on something else. Like, I don't know, small animals."

"Oh-kay." She elongated the word. "Do demons have a favorite small fuzzy animal?"

"To torture or to dismember?" He asked her curiously. "Because that makes a difference."

She sighed. "This might be beyond hellish radar, but one you think is cute."

"It would be a tie between two creatures." He responded, thinking it over in his head.

"Well?" She asked. "I'm waiting."

"The slow loris, and the honey badger." He told her with a nod. "One looks 'cute', as you would call it, but is highly venomous. The other simply could not give any less of a shit if it tried." He chuckled.

She smirked. "You almost quoted a really old meme there for a second."

"I have literally no idea what you are on about." He told her simply. "I haven't seen it."

She sighed a little bit. She didn't exactly have a phone to show him in this form "Alright then, when we are home and it is safe to do so, I order you to find the honey badger don't care video, and watch it.

Zangrunath chuckled at that. "Very well."

There was another long silence between them as Ellyria thought and Zangrunath transported them where they needed to be. "I don't want to live afraid forever." She admitted at a whisper.

A smirk took Zangrunath's face, even though they were mist right now. "Living afraid only leads to paranoia, which is more likely to kill you." He told her honestly. "That is a good thing you are trying to do. I approve"

"Thanks for being here for me. It really helps." She added.

"I am bound to you." He told her. "I have to be here for you." He reminded her. "Otherwise bad things would happen."

"You could be really malicious about it, though." She sighed. "Accept a compliment from someone besides the Prince of Darkness for once."

"He doesn't give compliments, unless of course he is trying to get something." He explained. "Besides, it doesn't help you get what you want if I just decided to put you down every chance I got."

She thought for a moment. "How do I find a place in Hell that isn't, well, that's less miserable."

"Make sure that, when you die, you have stopped at nothing to get what you want." He told her simply. "Hell is based on desires after all."

"And, if I sent others?" She asked.

"That would increase your chances, too." He told her with a mental nod. "You are helping the Prince."

"A contract lawyer goes to Hell. Starts like a bad joke." She mentally giggled.

"That is how the Keeper of Contracts got his job. He knew how to make sure things worked out for the Prince, so he got promoted." He told her honestly. "It did take time, but he got there, eventually."

She thought about that. "Any chance of honorary demonhood?"

"Let me let you in on a secret, demons aren't born. They're made." He simply told her.

"Oh." She drawled thoughtfully.

"Yeah." He mentally nodded. "What you did while alive affects what you become down there. Which is why some people think that, if you commit every sin imaginable, you go down there a god."

She shook her head mentally. "As if he'd let anybody unproven become that powerful." His words had her thinking, though. She wasn't particularly proud of the thoughts.

"No, he wouldn't." He chuckled. "But, he does find it amusing."

She sighed mentally. "You're giving me horrible ideas all in order to save myself."

He laughed at that, starting to angle towards the ground. "Good luck. Because, if you did, you would be the first to get out of an Annihilation Ritual contract."

"It's not to get myself out." She replied quietly.

"To get better accommodations." He deduced with a sigh.

"Basically." She responded.

They traveled for a few more minutes, continuing to descend, before Zangrunath spoke back. "You can do it." He told her honestly. "With how powerful you are, it shouldn't be too difficult."

"I'll burn that bridge when I get to it." She told him bluntly, but she felt encouraged by his words. If it could work in theory, she just needed time to plan for it to become reality. Well, she also needed a plan, too.

He chuckled. "I like that expression." They ghosted across a bridge. He saw their destination in the distance. "We are almost there." He told her, starting to slow down a bit.

"Ugh. I'm nervous." She groaned.

"That makes sense." He told her reassuringly. "This is a risky move, but a move we have to take."

"We need to know. We can't fly blind on this anymore." She agreed.

He stopped short of where the ley line was. "We need to be smarter, and we need to work better together in order to make sure we can beat them."

She agreed. "Let's do this."

Zangrunath pulled away, and their forms materialized fully side by side, letting her have her body back. "You do the ritual; I will be on guard. This one is pretty far out of the way, but that doesn't mean they won't come looking."

She nodded, starting to step forward, and feeling when the magic linked with hers. However, unlike the previous times, there wasn't a huge surge of power. "Zane?" She worried, turning to ask what was happening, but she didn't see what he saw. Her entire body glowed with intense magic.

"You are fine." He told her with a serious look. As far as he was concerned, talking would waste precious time. "Start the ritual. I am ready." He told her, becoming his demonic self. Ready for anything that might come.

She nodded, and turned to create the correct circle. For a split second, she panicked because she didn't have salt, but Zane had told her trueborn witches didn't need those things. A puzzled look settled on her face for a second before she waved her hand, and the proper sigil appear in a ring of lightning on the ground. It crackled dangerously, but she stepped inside, sitting down. She closed her eyes, and chanted for a moment, focusing quite a bit of magic into talking with her Dad.

Zangrunath watched as she began to cast the ritual, and knew that, if the Vatican was paying attention, this was what they were looking for. He began to make wide circles around the area. He didn't want to potentially ruin this. They needed to get this information.

After several minutes of deep concentration, a form a few inches taller than Ellyria appeared before her, fully formed but somewhat translucent. She opened her eyes after stabilizing the magic. "Dad." She sighed.

A smile cracked the man's lips as he saw his daughter for the first time in over two years. "Hey Elly, how have you been? You're looking good."

"Kind of terrible, actually." She gave him a bitter smile. "I hate to jump to the fun stuff, but I have the Vatican after me, Daddy."

He sighed, and nodded. "Sorry. I wish that I could've told you sooner, but they got to me before I explained everything."

"It's okay." She sighed, moving her fingers. "I can change things and remake them, and the one grimoire I found is incomplete."

"It seems that you inherited my abilities and, then, got some new ones of your own." He commented with a slight chuckle. "It is complete, you just have to unlock it at the right time." He told her simply.

She tried to think. "Is it an actual time or event?"

"An event." he started. "It is blood bound after all."

"It didn't unlock on my birthday." She thought for another minute. "Your birthday? Mom's? Your anniversary?"

"A blood moon." He told her. "One that is somewhat hard to predict, but gets the job done."

She thought about this for a minute, trying to do math, and failing in her hurry. "Zane! When is the next blood moon?"

"May of next year." He called back as he kept his eyes open, and thought he saw something in the sky. "You might want to hurry up!" He called out, readying himself.

She frowned, and turned back to her Dad. "I'm sorry. I don't have much time. Anything I should know? Anything that might help keep me alive?"

He looked at her and ,then, to Zangrunath. "Keep him close at all times, and, most importantly, do not try to destroy the Vatican. It's nearly impossible. Give them a win with you still winning." He told her seriously.

"I love you." She whispered, starting to stop the flow of magic.

"I love you, sweetie. Take care." He smiled at her as he began to disappear.

She didn't have time to watch her father fade away before she was sprinting to Zangrunath. She turned her head to see what was coming, and realized the mistake she'd made as she tripped on her way to the demon.

He felt a twinge of pain come from Ellyria, and quickly glanced back to see her getting up. He shook his head before he spotted three helicopters coming their way. He growled, and sprouted his wings. "Do you want to fight or are we running?" He asked, prepared for either outcome.

"My Dad says give them a win with me still winning." She repeated. "I don't know what that means."

Zangrunath shook his head, and grabbed her, quickly flying away with Ellyria in his arms. "It means we run away and figure out the cryptic shit later." He groaned, flying low to the ground and fast. He swooped as close to the cover of trees or other obstacles as often as possible, trying to stay out of sight of the flying hunks of metal.

"You want me to slow them down?" She offered.

"If you can do that without giving away our position, that would be great." He nodded.

She nodded, looking up to where she saw the blades of the helicopters in the air. It was beyond daunting, and she felt herself freeze until she forced herself to take a breath. With the clarity that the breath gave her, she came up with an idea. A crazy one. If she could pull this off, she really could do anything. "Here goes-physics." She mumbled as she started concentrating.

The helicopters were unaffected for several moments as Ellyria tried to figure out how to do what she wanted, making Zangrunath wonder what in the Hells she was doing before, suddenly, all three started to dip and drop in odd bobbing movements.

He looked back at the helicopters in shock and, then, to Ellyria. "Keep it up for a bit longer. We are almost out of their sight." He encouraged her as he continued to fly quickly amongst the trees.

She was concentrating hard, and couldn't respond. But, she kept following instructions. The only real indication that she'd heard him was that she nodded once for his benefit.

Zangrunath flew quickly for several more nerve-wracking moments, watching out of the corner of his eye as the helicopters dropped below the tree line in the distance behind them. He smiled at Ellyria. "Good job. You can stop, now. They won't be able to catch up to us."

She stopped concentrating, and sighed. When she looked at him, there was a little blood coming from her nose. "I think I used everything I got from the ley and then some."

"Well, you made it work." He smiled down at her. "Let's get you home so you can rest."

"Do I need to open my mouth for possession?" She asked quietly.

He looked up at the night sky, and shook his head. "No, not unless you want to. We will be fine."

She cuddled into his chest tiredly, and closed her eyes in exhaustion. "This is fine."

He gave her an odd look, and continued to fly home. "Just let me know if you need to stop for anything." He told her as he flew above the trees.

"I should be fine." She whispered. Her head rested on his chest, and she dozed off and on for the remainder of the trip, sleeping in the demon's arms throughout the rest of the flight.

He looked down at her, and shook his head at her. He just wanted to get her home. Zangrunath flew silently through the night, taking care not to wake her as he did so. He eventually got back to the house, and stealthily brought her inside without the lookouts noticing them. He brought her into her room, and laid her down. He tucked her in. She needed the sleep, and he would make sure to stand guard to keep her safe.

Tuesday, April 14, 2020

Ellyria awoke before her alarm, and sat up. She looked around to find herself alone. She sighed a little, getting out of bed, and heading to the kitchen. She started to make herself a quick breakfast as she asked the room, "Zane?"

Zangrunath appeared next to her. "Yes, Ellyria?" He asked.

"Sorry. Just checking." She responded. "The last few days, you've been pretty close when I woke up."

"I wanted to make sure that no one would suspect us of anything after last night." He told her truthfully.

She nodded, throwing veggies and some leftover meats together in a skillet to make herself an omelet. "People out front still?"

"Yes." He nodded before looking at her cooking. "Do you want me to finish that for you?"

Ellyria shook her head. "No. I'm fine. You've done this more than enough lately. Thank you." A little smirk came over her lips as she added a few more eggs.

He was going to reply, but thought it would be like a broken record at this point. So, instead, he left her to her cooking. "I will be on guard if you need me."

She nodded. "I will in about ten minutes. I have a plan."

"Oh, really?" He asked with a curious look.

"I'm making the stakeout car breakfast." She giggled.

"Stakeout car breakfast?" He asked, confused by her words, and unclear about her plan.

Ellyria smirked. "A peace offering."

It took him a moment to realize what she meant before he sighed. "Oh, you are making them breakfast. I thought we were doing the stakeout." He shrugged a little. "Oh, well. When the time comes, I can bring them over, if you like."

She was starting to take out paper plates as she folded the omelet, and cut it into thirds. "It's fine. Just make sure nothing weird happens while I go out there."

He made a face, but begrudgingly agreed. "I will do that."

"I know. It's dangerous." She told him as she pulled out a couple plastic forks, and walked towards the door. "But, I need to seem like a clueless eighteen year old."

"Just be careful," he warned her as he disappeared, "and, please, don't piss them off."

She shook her head. "Oh, no. Doing this nice and simple." She told him mentally as she walked across the grassy yard to the van that was watching her house. She balanced the plates on one arm, and knocked on the window. "Good morning." She greeted.

There was a moment of confusion and disarray as the men inside figured out what to do. They argued for a brief moment before the one at the window rolled it down. "Morning. How can we help you?" He asked, clearly confused.

She handed them the plates. "I saw you watching that drug dealer's place across the street, and thought you could use some breakfast." She lied with a little smile on her face.

The man gave a small smile, and nodded. "Yeah, thank you." He told her, taking the plates of food. "Just don't do this again, we are supposed to stay hidden." He blurted, realizing what he'd just said, and sighing.

"Oh." She looked around a bit. "I didn't realize I was blowing your cover. Be safe." She told them with a little whisper, scampering back into her house with a victorious smile gracing her lips.

"Will do." He replied, rolling up the window, and watching her as she made her way back inside.

She closed the front door, and pressed herself against it. "That went okay?"

Zangrunath appeared next to her, and nodded. "Yes, they are idiots."

"Won't fix the problem, though." She sighed, going to get dressed a bit better for the virtual school day ahead.

"No, it won't," he told her truthfully, "but it might help take the heat off of us."

"How do we fix this?" She asked as she started to dress. She paused to take a hurried bite of her portion of omelet, and went to go put on makeup.

"We need to figure out a way to make them think you are normal. Or, at the very least, not the one who caused this." He sighed.

Ellyria nodded, and whispered. "I hate myself right now."

"Hindsight is twenty-twenty." He reminded her with a little demonic chuckle.

"It's not hindsight." She whispered, applying the mascara to her lashes. "We could fix this, but-" Her voice caught, and her words hung in the air.

"But?" He asked her seriously.

She sighed, and one of her hands settled over her heart. "I have to make myself okay with human sacrifice."

He sighed. "Which I doubt you will," he commented, holding the bridge of his nose.

"Zangrunath. I-" She sighed, trailing off for a moment. "The only person that is close enough to the problem. The only person close enough to me is, is- She's my Mom."

"We will just do this the hard way." He told her, holding in a groan. "You can do whatever you want. I just have to help you. It's fine."

"On another note, did you ever find out if my applications made it to those schools?" She asked. "Stanford? Harvard? A clown college? Anything?"

"I found a few of them. Ohio State was one of the ones that accepted you." He informed her.

She sighed, shaking her way to keep away the thoughts of Corbin. "I don't think I can go there anymore. Was there another? Any other?"

He nodded. "Well, if you are going to be practicing law, then, Penn State might be your best bet as far as acceptances go."

"I think I'll go there." She responded quietly, feeling a little deflated. It wasn't her first choice, but it was out of state, which was good enough at this point. She tried not to sigh as she berated herself for not being better and letting this happen in the first place.

"Alright, then." He agreed with a nod. "I will do what I can."

Ellyria looked up at him seriously. "Did she throw any of them out?"

He nodded with a sigh. "Yes. The expensive ones."

"Of course." She grumbled. "All the ones I actually wanted in to." Part of her wondered if it was the drugs or just selfishness that had led her mother to so thoroughly sabotage what was supposed to be the exciting college acceptance process.

"Don't worry." He smirked. "You will be able to attend any school you want. I have a fair amount of leverage at the law schools." He chuckled.

She frowned. "Whatever. It's too late, now." Demonic contacts were great, but admissions to Ivy League at this point? Forget about it. "I just wanted to get in on my own."

"Let it be known that it was your own merit that got you accepted to them in the first place." He told her seriously. "I will just help get you through it all."

Ellyria nodded. "I trust whatever you think is best. I want to be the best contract lawyer that scholarship money can buy."

Zangrunath grinned at her widely. "You will be. That much I am certain of."

She smiled back, and went to go grab her laptop. "Let's try the school thing again."

"After you, miss." He bowed a little, letting her lead the way.

Ellyria walked to couch, and plopped down unceremoniously. "Thanks, Zane." She mumbled as she logged into Mrs. Dorsett's first period.

"Anytime, Elly." He replied.

ARTICLE VI

Monday, April 20, 2020

Ellyria was tapping her toes impatiently, waiting for calculus to start. She looked up at the ceiling more for the blank space to clear her mind than anything before she whispered. "Twenty-one days. Twenty-one days."

"Yes." Zangrunath sighed from his seat against the headboard beside her. "You just need to relax. Your feet have been doing that for five minutes." he told her annoyed.

She stopped moving. "Sorry." She mumbled. "Graduation is so, so close. And, we still haven't heard back about Harvard or wherever you decided on for me."

"I said Penn State, but, if you want to go to Harvard, I will give them a chat." He smirked.

"Just not Ohio State." She shook her head, and shrugged. She kept telling herself that she'd already given up on Harvard. "I don't care where I go anymore. Just get me where I need to be."

"Then, I will give Harvard a call." He told her honestly. "We have had quite a few of their lawyers work for us in the past. They do good work."

Ellyria nodded, opening her lips to respond when a new box and name appeared on screen. An unfamiliar face entered the virtual classroom.

The boy, whose name was Jack according to his username, gave the group a little wave, and typed something on his keyboard that must've gone straight to the teacher. A moment later, he unmuted. "Hi, there! I'm Jack. My family just moved into town, and I'm looking forward to getting to know you all."

Ellyria clicked off the video for a second, and glanced at Zane. She didn't like this one bit. It reeked of the Vatican's interference.

Zane nodded back, and reached over to turn the camera back on. "They can't do anything to you here." He reassured her mentally.

The math lesson started, and Ellyria watched intently, focusing on what she would need to know for finals. She was not looking forward to that. She knew that she could pass them, but it was not something that would be easy for her. This was not her best subject by any means. Luckily, she had Zane to help her, but she didn't want to use him as a crutch. She wanted to be able to do things on her own without help. It was a matter of pride.

Midway through the lesson, a notification appeared in chat, and a private message came through from the new kid, Jack, 'Hello. Who are you two?'.

Ellyria rolled her eyes, and let out a huff. This guy was either a morning person, and just trying to be friendlier than she cared for or a part of the Vatican. Regardless, she didn't like it. 'I'm Ellyria, and this is my cousin, Zane. Like the name we put into Zoom that you can see on your screen, and in this chat.' She replied quickly, trying to be cordial, but firm.

'Well, it's nice to meet you.' Jack responded. His image in the meeting looked almost puppy dog like.

Zangrunath's eyes narrowed, and he gazed at the little box on the screen that contained this Jack fellow, watching it with searing anger in his eyes. If he were in his true form, they would be wreathed in flames. He was internally screaming at the young man mentally daring him to try anything more.

"If he messages again, will you respond for me?" Ellyria

"By all means." He replied mentally.

A few more minutes passed before they received another message from Jack. 'So, what's your next class?' He typed conversationally.

Zane shook his head, and stole the laptop from between their laps, placing it only on his. Now, it was just him on the screen instead of Ellyria. 'Isn't it a little late in the year to be transferring?' He tapped out with a huff.

Jack looked a little startled on the screen, but smirked as he responded, 'Normally, yes, but I had most of my credits already, so the school made an exception, since I only needed a few.' He gave a small shrug after he hit send.

Ellyria wiggled in her place, and spoke into Zangrunath's head. "I don't like this."

"Agreed." He replied gruffly.

"Later, I want you to find out as much on this guy as possible." She told him. "It could be paranoia, but I'm not taking any more chances than we already have."

"Will do." Zangrunath nodded, noticing that Jack seemed to be intently staring at his screen. His nostrils flared in irritation.

'What's up buddy? Something wrong?' Jack typed with a small smirk.

'Not yet.' Responded quickly, grumbling several curses under his breath.

Ellyria huffed, and stole the laptop back from Zane. 'We're trying to pay attention to a lesson over here, and you're distracting.'

Jack shook his head a little, typing quickly. 'Then, why do you keep replying?'

"Is there a way to mute this guy?" Ellyria asked, searching all over the interface for a mute or block button that would keep communication from this guy silent.

"There better fucking be." Zangrunath growled, taking the laptop back to check for the tool himself.

As Zane was searching for a way to get this guy off their backs, another message came through. 'Calm down, man. You look like you're going to pop a blood vessel.'

Ellyria sighed, and tried her best to pay attention to the lesson that was still happening throughout the entire debacle. She knew that this guy couldn't do anything to them while online, but it was still annoying. This was supposed to be school. She let out a long sigh. "When we're done, save this chat. We might have to talk to somebody about this."

"Can I kill him? Pretty sure no one in the room would complain." Zangrunath growled.

She laughed at that. "You're not wrong, but no. We have to keep a low profile."

Zangrunath sighed deeply as Jack was getting progressively more aggressive in pursuing the conversation. He closed his eyes for a moment, and felt Ellyria take the laptop away from him. He opened his eyes, and was about to say something when another message came in.

'Hey there, beautiful.' On the screen, Jack gave a playful wink.

Ellyria growled in an almost demon-like manner. 'Okay, look, asshole. You haven't been here for long, but my boyfriend died two Friday's ago, so you can fuck right off with that nonsense.' She toggled the chat over to message Mrs. Dorsett. 'I'm sorry, but we're leaving. You can talk to Jack about why.' She scrolled up a little bit on the chat, and took several screenshots of the conversation before logging out. She closed her laptop, and started to get dressed properly. "I'm going to have a frank conversation with the Principal about this. Would you mind printing those screenshots?"

"Would you like me to help?" Zangrunath smirked, as he did as she'd asked.

"If the need arises." She nodded, leaving her bedroom to go grab the papers from the printer. She folded them, and shoved them into her purse. "I don't even care if we're supposed to have an appointment. I'm fine with just showing up and demanding to see him at this point."

"Good." He nodded, trailing behind her with the car keys, and grabbing their masks. He handed Ellyria hers.

She grabbed the mask, and shoved it into her purse. "I'll put it on when we get there." She sighed, shuffling out of the house. She plopped down in the passenger's seat of the car, and looked up at the roof of it. "I already didn't want to go to school. This thing is not helping me at all."

He sighed. "I literally have to do what you want me to do, so I can't make you go to school if you don't want to."

"Let's just get this done, and go home to lay low again." She groaned, closing her eyes, and resting quietly for the short drive down the road. When she felt the car park, she sat up properly, and opened her eyes. She begrudgingly put on her mask. It was just a prop to make others comfortable around her at this point. She got out of the car, standing up straight, and trying to exude a confidence that she didn't really feel. "Alright. I've got this."

"I'll be right beside you the whole time." Zane reassured her, putting on his own mask. He walked beside her, opening the front door to the school wide for her, and giving a playful bow. "After you, my lady."

Ellyria rolled her eyes at him. "Really?" She giggled, stepping inside, looking around for a moment, and keeping a respectable distance from the receptionist. She took a breath, feeling nerves hit her. She was supposed to be in her classes at home right now. Nor had she told her guardian where she was going. Then again, she was eighteen. "Good morning. May I please speak to Principal Jones?"

"Just give me one moment." The woman responded, typing something in on her computer. After a brief pause, she looked up from her screen. "You're in luck. He is available, and willing to make an exception to the in-person meetings policy. He can meet you in the conference room." She pointed at a nearby door. "There's more space for distancing."

She nodded, "thank you." She told the woman with a useless smile behind her mask, walking into the conference room, and taking a seat. She crossed her arms, and tapped a toe impatiently.

A shiver took her. "It's cold in here." She complained, rubbing her arms with her hands.

Zangrunath nodded, and sat down beside her. After a moment, she heard his mental voice. "It's a power move for negotiation tactics. You will be fine. Don't let the cold make you make hasty decisions you don't mean. We will likely be left waiting here for a while."

She groaned. "Alright. Fine." She complained, tapping her toe impatiently, but otherwise resigned to wait it out for the time being.

Nearly twenty minutes later, Principal Jones, who was looking a little bit more round than previously due to some quarantine weight, stepped into the conference room wearing a mask with the school logo proudly plastered across the front of it. "Hello, Miss Grant, Mr. Grunath." He greeted cheerily, looking between the two of them. "How can I help you today?" He asked, taking a seat at the other end of the long conference room table.

"Hello, sir." Ellyria replied coolly. He hadn't earned any brownie points with her leaving her to stew over the situation at hand in an uncomfortably chilly room. She took a breath to calm herself a bit before taking the prints of the conversation with Jack. "I'd like the new transfer student removed from my classes or my schedule changed." She stated simply.

Mr. Jones looked at the documents in her hand, and stood up, walking over to take them. "And, why is that? Is there a problem?" He asked curiously. He fidgeted slightly as he waited for her to hand over the documents. He seemed a little defensive or nervous about this situation, which was hard to read given the mask covering up his expression.

"Yes. I don't like being distracted and flirted with while I'm trying to learn. It's harassment, and I want you to remove the problem from my day." She told him bluntly, handing him the documents. Her tone was firm and angry.

Mr. Jones let out a sigh. "I won't be able to change it today, but it will be changed tomorrow. I will give him a call about this once this class is over, but you will have to deal with him for the day." He told her, sounding a little cross as he looked at the documents.

"I want the private chat function turned off in all of my classes, then." She demanded.

He nodded. "I will send an email to your teachers as soon as we're done here." He told her. "I'm sorry that this happened."

"Thank you." She told him. "And, if this happens again, I'm leaving class, and I expect that the absence won't be reflected on my records.

He let out a sigh. "I will make sure that this doesn't happen in your classes again. We value your education here." He reassured her. "You can relax, Miss Grant, we just want what's best for you."

She stood up. "Thank you. I'll go back home and log into my classes, now. However, I will be logging out if I see the private chat function working when I do." She warned him.

"Understood." He told her with a smile. "Have a good day."

"You as well." She waved, getting up, and heading towards the exit. When they got out of the office, she paused, looking to Zangrunath. "How about that for taking what I want?"

"Not bad." Zangrunath smirked. "Not bad at all." He gave her a smile before he turned his head to look back at the door, hearing an odd commotion.

"Will you please get that little prick on the horn? They paid us far too much for him to act this way." Mr. Jones grumbled to his secretary.

Ellyria did a double take, suddenly glad that they'd stopped before heading across the street to the parking lot. "You heard that, right?"

"Clear as day." Zangrunath replied with a growl. "We need to be even more careful."

She closed her eyes, and frowned. "How do we get out of this?"

"Very carefully." He told her as he began to slowly walk back to the car. "We need to find out how far this goes, and who all is a part of this."

"I could test out, and we could run." She offered half-heartedly.

He shook his head, marching the short distance towards the car. "No, that would only impede your goals." He was obviously thinking hard, pausing briefly to look at Ellyria. "What if we used him?" He asked curiously.

She followed him, and let out an exasperated breath at his words. "Oh, no."

"He is an idiot. It will be simple." He assured her, waving it off.

She made a face. "Please, don't make me flirt with him."

"No, that would be demeaning even for him." He told her seriously. "We will just use him to get information. Surely, you must have spells to make him tell us things."

"I've been on a strict no casting diet." She reminded him as they hopped into the car. "I haven't even been meditating. Well, you know." She sighed, thinking about what she'd found in her grimoire so far. "Yes, I do. Ones that are the same or better than the thing I did to Cor-" She paused mid-sentence, and didn't finish the statement.

He nodded, ignoring the annoying emotion, which seemed to be the best way to help her at the moment. "I know you have. But, this will only be a single spell. Nothing over the top." He reasoned. "It won't be enough to gain attention."

She nodded. "Which one do you want? I want to make sure I do my research properly."

"One that can gain information without him knowing he told us." He suggested, starting the car. "I have a suspicion he is a talker."

"I think that I know which one it should be. I just want to double check" She told him. "We'll just have to corner him during material pickup or something."

"Leave that to me. I think I might have a plan." He chuckled.

Ellyria nodded thoughtfully. They had a lot of work ahead of them. She just wished that it could be a little easier. "Do you think I could properly ward the garage without arousing suspicion or are we beyond that at this point?"

"It might take a day or two, but it is doable." He agreed.

"We both need a place we can do things without them sensing it." She sighed.

"Indeed. It is harder for them to track me, but I don't want them to start. Having the space will help immensely." He nodded, looking at her for a moment before heading towards the house finally.

She nodded. "It might take longer than it normally would, but it'll be worth it."

"Agreed. It is better to be safe than dead." He told her firmly. "Let's get you home."

"Thanks." She murmured tiredly. "You always take care of me."

"It is my job." He reminded her. "You just relax."

Ellyria nodded. "I still feel like less of a slave driver if I thank you. I don't like the servitude thing."

He gave her a small nod. "It is alright. I am used to it either way. It grows on you after so many millennia."

"What's it like? Living that long?" She whispered.

"Honestly," he started with a sigh, "it got boring after the first five hundred years. Everything after that is just a reskinned version of something you have already done before."

"So, you've done this before? High school with a witch?" She asked with a giggle.

"No, but I have dealt with schools." He chuckled, as they neared the house. "You still have the athletes, the popular ones, and the social outcasts. That much hasn't changed. The only thing that is different this time around is how fast technology has gotten in the short time since I was last summoned."

She nodded. "Even the things that have changed in my lifetime are insane."

"Now, imagine seeing it countless times." He told her seriously as they pulled into the driveway. "It would lose its allure and mystery."

She dropped her bag into the back seat. "Yeah, I get it now."

He nodded, and unbuckled without getting out of the car. "It gets boring. So, you either accept the bad and embrace it or you just have a horrible afterlife." He told her, suddenly opening up.

"I bet, after all of the stuff I still find fascinating becomes boring, murder, death, and dismemberment would be a nice treat." She commented. "Something to make me feel alive and in control."

"Yeah." He agreed with a nod, going silent for several long moments.

"What's it feel like?" She asked suddenly out of nowhere.

"What?" He asked curiously.

"Killing someone." She responded.

He thought about it for a moment. "It's like being a god." He told her simply. "Being able to take and destroy something that took so long to get where it was, only for it to be destroyed in potential seconds." He explained with a chuckle. "It is exhilarating."

She thought about that. "I could've killed everybody on those helicopters so easily, Zangrunath. Sure. I was concentrating. It took a lot of power to do, but it could've been like," she snapped in lieu of words.

"Isn't it exciting to think about?" He asked her seriously. "To have that much power in your hands."

She gulped. "I almost hate to admit it, but, yeah, it was."

"Give it time. You might actually learn to like it." He told her.

She thought about that for a second. "It's like, the longer we're bound, the easier the idea gets to wrap my head around."

He finally got out of the car, and walked around to get the door for her. "Absolute power corrupts absolutely." He quoted, offering her a hand.

She took his hand, and stood up, looking up at his eyes. "How did my Dad not succumb to it?" She tried not to look at the car with the guys staking out her house. "It would be so easy to just crush them with a thought."

"He must have had a will strong enough to deny the temptation or he had someone powerful to keep him focused." He told her.

"I don't think I'm strong like that." She murmured as they walked to the house.

"At least you have power. That might keep you from abusing it." He told her, following behind her.

She opened the door to the house, and walked in, seeing her mother at the coffee table. She was leaned over, ready to shoot something up. Ellyria threw her purse down, and growled, running over. Knocking the drugs out of her mother's hands. "Stop that!" She yelled, pushing her mother back onto the couch. "How long have you been back on the drugs? Tell me!"

Lynne looked to her daughter, but saw the abyssal glowing eyes of Zangrunath beside her. "Elly." She whimpered.

Ellyria bent over, scrambling to grab the items from the ground. She walked over to a closet, and grabbed the household mop bucket tossing the syringe in first. "Show me your stash. And, not just the main stash, but the side stash for when I find the main stash."

Lynne looked shocked, but followed Ellyria's orders, digging her stash out of her underwear drawer. She tossed the items into the bucket, and whined, "that's it. I promise. I only got a little."

Ellyria looked furious, and she waved a hand, casting a spell by pure instinct. She didn't even have any stones on her at the moment. "Tell me where else it's hidden." She demanded.

"In a coat jacket in the closet." Her mother blurted, suddenly covering her mouth in horror.

Ellyria walked around the corner into the walk-in closet, and Zangrunath looked at her mother. He shook his head in disappointment. "You chose wrong." He growled in a dark and threatening tone.

Before Lynne could even whimper in response, Ellyria came back around the corner. Her bucket was now much more full. She marched to the kitchen sink, and placed the bucket inside. She poured an entire bag of ground coffee into the bucket, and turned on the faucet. As it filled up, she reeled on her mother, and shouted. "If I ever find you taking this shit again, my response will be a whole lot worse than making it useless. Got it?"

Lynne jumped back in fear, and nodded meekly in response, holding up her hands in surrender. "Y- yes, dear."

Ellyria looked like she was about to say something cruel in response before she huffed, and stormed off to her room. She slammed the door behind her, and screamed until her throat hurt into her pillow. "I thought she couldn't do that anymore." She groaned.

Zangrunath quickly disappeared and reappeared next to Ellyria. "I'm sorry." He apologized, shaking his head at himself. "I should have done a better job."

"You did fine." She groaned back in frustration. "It's not the first time that's happened. I honestly should've expected it sooner."

"I still could've done better." He replied.

"It's fine." She sniffled. "In a month, it won't be a problem anymore. We can just leave."

"We can go wherever you want." He promised, sitting down on the bed. "You just say the word."

She rolled over, and looked up at him. "New York. I've always wanted to go."

"We will." He nodded. "Once we are done with this, we will go." He promised.

She sat up, and grabbed the laptop. "Ugh. I don't want to finish the school day."

Zangrunath sighed, and sat down on the bed beside her. "There isn't much time left, but we will do what you want."

Ellyria wrenched the laptop open, and jammed her fingers on the keys as she typed in her password. "I'll, at least, check to see if they did what I asked."

"That is a good plan." He told her in a placating manner.

She glanced at him with a fire in her eyes, but didn't say or do anything. Instead, she just clicked on the link to Mr. Harrison's class. When they popped into the meeting, she saw Jack's name on the screen, and groaned. She was just about to leave the class, regardless of the chat function being on or off, but she did say that she would check. She moved the mouse down to the button, and clicked it. When she did, she noticed that the chat was set to everyone only. A sigh escaped her. "Alright. I'll stay, but only because Mr. Harrison is awesome."

Zane nodded, happy seeing that she was already calming down. "Good. Things can only go up from here."

"I hope so." She murmured, listening intently to her classes for the rest of the morning. When all was said and done, she stood up, and grabbed her selenite wand. "I'm going to start warding the garage. I need a distraction."

"Alright. I will go check around the house." He told her. "Make sure there are no other surprises." He sighed.

"Of course not. I'm going to charge it over the next few days, so they won't notice it." She paused for a second as she walked out the bedroom door. "I hope."

He nodded and disappeared, going to make sure the house was safe. He saw the van still idly looking for something they weren't sure of, and checked around the backyard to make sure the seals were still intact.

Ellyria meticulously inscribed runes from her grimoire into the walls, floor, and even the ceiling of the garage. During her focus, she heard her mother leave, but ignored it. She didn't want to deal with that right now. It was bad enough that she'd cast a spell on her, and that she'd relapsed. Again. Shaking her head to clear it of darker thoughts, she took a place in the center of the room, and carefully infused a little magic into the runes. When she started to be able to sense it, she stopped. Tomorrow, she would add more, but, for now, this was almost too much.

When she left the room, she called out, "did you sense any of that?"

Zangrunath appeared next to her, and shook his head. "No, I didn't sense a thing." He told her honestly.

"Good." She smiled, taking a seat at the couch. "This no casting diet is making me realize how boring I am."

"This is what normal people do." He chuckled. "Though, most of them play games or something to alleviate their boredom."

"I honestly don't even know what games I like." She sighed.

"Well, if ever there was a time, now would be it." He offered halfheartedly. "But, to be honest, I don't think you would enjoy them nearly as much. You can already do more than any game can offer."

She nodded. "And, reading just makes me think too much right now."

"If you have a puzzle, you should do that," He suggested.

"I don't, but," she thought for a minute, "you did say that you'd help teach me Latin."

"If you want to start that, we can." He offered.

She smiled, and nodded. "Yes, please."

"Alright," he replied with a smile, going to go get paper. "Let's teach you Latin."

When night fell, Ellyria started to make dinner for herself, and she looked to Zangrunath. "Thank you." She smiled. "You can go find out about that jerk now. I would rather sleep with you here."

"Okay, I will go see if I can find out more about him online." He proposed, going to her room. "Surely, someone that idiotic would leave some form a of trail."

"I've still got a couple hours to go if it comes down to you leaving." She told him easily as she made mac and cheese.

"If it does, I will let you know." He replied to her. "Going to be honest though, it is pretty easy to find things out online. You would think that people would post less stuff about them, but it is the opposite." He chuckled, seeing the plethora of posts about Heather's less than stellar character even though she was dead.

She nodded. "This is why I don't have social media. It's way too easy to accidentally give away the secret." She commented, dragging out the word way for a moment to emphasize it.

"Or become someone else." He smirked, clicking a few links, and finding Jack's profile rather easily. "Found him. And, sure enough, he is an asshole."

"Details." She stated simply as she strained the noodles.

"Born in May. Is a Taurus, whatever that means. Likes soccer. He thinks it is the best sport ever. Has a collection of baseball cards, all of which are signed, by the way. And, lastly, which is my personal favorite. He likes to berate and potentially throw food back at fast food employees, if they get his order wrong, which, sometimes, he does on purpose." He groaned, and turning to Ellyria, "please can I kill him?"

She groaned. "I hate him, but none of that actually gives us a reason to kill the guy. Unfortunately." She added the noodles back into the pan, and started to add the cheese and milk. "Even though life would be way easier without him in the way."

"Well, if we do things right, he should just disappear either way." He chuckled.

"This makes me feel like some sort of tyrant. Considering his life worth less than mine." She told him.

"Oh, he won't die that way. That, he will do to himself." He told her honestly. "Once we get rid of the Vatican, he should just not show up anymore."

She plated her meal, leaning on the counter, and starting to eat. "I want him gone so badly."

"Don't worry. He will be." He told her firmly. "Just give it time."

She took a bite, chewing, and putting her fork down when she heard a shuffling coming from out back. "Do you hear that?"

He paused, and listened closely. "What is it?" He asked, trying to hear what she was hearing.

She turned around, and grabbed a kitchen knife. "This no magic thing sucks." She whispered. "It sounds like someone out back."

"Give me a moment." He spoke at a low growl. He disappeared, and travelled via shadow into the backyard, almost hoping it was an enemy.

Ellyria slowly crept to the back door, unlocking and yanking it open. She found a man with a scraggly beard wearing dark clothes there. She growled as she brandished the knife in hand. "Can I fucking help you?"

The man stopped where Ellyria caught him as he abruptly came to a stop. "Uh, I-" He gulped. "Hello, Miss Grant, I presume?"

"Get off of this property before I decide to call the cops." She threatened. When he didn't move immediately, she brandished the knife over her head in a stabbing motion. "Now!"

When all signs of the man out back were gone, she sighed, closing and locking the door behind her. "They're starting to get pretty confident."

"Yeah, they are." Zangrunath replied mentally as he stealthily watched the man leave the yard. When he was gone, he appeared next to Ellyria. "You did well, telling him off, I'm impressed."

"Thanks." She sighed, going back to her plate. "I'm not sure I can eat this anymore."

"Eat what you can, at least." He told her seriously. "Then, just save the rest for later."

Ellyria nodded, and took a few more bites before packaging it up. "This has me so on edge. How am I supposed to sleep?"

"You will sleep." He reassured her calmly. "Just relax. If need be, I will take care of them."

She yawned. "Thank you." Ellyria started to shuffle towards her bedroom.

"Sleep well." He whispered to her as she went to get some rest. "I will continue to do my research."

"Happy hunting." She mumbled. "If you need to leave, wake me, please. I'd rather be conscious in case they decide to get nosy again."

"Only if I need to." He told her honestly. "I would much rather you get rest than me get the information. You are my top priority, after all."

Ellyria nodded. "I trust you." She got changed in her room, and laid down to rest. She turned over after a few minutes. And again. She flipped her pillow and fluffed it up. After about an hour of trying to relax, she came back out to the living room where she laid down on the couch, and rested her head on Zangrunath's thigh. Closing her eyes, she finally found rest.

Zangrunath was a little surprised by her sudden intrusion, but let her sleep on his lap. Granted, he was now trapped on the couch, but he didn't have anywhere to go, so it was fine. He was just thankful that he never needed to use the bathroom. This would have been actual Hell otherwise. So, for now, he went about his research as she slept.

Tuesday, April 21, 2020

Ellyria stretched in her place as she came to consciousness. Her eyes fluttered open, and she saw a laptop close to her face and felt Zangrunath rather close to her. She yawned. "Good morning." She mumbled.

"Morning." Zangrunath replied simply as he finished up the last of his research. "I think I have Jack figured out pretty easily. I know just about everything there is to know about him." He smiled down at her.

She crawled off the couch, and started to brew coffee with what little grounds they had remaining. "Alright. I'm awake. Hit me."

"Well, he is allergic to bees as well as honey. Favorite color is blue. He has a stuffed animal named Mr. Flump-flump, and he also has two dogs and a cat. He's not a fan of lemons, and he would drink protein shakes every day if he could." He chuckled. "The rest is just minor little things, like his influencer status on TikTok." He scoffed a little, waving it off.

"The more you tell me, the more I hate him." She took the coffee pot off the heat for a second, and poured herself a cup. "Ugh." She glowered, glancing at the calendar. Tuesdays were the new material pick up day, which she was grateful for. Whomever thought to make Mondays worse than they already were hadn't won any awards at the beginning of the online schooling. "I don't want to go to classes or do anything."

"Then don't." He countered. "There are plenty of students who do that and still end up plenty powerful. There are less than thirty days remaining. Relax."

She sighed. "They were supposed to give me a new class schedule today. It's just senioritis. I can do this."

"Is that a new disease? Because it sounds stupid." He asked seriously.

Ellyria shrugged. "It's what society calls the phenomenon of seniors in high school slacking off because the end is in sight."

Zangrunath sighed a bit. "Of course, there would be a name for laziness. We just call it Sloth." He glanced at the time on the laptop. "Are we doing this?"

She nodded, taking a huge gulp of coffee as she moved to get out of pajamas. She got dressed, and looked in her mirror. "Forget makeup. I'm ready." She grumbled as she met Zangrunath in the living room.

"I prefer women without makeup." He smiled at her while giving her the compliment. "Most women who wear it are hideous without. You don't need it." He told her honestly.

Ellyria blushed. "Thank you. That's actually really sweet for you to say."

"You seemed like you needed the compliment." He responded simply.

"Didn't need it, but it's appreciated all the same." She smiled, sitting down on the couch, and placing the laptop in her lap. "Who knew a demon could be nicer than a human teenager."

"It is called the truth." He told her as he sat down beside her. "Most teenagers are also oblivious as to what is right in front of them."

She nodded. "I know you can't lie to me. I'll get rid of the makeup."

"Actually, I don't lie very often to begin with." He replied. "The truth is far more hurtful than any lie can accomplish. Most people don't want to hear it."

Ellyria thought about that for a minute. "You're right. Thank you." She moved her hand, and it bumped his. She blushed, and leaned away.

He shrugged it off. "No problem."

"Zane?" She whispered after a while, logging into her email to check for her new schedule.

"Yes?" He asked back.

She sighed, seeing that there were no new messages yet. "I don't know why, but I've just got a bad gut feeling right now."

"About what?" He asked curiously.

"Today." She explained simply.

"Would you rather not attend, then?" He asked once again.

Ellyria thought it over. "No. I don't really want to go, but something tells me, it'll be worse delaying it."

"Okay." He nodded. "Just remember, I will be by you the whole time."

"I know. Thanks. It helps me feel safe." She nodded.

"No problem." he nodded back. "Worst case scenario, we leave early."

"Worst case scenario, we summon the legions of Hell." She joked.

He laughed at that. "Under normal circumstances, the school might have enough people do that. The hard part would be starting that ritual. Probably not doable with just material pick up, though."

Ellyria raised an eyebrow. "That's actually a thing. Huh."

"Yeah, but it can only be used under very strict circumstances." He told her with a chuckle.

"I'm actually incredibly interested." She mumbled with a huge blush.

"Well, for starters, you need to break the seven seals, and, then, after the horsemen show up, you can cast it as much as you like." He joked.

Ellyria's eyes grew wide. "Uh, yeah. Not sure I want to actually start the apocalypse."

"Good. Because I don't want you to, either." He told her. "There is still a lot to get done before it gets to that."

She nodded. "It's not a parlor trick is what I'm hearing. Even if I probably have the power to actually do it."

"Could you do it, yes." He answered her back seriously. "However, humanity isn't ready for it yet. They would be destroyed."

"I agree. I don't even know how I would react." She shook her head. "Let's leave that to the antichrist or whatever the old prophecy foretells." Her voice full of sarcasm.

"Yeah, that would be for the best." He nodded.

She looked at him, impatiently hitting refresh again. "Is it normal that you tell me all of this?"

"It's not like it's a bad thing." He replied, taking the laptop from her, and closing it for a moment. "Using it is its own challenge."

"You're a mystery." She laughed.

"Not really." He shrugged.

Ellyria smirked at him, but was stopped in her tracks when her phone started to ring. She saw the number, and sighed. "Oh, no." She complained when she noticed the school's number. "Bad feelings." She muttered, answering the phone with a murderous, yet resigned, look. "Hello?" She greeted as pleasantly as she could muster.

"Hello, Miss Grant." Principal Jones's voice came through the line. His tone was lively and chipper.

"Somebody had his Wheaties today." Zangrunath deadpanned under his breath.

"Good Morning, sir." Ellyria greeted, giving Zane a playful smack on the shoulder as she tried not to giggle at his joke. A goofy smile plastered on her face.

The Principal didn't miss a beat, "good morning to you as well. I'm afraid that I am calling as the bearer of some unfortunate news regarding your schedule."

Ellyria sighed in frustration. "Alright. Go ahead."

"You see, we've tried to make adjustments to both yours and the other student's schedule, and there's simply no combination of classes that keeps you out of class with one another and gives you the remaining credits you need."

She sighed, looking at Zangrunath, and she spoke to him mentally. "This might seem contrary, but I don't like being manipulated."

Zangrunath sighed, and looked to Ellyria. "How badly do you want to change it?" He asked her seriously.

Ellyria sighed, and looked at the floor for a moment before looking up, pinching the bridge of her nose. "Alright. Fine. I'm about to be late for class, so how about I drop by the office this afternoon during my pickup time? We'll chat then, okay?"

"Very well, Miss Grant. I look forward to talking with you then." Mr. Jones responded. "Do have a lovely morning."

She sighed. "You as well." She responded, rolling her eyes as she hung up. "I can't believe this." She looked like she wanted to punch or throw something.

Zane sighed, and stood up, gently guiding her to her place on the couch. "We will get this figured out, but, in the meantime, there is no point in stewing over it when you have classes to distract you."

She groaned, but nodded. "You're right." She let out a little frustrated puff of air. "Sorry."

"You are fine. Just take deep breaths. You let yourself get so wrapped up in emotions that you stop thinking logically. Calm down, and we will get this fixed." He reassured her, opening the laptop, and logging into their first class.

During a short break in their schedule, Ellyria stepped away with a somewhat mischievous grin on her face. She grabbed her grimoire, and thumbed through the pages for a spell that she'd remembered seeing. She read it over, committing it to memory as quickly as possible. Now, she would be prepared for their meeting this afternoon.

Come material pickup time, Zane gently rested a hand on the small of Ellyria's back, and guided her into the front office. They were both followed by the eyes of several different students and parents, but he ignored them. They had an appointment, and belonged here just as much as any of them.

Back behind them, a small, but distinctly male voice, called out, and the familiar face of Jack rushed over to them. He wasn't wearing a mask, and was holding his phone in his hand. It looked like it was recording. "Hey, my dudes. It's ya boy, Jack coming at you live from my new school. I'm about to talk the hottest chick in school, and, I'm tellin' ya, she's going to be my girlfriend. Let's see how it goes."

Ellyria stopped before they could make it into the building. She sneered behind her mask as she saw the boy wearing a supreme t-shirt, and, over top, was a hoodie that just looked like a piece of pizza. "Go away." She told him simply, turning around to head inside.

"Wait up just a minute, sweetheart. Give me a chance, and I'll give you the world." He simpered, still holding his phone like it would help change her mind.

She turned back around, and glared. "There is only one person who is allowed to call me that, and I buried him two years ago." She muttered darkly. "Do. Not. Talk. To. Me."

He laughed a little bit at the fire in her eyes. "Alright, I like that. You're spunky." He made a kissing noise, gesturing with his free hand to 'send' the kiss her way, and gave her a nod with a bright smile. "Talk to you later, baby."

She growled, and shook her head, grabbing his arm to keep it out of her way, and punching him in the face with all her might. She shook her hand as she pulled it away. That had stung. "That was because you seem to only learn the hard way." She stated simply, turning around, and marching inside on a warpath.

Zane's eyebrows rose in surprise. Even he hadn't expected that impressive show, and the people lined up for material pick up were laughing and taking pictures all around. He could see the screen on Jack's phone lighting up with commentary on the epic fail. A chuckle escaped him before he joined her inside. This witch was full of surprises.

"Principal Jones should be expecting me." Ellyria stated quickly to the receptionist, walking into the conference room.

Zane gave a shrug, and pointed at Ellyria, shaking his head at the receptionist. "Sorry about her, ma'am. We had a small issue with some refuse outside, and it set her off." He smirked before following Ellyria into the conference room.

A few moments later, Principal Jones joined them in the conference, looking a bit irate. "Miss Grant, now, what is this I hear about you punching our newest student right in front of this very office?" He demanded.

She sighed, looking down at the ground for a second before looking up. After a moment of intense focus, she tapped into the ley lines, which she was starting to feel was happening easier and easier from her earlier struggles. Mr. Jones's eyes glazed over in an instant as the spell took its effect on him. "Why are you doing this?" She asked him quietly.

"We were paid very well to make sure that he stayed close to you." He told her without thinking.

"Did the Vatican send him? What's their goal?" She asked, standing up, and grabbing his hand to keep him under the effects for longer.

He nodded. "Yes. They sent him, but I don't know their goal. They just want to keep an eye on you." Mr. Jones told her simply.

"Where can I find them? What do they know about me?" Ellyria's voice soothed as used a little more magic to influence him.

"They know you can cast spells. I don't know where they are. They just pay us money." He explained.

She sighed. "If I asked, would you let me test out of the rest of the year?"

"Of course." He nodded. "All students are able to do that, if they ask."

Ellyria looked to Zangrunath. "Any questions before I put him under?"

"No, I'm good. You covered all of the bases." Zangrunath smiled.

"Alright, Principal Jones. Sweet dreams. You won't remember this when you wake up." She smirked, moving her hand to his temple, and removing the conversion from his mind. She watched as his face fell, and felt a moment of panic as he started to slump over right in front of her.

Zane poofed beside her, and effortlessly picked the man up, placing him down in a chair. He arranged him to look like he was deeply thinking. "So, we head home and come back tomorrow then?" He asked her seriously.

"I'm done with this dump." She muttered. "Let me just test out of this place. I can't take it anymore."

"Then, do you want me to take the test for you?" He asked. "I would make sure that you passed no matter how hard they tried to make you fail it."

Ellyria sighed, closing her eyes. "They would do that. Wouldn't they?"

"At this point, I wouldn't hold it against them." He replied.

"Yes." She whispered. "I hate doing it, but yes. I'd rather be hiding at home than dealing with all of this."

"Then, I will make sure you pass." He told her with a nod, opening the door for her.

She stopped at the assistant's desk on the way out of the conference room. "I'm going home today. Tomorrow, I'm coming back to take my finals early. I don't feel safe here or in classes with Jack." Ellyria told her bluntly.

The assistant nodded. "Okay, have a good day. I will put you on the calendar for tomorrow."

Ellyria walked out the office door, and looked to Zangrunath. "I hope this place burns." She muttered as a few students and parents took steps back to give them a wide berth.

"Do you hope or want?" He asked with a grin. "Because I can arrange that."

"Let's wait until it doesn't look suspicious. Maybe, in a week." She chuckled at his mischievous grin.

"Sounds good." He smiled back at her as he led her to the car. "Let's go get you home."

She nodded. "I can keep working on the garage, and check on Mom."

"I will also check on the car. Surely, the police will be done with the investigation."

She smiled. "I learned how to fix it just in time."

"And, when you get it fixed, you will have a sweet ride." He smiled back at her.

"That was kind of the plan." She smiled.

"A good one, at that." He nodded. "There are people who would sell their soul for that car."

She sighed, getting into the Grand Prix. "I mean, in a really roundabout manner, I have."

"You are getting that car and so much more." He told her. "It's just the tip of the iceberg."

"I figure that no self-respecting Harvard educated lawyer is going to drive a Pontiac when given the choice otherwise." She smirked.

"The choice is tough. A muscle car or a Pontiac." He chuckled. "Could go either way."

She smiled. "Nothing wrong with the Pontiac, but I want to drive to contract negotiations in style."

"It's the work car." He nodded.

As they started to drive away, she closed her eyes, and shook her head. "I feel like I'm quitting."

"You are not quitting. You are beating the system." He told her honestly.

"Thanks." She replied with a smile. She looked at him for a little longer than she meant to before turning her attention to the road. "Tomorrow, at least, the school thing is over with for a while. Then, we just have to figure out Harvard, The Vatican, and my Mom. Ugh. When did life become this stressful?"

"I believe that it's called growing up." He replied.

She giggled. "You're right. At least, I won't have to worry too hard about school for a couple months. And, the house should have wards in the garage by tomorrow at the latest."

"The wards are going to be helpful. Once they are done, things will get better. As for school, it's fine to take a break to figure out the Vatican mess." He told her as they drove.

"I still have so much to figure out." She sighed. "It's kind of overwhelming.

"It will be fine." He told her calmly. "You have time to figure it out, yes there is a learning curve, but I will be there to help you. It is my job after all."

Ellyria smiled. "Thank you for being there. It's like you're the only one I can count on in that regard. I was feeling alone for a long time before you showed up. It's nice to have someone to rely on."

"Thank you for summoning me." He smiled back at her. "It has been too long since I was last back here. I was starting to worry that we were losing our grasp, but you came along and changed that. There's a chance for things to look up for Hell." He smiled. "Pun intended."

She started to laugh at that. "Sorry it wasn't for a war, but this is a battle of a different type. I hope you don't mind too much."

"It's fine. It doesn't matter if it is one versus one hundred or thousands versus thousands. War is war." He told her with a smile.

"Well, you're my general." She smiled.

"Yes, I am." He nodded.

Ellyria eyed him up and down for a minute before looking away with a bright blush. "Oh." She let out a little sound of surprise. "Sorry." She mumbled. Did she just flirt with Zangrunath?

"Sorry for what?" He asked her curiously. "It's true I am a general, and I am yours." He explained. "There is nothing to be sorry for."

"Uh, just had a moment there, is all." She whispered. She couldn't flirt with a demon. She loved Corbin. He was dead, but her feelings were the same. This was business.

He looked at her curiously. "Let's get you home to rest."

She nodded. "Yeah, I'd like to use some magic today. Might help me feel better."

"Alright, we are almost there." He told her.

"Thanks." She whispered with a small smile on her face as they parked in the driveway. She looked over to her Mom's van beside her car. "I have no faith that she's not using again, right now." Her smile faded, looking to Zangrunath. "I trust you to decide what to do. I don't care what happens to her anymore. That's not my Mom. It hasn't been for a long time."

He gave her a silent nod. "I have a plan. It won't be today, but it's a plan nonetheless." He assured her.

"I trust you." She told him again. "Do what you need to do. I support whatever your decision is on this one."

"Are you sure?" He asked her seriously. "Because you will never see her again after my plan."

"I haven't really seen her since my Dad was alive." She replied bluntly.

"Okay." He nodded. "I will let you know ahead of time when that happens."

She got out of the car, and muttered, "thank you," one more time.

"No problem." He responded quietly, following her into the house.

Ellyria let them in, and ignored her mother on the couch, shaking her head. Instead, she walked directly into the garage to start adding more magic to the wards. She needed to use some magic before she decided to blow something up.

Zangrunath looked at Lynne, and sighed. How could someone have such little regard for others? He shook his head, and went about checking around the house for intruders. He could still see the van across the street as well as a few other people milling about acting 'normal'. He thought his plan over in his head. It would need to be soon, but it had to be at the right time. For now, he would wait. Then, all their problems could be relieved in one fell swoop.

Ellyria opened her eyes just after lunch time. The wards were almost done. She could tell that stronger magic could be used in the room, but knew it would be best not to test that until after she could finish it tomorrow. She got up, and started to move towards the kitchen only to have Zangrunath hand her a plate at the entrance to the living room. He was body blocking whatever was behind him. "Oh. Thank you."

"No worries. I hope you enjoy it." He told her honestly, trying to make sure that her day would be better for as long as it could be.

She took the food, and went to her room. "You mind working on the Latin again tonight?"

"I don't mind." He told her as he followed her to her room. "How far are the wards coming along?" He asked her curiously, needing the garage for his plans.

"It should be done tomorrow. I don't want to put too much in too fast." She sighed. "It would look suspicious."

"That's good." He nodded. "And, I agree, it would be silly if it were done in a day. They would definitely know something was up."

She took several bites of food, and changed the subject from one stressful thing that she couldn't control to one that she could. "I want to make sure that the school has no reason to disqualify me from taking or passing the test tomorrow. Do you have any thoughts? Because I have several."

"I am not worried, but what troubles you?" He asked her back.

"I want to get there early, in case they decide to be manipulative, and I want a way to prove that they didn't change my answers. So, I'd either like you to keep a separate page to log those or take a picture after it's all over." She told him. "Call it paranoid, but I've got no confidence that they won't do it."

"I can do that. I will keep the separate page. That way, it will look like I am working harder, and, if they do switch the answers, I will have a backup." He chuckled. "Though, I am not too worried. There is not much that they can throw at me that I can't handle."

Ellyria nodded, taking another bite. "Thank you." She sighed. "I really appreciate it. Kinda hate not doing it myself, but," she left the sentence hanging in the air.

Zangrunath placed a hand on her shoulder. "It's fine." He told her. "I am here to help make you succeed by any means necessary."

"How long will you be around after I get what I want?" She asked suddenly.

"After you finally achieve your dream, I disappear. Simple as that." He told her simply.

She frowned. "No goodbye?"

"No, that isn't up to me." He shook his head. "Once the deal has been complete, the ritual brings me back to Hell. It is beyond my control."

"Well, that kinda blows." She took another bite and sighed. "After all that time together, I'd want to say goodbye to my closest companion for years."

He nodded again. "I agree, there were a few witches over the centuries that did leave an impression or two."

She finished her plate. "I guess that we'll know when it's getting close to the end."

"More than likely." He told her simply. "Given how you stated your idea, we will walk into a room, and I will just vanish." He explained, thinking over her words from weeks earlier.

"I could've worded that better." She facepalmed. "I'm going to regret that."

"It is what it is." He shrugged. "Only a handful of people ever make their idea foolproof."

She nodded. "I doubt any of them were seventeen at the time, either."

He shook his head with a chuckle. "No, you are the youngest by a large margin. Most of my contracts were with people in their mid-forties."

"What was the youngest summoner that you know about?" She asked.

"That I know about?" He asked, thinking hard on that. "I don't know of all of them, but I have heard of one who was twenty-five." He told her, confident in his response. "He was an odd one."

"Wait. So," she gulped, "I'm the youngest you know about?"

He nodded, giving her a deadpan stare. "Yes, I am certain that you are the strongest one I have ever met. Maybe, even, the strongest there has ever been."

"That's a lot of pressure." She closed her eyes. "I'm just, Hell. I can't even say a kid anymore. I'm an adult. How can I be this strong when I have no idea what I'm doing?"

"I chalk it up to your father." He finished, and gave a little sigh as he looked in the general direction of her mother. "He must have been pretty strong for you to have such intense power."

"That's the thing. I hardly ever saw him casting. He'd barely started to teach me. I just don't get it." She flopped down onto the bed dramatically.

"Then, he must have been hiding it so that the Vatican didn't find out." He told her. "Otherwise, you would have been much better trained."

She sighed. "I do remember him doing something when I was really little. I snuck up on him in the garage, and he was making a gold necklace chain out of something. He sold it. I think that's how he kept us afloat when money got tight."

He raised an eyebrow, and looked at her. He shook his head lightly. "The more I hear about this man, the more questions I have about him." He commented with a sigh. "He was hiding something big. That much, I know. If it was you or something else, I don't know, but, someone who has nothing to hide and that much power, does not live in a life like this." He gestured to the house.

"I don't know." She shrugged. "I guess, we can ask in six months."

"Or go on a trip." He sighed, holding his head in his hands. "Realistically, we should wait. No point in going through all this trouble to get rid of the Vatican only to get their attention back a few minutes later."

"I can wait. We need to lay low." She sighed. "I get it, even though I hate it."

"We will manage." Zangrunath told her. "Besides, I have a plan to get them off of our back."

She nodded. "You've done this far more than me. Do whatever you think is best."

He nodded, and sighed. "Yeah, more times than I like." He told her, looking at her seriously, now. "You will need to go somewhere tomorrow." He told her bluntly.

"Okay." She hummed. "I guess, I'll go get a coffee at the bookstore or something."

He made a face. "I would prefer it if it was somewhere more-secluded." He told her, not wanting to go into the details.

She winced. "Do I need an alibi?"

"No." He shook his head. "I just don't want you to be around people when you feel what happens tomorrow." He explained with a sigh.

"I'll drive out to the truck stop nearest to town, and look at memes on my phone or something." She corrected.

He sighed, and nodded. "Alright. Just let me know when you get there. I don't want you to get hurt while driving."

She shook her head vehemently. "Please, no. I have enough issues with cars. They are starting to be nerve wracking to be inside.

"Give it time. It is a phase. After some time, you will be fine. Just let me know when you are parked and safe. You will know when you can come back." He groaned, glancing in the general direction of her mother. "All will be fixed after I am done."

"I don't think I want to know until it's done." She admitted. "Will you distract me with Latin, now? I don't want to think about any of this for the night."

"Of course." He nodded, standing up, and getting some paper. He placed it between them, and grinned. "Let's get to it."

"Thank you." She smiled, sitting up straighter. Ready to learn.

"Let's continue where we left off." He resolved, starting to give a brief overview of the previous lesson in order to build on what she needed to know next in learning the dead language.

ARTICLE VII

Wednesday, April 22, 2020

As Ellyria slept, Zangrunath was busy making sure that things would go smoothly for the day. He needed to take the test for her, which he wasn't worried about, but, what he was concerned for, was his plan for after the test. He was going to get the Vatican off their backs. All this sneaking around was holding them back. He wanted to make sure Ellyria was okay. She was his summoner; she would always come first. With that in mind, he went to make breakfast for her. She was about to have a long, tiring day, so, when she awoke, he had a nice breakfast and coffee waiting for her.

Ellyria's alarm went off earlier than usual, which was jarring. She automatically rolled out of bed, going about her routine. Once she was cleaned up and dressed, she went to go grab a breakfast bar only to find a full English style breakfast on the counter with coffee. "Woah." She gaped, looking at the spread. "What? No blood pudding?"

He chuckled. "Sorry. I couldn't leave the house to get the pig's blood." he joked.

"Yeah, no. I wouldn't have eaten it anyway." She made a face, starting to dig in. "Oh, this is perfect. Thank you."

"Good. I am glad you like it." He gave a nod, and watched her eat for a moment, turning to clean the few dishes as he spoke to her. "You will need to have a good amount of energy for today." He told her, trying not to explain any more than he needed to.

"Alright." She nodded. "I bet it gets distracting to be hungry while possessing someone."

"It can, but I won't be possessing you today." He told her simply, "You will be here finishing off the wards in the garage."

"W- what?" She asked as confusion struck her.

"I will be going to the school, looking like you, to take the test. You just have to tell me to go." He shrugged.

She chewed another bite of sausage. "I didn't know you could do that. You're full of surprises."

"You think this form is my only one?" He chuckled, gesturing to himself. "I choose this one to blend in at the school. I could literally look like anyone." He smirked.

She nodded. "Wow. Alright, then." She finished another bite. "I want you to go to the school for me to take that test like we discussed."

"As you wish." He replied with a nod, becoming shrouded in mist in an instant, and appearing as Ellyria a moment later. Upon further inspection, it was accurate down to the clothing she was wearing except for, in her opinion, one glaring omission.

She looked Zangrunath's disguise over, and waved him to her side. "You're missing something."

"What's that?" He asked in her voice.

She pulled her quartz necklace from around her neck, and put it over his. "There." She touched it, and carefully charged it. "Much more accurate."

"Thank you. It should help me get this over with quickly." He smiled back at her. "Will you need me to get anything on the way home?"

"No, but, if you could turn my books into the office, that would be helpful." She smiled.

"Of course." He nodded at her. "I will do that after the test so that I don't raise any suspicions."

She nodded. "Good." She finished her meal, and looked at the clock. "You do that, and the garage will be done by the time you get back."

"Perfect. I will need to put a sigil down when I do." He explained, making a face. "We will worry about that when I return." He told her. "For now, I will be off. I will see you later." He waved, making his way to the door.

"I don't feel like good luck is the correct thing to say in this situation, so break a leg." She offered.

"That could be done easily enough. Maybe, I can arrange it for somebody to 'trip'." He smirked. "Be back soon."

Ellyria nodded, and cleaned up her dishes. When she was done, she made her way into the garage to finish infusing the wards with magic. She took a deep breath to focus, and connected to the earth. She was starting to notice that, even away from a ley line, it was similar. It just didn't react as quickly. After a few hours of concentration, the wards felt complete, but she moved to touch the wall. Her father had found a way to hide their grimoire behind thick concrete, but that wasn't practical for an entire garage. She looked at the drywall, and focused hard for several more minutes, feeling quite a bit of power being used as she focused on manipulating the matter inside of the very walls. When she was done, she slid to the ground to rest in the now magically warded and lead lined room.

Zangrunath quickly made it to the school, put on a mask, and grabbed her backpack out of the back seat of the car. He needed to look the part today. He walked to the office, and smiled sweetly. "Good morning, Mr. Jones. I'm here for my finals."

Mr. Jones gave a nod, and made a show of going to the receptionist to retrieve four packets that were stored in manila envelopes, and sealed shut with special labels. He smiled, and walked her over to the conference room, which was even colder than her last two visits. "This will be the best room for it. We don't have anybody to proctor the test at the moment, so, when you're done, just bring your papers up to the front. You'll need to leave your backpack out here. You can't use a calculator or any notes. Time will be up when fourth period ends." He informed her seriously, handing over the four envelopes, labelled for each of her classes.

Zangrunath made a face to make her seem overdramatic. "Alright, fine." He scoffed, grabbing a couple pens and pencils from the backpack, leaving it on a chair just outside the door. He grabbed the envelopes from the Principal's hands, and crossed his arms. "Let's get this over with so that I can be done with this place." He demanded. He was having fun pretending to be Ellyria.

Mr. Jones nodded. "Okay, good luck. See you in a few hours, and, if you need to use the restroom, you can use the one for staff two doors over." He smiled at her victoriously, knowing these tests would be next to impossible to pass. He stepped out of the room, and closed the door with a resounding click, strolling off to his office with a swagger about him.

Zangrunath sat down, and opened the math test first. This test was Hellacious just to look at. He knew he could do it, but these were concepts and topics that required years of college to be able to solve. He made a face, and picked up his pencil, shaking his head as he began to take the test.

Thanks to the level of difficulty behind each question, it took him much longer than he'd originally expected to complete the test. Luckily, he still finished it before the end of fourth period. Barely. Thanks to demonic magic, the hardest part was making sure that he copied everything down on a separate page. He made sure to get a few of the questions wrong, just for posterity's sake, but it would still be a ninety or more on the test.

He strode out of the conference room with ten minutes to spare, and handed the papers to the receptionist. A wide smile on his disguised and masked face. "Finished." He announced.

The woman took the documents, and nodded, typing something in her computer. "Thank you, dear." She smiled sweetly.

He nodded, and watched as, a moment later, Principal Jones came out of his office. He took the papers from the woman, and looked them over, shocked that they were completed at all. "Give me just a moment to get my answer key." He murmured, walking back into his office, and returning a moment later with a neatly typed document with the answers, and special rubric for simplified grading percentages. He took a red pen out from his breast pocket, and started going over her test right there on the counter of the reception desk.

Zangrunath sat there with his arms crossed. He was half tempted to yawn; he was so bored with the whole thing. "Is it alright to turn in my books?"

"Do you want to get your results first?" Mr. Jones asked curiously. "What if you don't pass?"

"Then, you can give them back to me." He responded, quickly going over to Ellyria's discarded backpack, and pulling out her textbooks. He carried them over to the front desk, and placed them in front of the receptionist. As he did, he saw Mr. Jones starting to look pale as he started grading the second packet. "So, how did I do?" He asked innocently.

"So far, so good." He responded with a nod, going through English next.

Zangrunath waited several more minutes as the Principal began to sweat with each new red checkmark. After he got to the last page of the home economics documents, which were the easiest test of the bunch, he asked, "did I pass?"

Principal Jones nodded in defeat. He looked like he'd just seen a ghost. "Y- yeah. You did great." He mumbled hollowly.

Zangrunath made a happy face, and jumped around with faux joy. "Yay! Thank you so much!"

"The pleasure was all ours." He replied with a little sigh. "You enjoy the rest of your day. Thank you for attending our school." He congratulated, giving her a fist bump in lieu of a handshake. "We will send your diploma in the mail."

"I will." Zangrunath replied, grabbing the backpack, and heading towards the door. "Thank you again." He smiled widely as he forced a few joyful tears to come to his eyes. He quickly made his way back to the car, and headed back home.

Ellyria came to with a little snort when she heard someone enter the garage. She looked over groggily. "Huh?" She grunted.

Zangrunath smiled at her. "Congratulations. You passed with flying colors." He announced, still looking like her for a beat before turning into his human form. "You are done with high school."

She smiled tiredly. "Thank you."

"It was no problem." He smiled back, moving over to pick her up, and bring her to her room. "Let's get you a better resting spot."

She leaned into him. "Kinda passed out." She admitted. "Should've taken more stones."

"It's fine." He told her as he gently laid her down on her bed. "We won't have to worry about prying eyes anymore, now, thanks to you."

"Good." She sighed, closing her eyes. She pointed to her jewelry box. "Can you bring me the third drawer?"

He turned, and grabbed the drawer like she asked. "Here you are." He said, placing it next to her.

She grabbed several different stones out of the drawer. All in whites and greys. He recognized a few as hematite and painted Jasper. She started arranging them and drawing magic from them. "Thanks." She muttered tiredly.

"No problem." He replied with a nod. "I am going to put a glyph in the garage. It will take me a bit, but I will need it for later." He informed her, making his way to the door.

"Okay." She murmured, closing her eyes, and falling into a deep sleep.

Zangrunath nodded, and let her sleep. He returned to the garage, choosing a wall. He began inscribing a demonic glyph on it that he would need for later. He wasn't looking forward to it, but there really wasn't any other choice. He was going to die tonight, and he needed this to get back quickly after the job was done.

Ellyria slept for a few hours, and, when she woke up, she found Zangrunath beside her on the bed. She sat up. "I need to go, don't I?" She murmured, rubbing sleep from her eyes.

He nodded. "Yeah. It's about that time, and you don't want to be here for this."

"Alright." She nodded, grabbing her car keys, and looking at him. She took a breath, and grabbed his hand. "I can only guess what you're going to do, but thanks."

He nodded, smiling back at her. "No problem. Just go relax as best you can, and, as a heads up, I will let you know before anything happens."

She let go of him, and made her way out of the house. She got on Grand, and took the sixty-four over to a little shop along the highway that was run down, and had only a couple cars parked out front. She wheeled around to the side, parking behind one of the storage pods, and put up the shade screen for a little more privacy.

Ellyria got out of the driver's seat, hopped into the backseat, and laid down. She wasn't exactly sure what was about to happen, but she remembered the pain of Zangrunath being shot last month. He had told her to be alone and prepared for something, so she was ready for the worst. "I'm ready, Zane." She whispered into his head.

Zangrunath let out a sigh as he heard her voice. "Thank you. I will try to make this quick." He pledged, making a beeline to her mother on the couch.

Lynne's eyes looked at Zangrunath in a foggy, glazed over state before she shot upright as if possessed, somehow, by another demon. She attacked him with a flurry of terribly ill placed and weak punches. She screamed. "No!" Her voice was desperate, but her mouth, thick with saliva as spittle sprayed out on the demon.

He sneered at the disgusting display, and easily dodged the punches. A hand effortlessly pushed her back onto the couch.

"You had your chance, and you blew it." He told her simply. "I hope it was worth it." He menaced darkly, letting his humanoid illusion fade inch by inch until there was nothing left besides a demon standing there.

"Elly! No. No. Elly!" She whimpered, backing away, and falling into the couch in a useless heap.

"Be quiet!" He told her firmly. "You did this to yourself. Now, instead of being a useless piece of shit, you are going to do one final act to help your daughter." He informed her with fiery red eyes.

She curled into a ball, sniffling, and looking up at him. Her eyes were still glassy, but she looked at him seriously for a minute. "Elly." She eventually murmured. Her thoughts were unreadable on her face.

Zangrunath looked her over with scorn. He would not relish puppeteering this woman. He turned his body into mist, and rushed inside her mouth and nose, possessing her body. She tried to fight it off, but, in her drugged state, it was useless. A smugness washed over him. Perhaps, if she were well, she could have fought him but not like this. When he had full control, Zangrunath groaned. "Ugh. It figures you would be this high." He complained, feeling the drugs in her system, but shrugging it off thanks to his Hellish constitution.

"What is this? I don't like this. Get out." Lynne's voice weakly argued from somewhere deep inside of him. His personality almost completely blocked her out, unlike her daughter.

"Be quiet." He ordered as he walked to the door, stumbling a bit thanks to the drugs. "You are going to help Elly, by dying for her." He told her emotionlessly. "You will make her life easier without your addiction, and without the fear of being chased by the men who have been stalking your house for the past few months." He stepped outside, and glanced over at the van. He raised a hand, and used demonic magic to start casting spells haphazardly. Thanks to this drug addled body, his aim was off, but, luckily, fire tended to make a big splash on its own. Making sure to draw attention, Zangrunath made some of the spells get close to the stakeout van.

"Elly was chased? What are you doing? That's not normal." Lynne's tiny, foggy voice suddenly sounded completely sober in his head. "What did you do to her?"

"It's not what I did to her. It's what she did to me." He replied gruffly. He didn't have the time nor the crayons to make that elevator go all the way up to the top. "She summoned me using her powers, not that you would know about that. You were too high most of the time to notice." He chided, throwing a few more spells all about. "And, yes, she is being chased, but not after tonight. You are going to die taking the blame for her. A mother should protect her daughter. Right?" He growled at her as he saw men start to approach quickly with weapons drawn.

"No, no. She's not mine. She's theirs." She whimpered. "They just put me in charge of her. She wasn't supposed to be mine. I don't want to die."

He gave a slight pause at that, but continued to cast the spells wildly, aiming at the closest man with a gun. "Who are 'they'?" He asked. Now, morbidly curious.

"Her father and mother. I never met her. She was never around from the beginning, so he asked me to formally adopt her. It wasn't so bad while he was around. He did most everything, and I just did typical Mom things for him. When it started out, it was just business, and, then, he left her behind with me. It was just so hard that I-" She trailed off. "Please, I'm not her Mom."

Zangrunath growled at her words. He knew she wasn't lying, but this meant things were not as he thought they were. He threw a few more spells at the men who were coming towards them, hitting a few of them. "You could have been there for her, but instead you chose to get high, making her life a living Hell." His voice stern and judgmental as bullets were flying, now. "Just be quiet, and let me worry about her from now on. I have to protect her even if that means killing you." He sighed before he mentally told Ellyria. "Be ready for pain. I am sorry." He fired a few more spells, and the first bullet hit his chest, searing it with a little holy magic along with the stopping power of the hot lead.

Even from afar, Ellyria heard Zangrunath's words. She covered her mouth seconds before she felt it, and she couldn't help convulsing and screaming. Whatever was happening was more like a warzone than she could've even guessed at. She started to cry.

Zangrunath felt the wounds start to overwhelm him, and he fell to his knees as her mother's body began to fade away with him in it. He threw a few more fireballs to sell the farse before he felt one final volley of lead end him and Lynne.

Ellyria felt the moment Zangrunath left her. She mentally called out even though agony lanced through her body. "Zane! Zane!" She screamed to no avail. In a panic, she climbed into the driver's seat, and started to speed back into town. "What the Hell?" She muttered to herself.

She made it home in record time, and found a police line all around her street. She parked, ducking under it before a pair of strong arms stopped her. "No! That's my house! What happened?" She screamed, struggling to move forward into the bloodied and scorched yard.

The officer that held her sighed deeply, and used his superior strength to place her on the ground and turn her around. "We are still investigating, miss. This is an active crime scene, but I'm glad you are safe. We were worried when records showed there might have been somebody else home." He informed her. He turned his head, and saw all the blood and scorch marks. "I'm sorry, miss." He quietly apologized.

"W- where am I supposed to go?" She mumbled. "I don't have anybody or anywhere else."

He looked at her sadly, "once we get the investigators and the coroner here, you are free to go into the house, if you want." He offered.

"Okay." She sniffed. "I'll go sit in my car, I guess."

He nodded, and placed a hand on her shoulder, "if there is anything you need, just ask." He told her as reassuringly as possible.

Ellyria shook her head, and let her tears fall as she slowly made her way back to the Grand Prix. She cried for a little bit, whispering to herself, "I killed her, I did this," more than once before she noticed the stakeout van nearby. It was empty, and looked battle damaged. She did a double take, checking that everybody behind the police line looked busy before she climbed out, and snuck over to it. It was well organized inside. A tiny smile pulled at her lips when she easily found several piles of scattered notes. She greedily grabbed it all, and brought it back with her to the car, starting to look it over piece by piece.

Zangrunath let out a roar as his head breached the surface of a pool of blood that seemed to magically shift between demonic black ichor and bright crimson red. His lungs gulped in air, and, after taking a moment to reorient himself, he straightened up and stretched, spreading his wings across the width of the ancient mausoleum. He waded out of the basin, and the liquid sloughed off behind him. There were several odd looks at him as he did so, but he gave them a glare. As always, the lesser demons turned away. He groaned as he made his way out of the gates of Hell. Reforming was never a comfortable task, and, partially thanks to Ellyria's power, he had done so in record time. As he passed through the gates, demonic symbols wrapped around his body, and, instead of walking or flying, he began to crawl out of the sigil he had carved into the garage. He was grateful to find that the room was empty at the moment, and took a moment to orient himself. Now that he was in the material realm again, he could feel his connection with Ellyria much more strongly, and he turned into a shadow to find her.

She felt Zangrunath appear beside her in the car rather than seeing him there. She handed him some papers as she silently cried. "I feel used."

He looked at her oddly and, then, to the papers. He read them over once and then again to make sure he had read them right. Part of him was simply impressed that she'd gotten her hands on them at all, but she clearly needed more than an impressed response right now. He looked back at Ellyria; his face mixed with emotions. "I'm sorry." He apologized sincerely. He looked back down at the paper in his hand, and felt anger rise. Corbin's name was on the paper. He had been working with the Vatican for a long time, apparently, since he was born. He looked over all the information she had gathered, and gave her a very puzzled look. "This is wrong." He told her simply as he started to take a closer look at each of the reports one at a time.

"Yeah, it was. The Vatican planted someone in my life just to spy on me right from the beginning. He got close to me, told me he loved me, and I loved him." She looked away as she sobbed harder. "I feel like an idiot."

He nodded, but drew her attention to one of the papers. "I know that this is fucked up beyond reason." He told her before pointing to the page in his hand. "But, this is wrong. It says that you have a small chance of magical power." He told her. "The date is after your time together at the ley line."

She wiped her eyes. "W- what?"

He sighed, and handed her the paper. "His accounts of what he learned about you are wrong. There are records of him saying he was going on a date with you, and all that stuff. But, it only mentions small spells. His accounts are nothing like what you can actually do." He told her seriously. "There isn't even a mention of me."

She gulped, and started to cry again for a different reason. "Corbin," she muttered brokenly.

He sighed, and put the papers down as she began to cry. Pulling her into his arms, he gave her what she needed right now, and just held her. "I knew he wasn't a bad guy, but this is something even I never expected."

"He protected me." She whispered as she cried into his shoulder. "I miss him, Zangrunath."

He nodded, and rubbed her back. "I know you do." He told her, looking at the papers idly as she cried. "He was a good guy." He sighed, shocked that he would defy the Vatican to keep her safe.

Ellyria cried for quite a while longer before she eventually had nothing left in her. "Mom went quick, right?"

He groaned, and nodded. "Yeah, I made it as quick as I could." He told her honestly.

She sighed. "Thanks." She looked all around at the street, and sighed. "When can we go back in?"

"As soon as they get all of the information they need to figure out what happened." He told her honestly. "I give it about an hour more." He guessed, looking at the activity around them.

"I'm sorry. I heard 'as soon as the Vatican confirms what they think happened'." She groaned. "I'm hungry, and exhausted."

"More than likely." He sighed, looking at some of the figures, and guessing they were the ones in charge. "If I did it right, they will think it was her causing all of the issues, not you." He told her simply. "And, given what we found here," he paused, looking at the papers, "it might have been the best bet."

She looked at the roof of the car. "Give them a win while still winning yourself."

"Yeah." He agreed, thinking about what Lynne had told him before she passed. "Your Dad was a pretty smart guy." He decided, looking at Ellyria a bit more critically now, and noticing that she didn't really resemble her 'mother' very much at all. The closest she had was somewhat similar height. He let out a sigh. This was getting even more complicated.

"I still have so many questions for him." She sighed, looking at her hands. She looked up at her house. "When all the paperwork is through, I want to sell the place."

He nodded. "That's fine." He told her, looking at the house as well. "I don't blame you for not wanting to be here anymore."

"We'll rent a place in Massachusetts until I get my law degree, and, then," she paused, "wherever that takes us. Maybe that penthouse you suggested."

"We can do that." He told her, thinking it over in his head, and nodding. "I will need to use some of the money from the sale and whatnot to make sure we have a way to afford it, but it won't be much." He told her with a small smile.

"You can have whatever you need. If her life insurance policy is the same as Dad's, we'll be pretty set for a while." She sighed, frowning. "I don't have any family now."

He placed a hand on her shoulder. "You are strong. You will be fine on your own." He replied comfortingly. "And, you won't be alone; I will be right by your side."

She smiled. "You will be." Ellyria took his hand, and squeezed it. "Thanks. I know I can always count on you."

He nodded, and squeezed her hand back slightly. "I will always do as you ask." He smiled at her.

"I've got a fun one for you." She offered.

"What is that?" He asked her curiously.

She smirked. "When things settle down, go break our old friend Jack's leg, and light the school on fire."

He chuckled at first, and then laughed. "Oh, with pleasure." He smiled widely at her. "I will make sure that you can see the smoke from here."

"I would be able to see the smoke almost too easily from here." She chuckled, "Oh, and throw Heather's head into the inferno for good measure." She added.

"Are you sure?" He asked her, a little sobered. "That might cause suspicions to be raised again."

She sighed. "No."

"If you want, I could try to make it look like Principal Jones was involved and do it that way." he offered.

"Don't tempt me with a good time." She chuckled darkly, feeling murderous instead of sad, which was an unfortunate improvement. "Do it. He was an easily manipulated pawn at best."

"Alright. I will make sure it is the scandal of the decade." He chuckled. "'High School Principal Caught Taking Bribes and Taking Heads: Burns Down School to Cover Tracks'." He spoke in his best radio show announcer voice, waving his hands to mimic a headline in the air.

Ellyria giggled, and spontaneously leaned in to peck him on the cheek. "That is phenomenal. Thank you." About two seconds after she did it, she blushed profusely, and looked out the driver's side window. "Sorry." She added at a whisper.

Zangrunath was smiling when he gave the headline, and, then, stopped to look at Ellyria with an odd face. He processed what had happened for a few moments, and turned to face her. "What was that?" He asked her seriously.

"Wasn't thinking. Just acted. Sorry." She replied, continuing to look away as she crossed her arms over her chest.

He thought about her words for a moment. "Well, that was a first." He mentioned, watching her curiously. "No summoner has ever had the wherewithal to kiss me before." He chuckled.

Ellyria glanced over at him. "Please don't add me to some imaginary list of weirdos."

"I never said I would." He stated, giving a small pause. "I just said it was the first. In the past, I have been asked to seduce someone for them or something akin to that. It is simply different, is all."

"Well, you know me, always breaking all the rules." She blushed. "I'm sorry if I made this weird. We can just pretend it never happened."

"If that is what you want." He shrugged, and sat back as he watched the activity finally starting to die down. "You didn't make that weird. Just wasn't expecting it." He idly commented.

"It's your own fault, really." She replied defensively.

"And, why is that?" he asked her seriously.

She looked down at her feet. "Your chosen form for walking around humans is cute."

He scoffed lightly at that. "This is tame." He told her simply. "I could turn into a person who you wouldn't be able to look at without questioning your own sexuality."

She made a face. "I don't think I want to know."

He shrugged. "Suit yourself." He replied simply. "I'll just stay as your 'cute' for the time being." He teased.

She blushed deep red again. "You're mocking me."

"You make it too easy." He retorted. "You have barely seen what I can do. Yet, you are impressed." He smirked. "Be warned, there is a lot more that you are going to see as time goes on."

Ellyria audibly gulped. "Noted." She looked over at him to speak as a knock came at the window beside her. She hurriedly put on her mask, and rolled the window down as the cool evening air rushed into the car. "Yes, officer?"

"The house is clear to enter again." He told her, looking to Zangrunath, and, then, back to Ellyria. "If you need to, we can have somebody drive by the house in case something happens."

"Thanks." Ellyria sniffled a bit for his benefit. "But, I just kind of want to mourn," her voice broke, "in peace."

The officer nodded, a soft smile present behind his masked face. "No problem, miss. Try to get some sleep tonight." He instructed, tipping his hat, and leaving them.

She looked over to Zangrunath. "Let's revisit this conversation after I've eaten and slept. Now, I'm frazzled."

"As you wish." He submitted, waiting for the police to scatter some more before he got out of the car, and went inside to start making food for her.

Ellyria looked around the place to basically find it ransacked. "My room is going to be trashed." She groaned.

Zangrunath sighed as he went about the kitchen. "Yeah, they did a number in here as well, but I doubt they actually found anything of value to them." He surmised as he put something together.

Ellyria looked towards her room for a minute before finally working up the energy to go in. She looked around for her magic items, and started to get upset when most of it was missing. She went to go sit on the couch. "I can't believe this." She grumbled.

"What's wrong?" He asked as she fell onto the couch.

"Probably have about a quarter of my stones left. No incense or sage to bless the house or meditating. The salt is gone. Heather's grimoire is gone. They probably only left Dad's probably because they couldn't see what it was." She covered her eyes. "I know that you said I don't need that stuff, but I learned how to use magic with it. I don't know if I can do without it yet. It's like starting back at square one."

He continued cooking for a few moments before he looked at her. "We can get more of those things. That isn't a problem." He told her as he put the food in the oven to broil for a few minutes. "We can get the book back. It will just take some time, and, now that they are more lenient with us, it will be easier." He told her honestly.

She nodded in resigned agreement. "It's fine. The wand was probably the most important thing they took, but it can be replaced. Might cost a small fortune, but," she shrugged, "I don't need Heather's grimoire."

"Then, we forget about it." He told her as he pulled the food out of the oven, and plated it up. "We just focus on getting what you need, and go from there." He walked over, and handed her a toasted sandwich.

She took the food, and started to ravenously eat, realizing that it had been more than twelve hours since her last meal. "Yum. Thanks."

He shook his head. "Don't worry about it. I just threw it together." He responded before starting to clean up all the mess that the Vatican and police had left behind.

When she had her meal finished, Ellyria laid down on the couch. "Don't kill yourself cleaning up. I want to help when I have the energy."

He made a face. "I already died once today. I don't intend on doing it a second time." He told her seriously as he continued to clean.

She closed her eyes. "Let's not do that again. It hurt."

"Sorry about that." He told her honestly. "I didn't want to tell you since I thought you might have more than a few reservations about it." He stopped to look at her. "It was the only way I could think to make it work. Sorry." He apologized, going back to cleaning.

Ellyria started to drift off. "Could you do Mom's room?"

"Yes, I can." He replied as he finished up the worst parts of the kitchen. "Sleep well." He told her before he went to clean her mother's room. He cleaned up quite a few discarded pieces of trash and clothing for a while, but, when he came upon an unlabeled file box full of documents, it gave him pause. He went through each item carefully, and it confirmed his suspicions. He found a marriage certificate as well as adoption papers for the woman known as Lynne, to be Ellyria's legal mother.

In Zangrunath's effort to avoid missing something, he found what, he decided, intrigued him most. He carefully picked up Ellyria's birth certificate. Her father's name came first on the paper in all capital letters, 'GRANT, SAMUEL W.'. However, just below it, the woman's name was not a normal one, 'DOE, EIAEL'. "The Hell?" He muttered to himself as he checked for any other references to the name in any of the other documents, coming up short. There was nothing. Just the name in this one spot.

He sighed, and placed the papers on the bed. He knew Ellyria would want to see this when she awoke. There was no way he would be able to hide this from her.

Thursday, April 23, 2020

Ellyria slept for a long time, coming to at around nine in the morning. She stretched and groaned in pain from laying on the couch for such a long time. She looked around to see the house near spotless. "Zane?" She asked.

"Yes?" He asked as he heard her call out.

"Sorry. I dreamed that you hadn't reformed yet." She yawned. "Thought it took longer."

"I am no weak demon." He told her, leaning on the couch to look down at her. "At most, it only takes an hour or two for me to come back." He told her honestly.

"Oh." She sighed, getting up and dressing for the day before she made a quick breakfast of cereal. Holding the bowl in one hand and the spoon in the other, she casually made her way into her Mom's bedroom. It was clean, and Zangrunath had started to move things into a few different boxes that they had on hand. She looked at one full of clothes. "We can just donate these. She wore different sizes than me."

"Yeah, she did." He nodded, looking at the papers still on the bed. "That's not all that was different about her." He informed her, pointing at the documents.

Ellyria put her bowl of cereal down on the dresser, and started to look the documents over. Marriage certificate. Death certificate for her father. Birth certificates for all three of them, and she cocked her head to the side. "Adoption papers."

"Yeah." He sighed. "This goes much deeper than I thought it did." He told her, shaking his head. "It deals with your father."

Ellyria flipped back to her birth certificate, and sat down on the bed. "What am I?"

"Well," he trailed off, sitting down opposite her on the bed, and looking over the papers. "I am still not sure myself." He told her bluntly. "Your father is your father, but your 'Mom' was hired by your Dad and this Eiael person to take care of and look after you." He explained what he had discovered as best he could.

"What a great job she did." Ellyria responded sarcastically.

"Oh yeah, wonders." He sighed, looking at her seriously. "When Samhain comes, we need to have that talk with your Dad because this is starting to have more layers than Hell."

"Some powers of your own as well." Ellyria murmured, looking at nothing as she remembered what her father said during the Articulation Ritual.

Zangrunath looked at Ellyria. "You have a very weird family." He commented, looking at her actual mother's name. "Eiael." He tested the name aloud, trying to place the origin, and coming up short.

"Sounds Latin." She commented, not believing her own words.

"Partially. However, I can't place it specifically, and I should be able to." He grumbled.

"Who am I?" She whispered, closing her eyes, and staying stock still.

He looked at her, and placed a hand on her shoulder. "You are you." He told her seriously. "It doesn't matter where you came from. It matters what you are doing, and what you leave behind after you die." He pointed out from experience.

Ellyria looked at shaking hands. "My magic is stronger than my Dad's, and we don't know what all it can do." She looked at him. "I could be dangerous."

"You have restraint." He responded confidently; his expression serious. "You know how to control yourself. Besides, you don't want to use all that power you have. You just want to use enough of it to become influential." He reminded her.

She shook her head. "They've trusted me with too much. It's so easy, Zangrunath. I could, I could-"

"Yes. You could turn this town into a crater." He mentioned, giving an example. "But, will you actually do it?" He asked, leaning closer to her with an expressionless face.

"No." She whispered.

He moved back, nodding, and looking satisfied by her answer. "Exactly. You don't have the heart to do it." He looked her over. "You might in time but not now. By the time you do get there, you will have learned how to exercise even more restraint, and that will make you even more terrifying." A devilish smirk pulling at his lips.

"I want to be normal." She whispered sadly, getting up from the bed. "I'm going to clean up my bedroom. I need-" She didn't finish the sentence.

He gave a sigh. "I hate to say this to you, but normal is gone." He informed her as she left the room.

Ellyria went to her room, and started to pick things up, packing things she didn't need immediately. His brutally honest words resonating in her mind. She knew he couldn't lie, but she wished that he could, at least, sugarcoat some things. "I want out of this hellhole." She murmured, knowing he'd hear it.

Zangrunath heard the words and nodded without her seeing it. "I will get started on it." He told her, moving to the laptop, and searching for modern practices for home sales.

"Just have to wait to own it first," she sighed, "but we can leave it vacant until then. I don't care."

"It will take some time, but it doesn't hurt to know what needs to be done." He replied. "We also have to get a car towed, too. You are now the proud owner of the Shelby even if she's not the prettiest at the moment."

"Just get it into the garage, and I'll do the rest." She told him somewhat confidently.

"No problem. It will be here next week." He told her. "I will make sure it is clean before you start working on it." His voice reassuring, though, he was hoping that the police had mostly cleaned it up.

She processed his words, and got a little excited. It was bittersweet, though. She missed the car's former owner, and dared not think about him too hard at the moment. "Thanks."

"You asked me to get the car. Don't worry about it." He waved her off a bit.

"Still appreciate it." She grumbled back. After a while, Ellyria ran out of boxes. "We're gonna need more packing supplies, and we'll probably want to sell Mom's van too."

"I can put an ad up online." He told her as he put a few packed boxes in the corner. He looked around, inspecting what else needed to get done.

"Furniture," she hummed, "I think we'll take. We should look at houses for rent in the Harvard area, assuming that I'm in."

"I have been in contact with a few, let's call them contacts, up there. Haven't gotten a letter yet, but Harvard will want you." He informed her.

She nodded. "What do you need from me for that?"

"Nothing at the moment. I will take care of most of the work." He told her, noticing the time, and moving to the kitchen to make her some lunch.

"I meant if I needed to fill an application." She laughed.

"You won't have to do much. Maybe an introduction letter." He told her. "I'll need a signature, but I can fake that for you."

She laughed. "I don't need you to forge my signature. I want to go."

"I know you do. I am just saying that I will take care of most of it." He assured her. "If I need you to do something, I will let you know." He explained, turning back to make her food.

Ellyria grabbed her Mom's purse, and started to go through it. She found some cash, which she took out, and her debit card. She pulled out her phone, and dialed the number on the back of the card, following the prompts on the recording. After a few minutes, she hung up. "Well, she didn't blow her entire paycheck on drugs."

"At least, she did something right." Zangrunath sighed, pouring her a drink while the food cooked.

Ellyria raised an eyebrow at the liquor he poured for her. "Well, I won't say no, but it's not even one in the afternoon."

"We are not dumping alcohol." He told her seriously. "That is a waste."

"Well, alright, then. I'm going to be busy." She paused significantly before saying the last word as she looked at the several opened bottles on the counter.

He looked at the bottles as well. "There will be time to finish it. Worst case, I drink it, and get it over with." He decided, pulling the food out of the oven, and letting it rest.

She took a big gulp of the drink. "Wouldn't I feel it if you did that?"

"Yeah. The only difference is that I would still be able to function afterwards." His tone lighthearted. A small chuckle escaped him.

"But, I'd be a helpless mess." She responded.

"Exactly. You would sleep it off, but I would be fine to clean the place." He told her, plating the food up, and handing it to her.

She shook her head. "Let's see how much I can whittle my way through."

"I will make sure you don't puke on yourself." He promised while giving her a look of doubt.

"I feel like I'm going to wake up in a bathtub with no memories of how I got there." She laughed as she started to eat and drink.

"I will make sure to sell your kidneys for good measure. That way, you really get the whole experience." He joked.

She made a half-hearted swat at him. "Oh, hell no!" She laughed.

He easily dodged out of the way. "Naked in the tub it is." He joked, starting to clean up the few dishes.

Ellyria chuckled. "All this while I'm going to have a hard time getting a buzz as it is."

He turned to her, and nodded. "You could down that bottle and still be fine." He told her honestly.

"Give it to me straight. If I do that, is my liver toast?" She asked.

He leaned against the counter, and looked at her. "Not much. We are bound, and, as such, if you ingest poison, I take the brunt of it. Same applies to alcohol. Hell, if you had cancer, my constitution would slow the effects of it dramatically." His statement matter of fact.

Ellyria picked up the bottle of vodka, and looked at him. "Well, here goes something. This week has been one Hell of a year." With that, she upended the bottle, and started to drink deeply.

Zangrunath leaned on the counter, and watched as the contents of the bottle began to slowly disappear. "Just be sure to come up for air." He commented.

After about twenty seconds, she did just that. She winced. "Oh, that burns."

He chuckled at her as he went back to cleaning. "It isn't that bad."

"I need a subject change." She paused, thinking for a moment. "Can you tell me about them?" She asked curiously. "Your former witches and their orders?"

He chuckled at that. "Yes, I can. There were several who were odd. One wanted to make sure that his flowers were protected. One asked that I sing him to sleep every night. The worst one was one who insisted I bathe him every night." He groaned.

She shivered. "Okay. That's disgusting. I will not insist that you bathe me."

"Thank you. That would be appreciated." He replied with a sigh of relief.

"In fact, I will comfortably tell you that you can hold off on doing that unless I'm completely out of commission for some reason, like when you harvest my kidneys in the bathtub." She giggled.

He chuckled as well. "If you ask, I will do." He reminded her calmly. "If you are ever out of commission, I will make sure you are taken care of."

Ellyria finished her meal, and carried the bottle around the house. She finished it while she was cleaning, and staggered through the room over to him. She put it down, nearly knocking it over in the same motion, and kissed him firmly on the lips. "I'm ready to revisit that, that conversation." She hiccuped, and stammered.

He pushed her away gently. "You are drunk." He sighed, helping her down onto the couch.

"So? My answers will be honest." She smiled a little goofy grin.

"Fine." He sighed, moving to sit across from her. "Where did we leave off?" He asked.

"A look that would have me question my sexuality, and powers you have that I haven't seen yet." She replied with a surprising amount of lucidity given her inebriated state.

"I thought you said you didn't want to see that?" He asked with a small amount of annoyance in his voice.

She blushed. "Thing is, I did. It's embarrassing."

He pinched the bridge of his nose. "Right. You were a virgin up until not that long ago." he sighed.

"Yeah, I'm not used to- to this." She pointed between them.

He blinked at her, and sat up a bit. "Okay. First, let me just say this real fast. I don't care if you are interested in me." He told her bluntly. "It is my job to make sure you get what you want. Secondly, I am the worst person to talk to about all of that. You know that, right?" He asked her seriously.

"You're the only person I have to talk to about all that." She frowned, moving to get more liquor. When she didn't get up fast enough, she used a little magic to float it to her. She drank more. "And, I don't know how I feel about," she pointed between the two of them again.

He gave another sigh, and covered his face a bit. He leaned back on the couch, and let out a groan. "What do you want to know?" He asked.

"I want to see the full force of your charms." She muttered.

"Alright." He agreed, standing up, and turning to face her. A mist surrounded him for a moment, and, when it subsided, there stood a figure that was an Adonis compared to what she had seen before in her lifetime. He leaned close to her, and smiled. "How is this?" He whispered lustfully into her ear.

Ellyria eyed him up and down. She gulped as she looked at him. "Oh, fuck me." She grumbled before looking away.

"That's about what I thought." He told her with a smirk, turning back into his usual human self. He sat down again. "What next?" He asked her nonchalantly. This was all parlor tricks for him really.

"Well, I already knew I was straight." She replied.

"So, a woman next?" He asked.

She nodded, taking another drink, and burping.

He didn't stand this time, but his body did change. The new illusion shimmering into place. He looked like the most beautiful woman she had ever seen in her life. He teasingly brushed her leg with a hand. "How does this work for you?" He asked with a smile that invited much more.

Ellyria breathed out as she saw this new form. She fanned herself, blushing deeply as she did. "Oh." She whispered.

Zangrunath smirked, and turned back into himself. "Well, apparently, you swing both ways."

"Apparently." She adjusted in her seat, moving away from him a little. "I- wow."

"Nothing wrong with that," he told her. "Technically, so do I." He shrugged.

"How so?" She responded.

He raised an eyebrow at her. "You think I can look like them just to feel pretty?"

Ellyria blushed even more. "Okay. This was a terrible alcohol fueled idea. Now, I'm confused and uncomfortable."

"That sounds like your problem." He laughed at her.

"I could make it your problem, too." She suddenly threatened.

His eyes narrowed at her. "If you do that, I promise you will regret that decision." He grumbled in a threatening tone that didn't promise fun.

She sighed, standing up, and starting to stumble away. "I'm sorry, okay? I don't know what I'm doing. I've got this hot demon around me all the time. I'm all alone with no family left, and all I know is that I want to be happy with whatever this is for the next few decades." She pointed between them.

He stood up, and put his hands on her shoulders as he started to guide her to her bedroom. "I don't like getting threatened." He told her in a somewhat calmer manner.

"I wouldn't actually do it." She told him. "I could have literally crushed helicopters to the earth weeks ago and didn't. I don't abuse power. I don't think it's in me." Her voice caught. "I'm sorry."

"I know." He told her as he laid her down in bed. "You wouldn't force me to do something like that, and I am glad." He told her honestly. "If you asked, that is a different story altogether."

"I might, one day. I don't know, but I would want you to choose." She rolled over onto the bed, and closed her eyes.

"I probably wouldn't say no." He told her, tucking her in. "Sleep well."

Ellyria didn't respond. She was already unconscious.

He gave a small chuckle as she slept, shaking his head. "You really are something else." He hummed, getting back to work while she got the rest that she needed.

ARTICLE VIII

Saturday, October 31, 2020

Ellyria was behind the wheel of the Shelby as she turned off the highway towards a ley line. The closest one to Harvard that was remote enough for their needs was in New Hampshire. She hadn't visited one since before they'd left Oklahoma, and the anticipation was killing her. She looked over to Zangrunath. "Can you turn off the super hearing for the conversation with my Dad? I've got personal questions."

Zangrunath chuckled. "I can if you want." He told her, keeping an eye all around them for any danger.

She parked the car right around the time the sun set. "I'll tell you when, though. I've got one other person that I want to see first."

He looked at her curiously. "Who?" He asked her seriously.

"Corbin." She told him. "I just want closure."

"Oh, okay." He nodded simply, thinking it over in his head a bit. "It has been a while since you mentioned him." He stated quietly without prying any further.

"I know." She smiled as she threw her flats into the back, and grabbed a heavy jacket to spend time outside in.

He nodded at her, and got ready to follow her. "Well, I am ready whenever you are."

She nodded, hopping out of the car, and instantly connecting with the nature around her. But, this time, she controlled it. She pulled it into herself, and used it as she set up the ritual. Unlike months before, the ritual didn't take large amounts of power to activate and stabilize. Samhain made it different. She looked up to see the specter of Corbin, standing to speak with him, and smiling. "Hey, you." She whispered.

"Long time, no see." Corbin smiled back. "You're looking good." He commented, looking her over appreciatively.

She looked down at herself. "Yeah, I kinda put on the freshman fifteen." She laughed. "I actually kinda like it."

"It suits you." He told her honestly, looking over to see Shelby sitting off in the distance. "I'm glad you fixed her up."

"It took about twenty tutorial videos and several days of trial and error." She informed him. "It was worth it to have a little reminder of my first love."

"That's fine." He smiled at her. "I know you will take good care of her."

"I will." She promised. "I wanted to thank you," she told him, getting a little quiet, "for protecting me."

He let out a little nervous chuckle. "They wanted me to get close to you, and to report everything I saw." He started. "What they didn't account for was that I actually fell for you." He smiled at her longingly. "It was worth it in the end."

"I wish you were here." She told him, wiping away a few tears. "You promised to be here when my dreams come true."

"I hoped to be there when they did." He corrected her with a sad smile. "I had a feeling that I wouldn't, but I know you will get what you want. You have the power to do it."

She frowned. "It's too bad that I was starting to have a second dream that involved you." She sighed. "Moving on after knowing what you did for me has been hard. How could anybody hold a candle to that?"

"You have a pretty good dream in mind." He smiled at her. "You will manage. Besides, you have someone to look after you." He glanced at Zangrunath. "You can be happy without me. I know you can."

"I am." She smiled bitterly. "Corb?"

"Yeah, Elly?" He asked her back.

Ellyria stepped a little further back. "I wanted to let you know that, the next time you see me, it's going to be because that dream came true."

He smiled back at her. "I look forward to seeing the day."

She moved as if to touch him before thinking better of it. "I love you." She whispered, preparing to end the ritual.

"Love you, too." He whispered back before his form faded before her.

Ellyria sniffed a bit before looking to Zangrunath. "Dad's next. You'll probably want to hear the first part."

He nodded at her. "I plan on it; I have questions."

"Then, get over here before I order it." She chuckled, starting to summon her Dad, now.

He chuckled, and walked next to her. "Well, now, I'm waiting on you."

After a minute, she opened her eyes, and looked at him. "Oh, very funny." Then, she looked to the ghost of her father. "Long time no see, Dad." She greeted. "Good news. We have more than five panicked minutes this time."

Sam chuckled. "I figured as much. You look far more comfortable this time around." He smiled at her. "It is good to see you, too."

She took a seat, and looked at him. "Now that we have time, I'm not really even sure where to start."

"Well, what questions do you have?" He asked her seriously.

"I guess I'll start at the beginning." She shrugged. "Who's Eiael?"

He raised his eyebrows a bit. "Ah, right to the big questions. Okay, well, she's your mother." He told her simply.

"I saw my birth certificate. I know that, but can you tell me about her?" She asked.

"Well, she oversees the things we do, so it only made sense that we got together. Though I was surprised that we did." He explained with a nod.

She thought about that. "Oversees us? Like, witches?"

"Yeah. She is good at making sure that people don't get too carried away with magic." He chuckled.

"But, we can change- we can change the makeup of things." Ellyria started loudly before restarting quieter. "That's not carried away?" Her words slow and deliberate.

"That is something you picked up from her." He told her honestly. "I didn't change the makeup. I just changed things around and reorganized it."

Ellyria sighed again. "You guys trusted me with way too much. I could do so much evil with what I can do."

"We know you will do what is right in the end." He smiled at her. "You are our daughter. You are incredibly strong willed." He chuckled.

Ellyria nodded. "So, the gravity thing isn't you either, then? I'm assuming."

"All her." Her father chuckled. "She's a strong one."

"The thing is, it's your power just stronger." She took out a ball of aluminum foil from her pocket. "I can turn this to gold." She explained as she did just that. "I can make it lighter than air." She let go of it, and it floated. "Or, I can make it so dense that it pulls Zane in." She started to do so, stopping when he started moving.

Zangrunath shook his head at her, and righted himself. "Yeah, all of that." He grumbled the words, punctuating the sentence with a growl to show his displeasure.

Her father let out a sigh. "Your powers are the byproduct of two powers colliding. It's like taking potassium and throwing into water. It explodes violently." He explained. "You're more like magnesium, though. You burn white hot, and no amount of water is going to put you out." He told her.

"Is my Mom, Eiael, still alive?" She asked.

"She is always watching over you." He told her simply.

Ellyria frowned. Of course, she wasn't around anymore. "Okay. Uh, Zane. I know I'm missing things.

"What was she like?" Zangrunath asked him curiously. "There must have been something wrong with her if the two of you asked Lynne to fill in to be her Mom." He added seriously.

"An angel." He smiled at the demon before he turned to Ellyria. "Sadly, we both knew that she wouldn't be able to see you grow, so that was when Lynne showed up." He told her honestly.

"Why not tell me that she wasn't my Mom? Why the cloak and dagger?" Ellyria asked.

"We were going to tell you on your eighteenth birthday." He began, trailing off.

Ellyria dramatically fell back onto the cool Massachusetts ground. "Oh, you've gotta be kidding me. You mean, you were going to let me blow up the house and, then, tell me that my parents are both incredibly magically gifted and oh by the way you're adopted?"

"We had a plan. We were going to take you somewhere safe and tell you a few days before it happened." He sighed. "We both know how well that ended."

"So, you knew I would do that whole explode-y bit when I turned eighteen?" She asked.

"We had an idea of what would happen, but we didn't know it would be that strong." He told her honestly. "I'm glad he was there to stop you." He pointed to Zangrunath.

Ellyria looked to Zangrunath. "I don't know what would've happened had he let it keep going."

"Unbridled chaos." Zangrunath told her father. "Where were you planning on taking her?" He demanded. "Seriously, it would have been like a nuke going off had no one stopped her."

"New Mexico." Her father deadpanned.

"You have got to be kidding me." Zangrunath facepalmed.

Ellyria's mouth fell open. "Great. I'm a nuclear weapon."

Her father shook his head. "You are not a weapon." He said in a quiet, reassuring manner. "You are whatever you want to be," he looked at the two of them, now, "a weapon of destruction or a tool for creation. The choice is yours alone to make."

"You were going to take me there to blow up." She frowned. "I don't want to think about it."

"We were not going to let you blow up." He told her with a chuckle. "I was going to make sure you had more practice before you went there and that you were in a good mental state." He sighed.

"Yeah, I was not in a good place or well trained." She sighed. "I am getting better now, though." She gestured to the clearing. "I'm at a ley line, and there's no weirdness in sight."

"I noticed." He smiled at her. "Remember, having an image in your head when you cast a spell is key to making it become real." He instructed, pointing to his temple. "If you are not at one hundred percent, it can crash and burn."

She started to laugh hard at that. "How else do you think I summoned him?" She pointed at Zangrunath.

Sunday, November 1, 2020

"Fate." Sam halfheartedly chuckled.

Ellyria took a deep breath. "Do you have any more questions, Zane? I want to speak with my Dad privately for a bit."

Zangrunath shook his head, and began walking to the car. "I will wait here." He told her before hopping inside.

"Please don't listen. It's personal." She ordered with some regret.

"I won't." He responded honestly.

Ellyria looked to her Dad, and gave him a little smile. "Fate?"

"Your mother and I knew long before you were born that something was going to happen." He told her seriously. "We both knew that you would be fine. You would become stronger because of it."

"Dad, I'm going to Hell. I made a literal deal with the devil. You're fine with this?" She asked, looking at the stars.

"No, it took me a long time to come to terms with it when I found out, and it pissed your mother off way more." He informed her. "But, there was nothing we could do to change it." He sighed deeply.

She sighed. "I was trying to talk to you."

He took a breath. "I'm not okay with the deal, but, like father, like daughter, I guess."

"What in the world is that supposed to mean?" She asked.

"You inadvertently made a deal to see me. I made a deal to make sure you grew up to be strong." He told her simply.

"Well, you got it." She sighed. "I could start and end wars if I had it in my heart to do so."

He nodded, and gave her a smile. "You got that from your Mom."

She shook her head. "I guess I'll never meet her." She frowned.

"She loves you very much, and, no matter what happens, she always will. The fact that you are alive makes her happy." He told her.

"Can I ask for some advice?" She asked quietly.

"Always." He smiled softly at her.

Ellyria looked over her shoulder at Zangrunath to make sure he wasn't listening. "Things are complicated with him."

"Well, yeah, things are always complicated with demons. It's how they work." He told her simply. "I take it that this is a closer matter?" He asked.

"He takes care of me." She sighed. "I have feelings, and, while I know he can't really return them the same way," she trailed off.

Her father gave a sigh, and nodded slowly. He thought it over in his head for a long moment before he replied. "You like him, right?" He asked her seriously.

"I don't know if I can. Can I?" She shook her head. "This isn't normal."

"Elly, nothing about our family is normal." He told her bluntly, glancing at Zangrunath in the car, and sighing. "If it's meant to be, I say go for it." He sighed nodding. "If angels and demons can love, why can't you love a demon?" He asked rhetorically.

She took a deep breath. "I know I don't need permission, but that does make me feel better."

"I'm glad I could help." He smiled at her softly. "My little Elly."

"I'm not so little anymore." She smiled. "I'm trying to decide on my undergrad degree. That counts for something. Right?"

"My little lawyer." He chuckled. "You will always be my little girl." He smiled at her.

She smirked. "Contract lawyer."

"Well, as they say down below, give them Hell." He laughed.

Ellyria looked up at the sky. "I wish this were more than once per year."

"Same." He sighed, looking at the sky. It was starting to look like the sun would be coming up soon. "The fact that I can see you at all is magic." He told her honestly.

"I'll be able to tell you what degree I'm actually going for next year." She smiled. "I love you, Daddy."

"I love you, too. Sweetie." He smiled back. "I can't wait to hear what you choose."

She thought for a minute. "Send love to Mom. Tell her," she sighed again, "sorry I never met her in order to summon her on Samhain."

"I will pass the message along." He chuckled. "Love you."

Ellyria stood up, and reached out. When her hand passed through her father, she groaned. "I miss your hugs the most."

"Same." He sighed, looking at his hand.

"See you next year." She smiled.

"See you then, sweetie." He smiled back.

As the sun rose, Ellyria's father disappeared, and she yawned as she walked towards the Shelby. She hopped into the passenger's seat. "I'm ready to go home, now."

Zangrunath smiled at her. "Have a good talk?" He asked as he started the muscle car.

"I did." She smiled at him. "Needed some advice from my Dad."

He raised an eyebrow at her. "Did you find the clarity you needed?" He asked jokingly.

"Yeah, I think I might've decided my major." She chuckled.

"Good to know." He nodded as he began to drive them back to the house.

Wednesday, May 26, 2021

Ellyria finished her first year of college a week prior; that meant now, she could stay up late tonight mostly consequence free. She sat at the kitchen table, thumbing through her grimoire. She glanced to Zangrunath, "Zane?" She murmured.

Zangrunath looked at her as he was cooking. "Yes?"

"Do you know how getting the words on these pages to appear this should work or am I winging it?" She asked.

"My guess is that you need to be outside, at least." He concluded, waving a spatula at her. "After that, your guess is as good as mine." He shrugged.

She nodded. "I've still got a solid hour before it starts, and another two before it hits the maximum eclipse."

"You can eat first." He decided, moving the burger and fries he made in front of her. "That should kill a few minutes."

She closed the grimoire, and dug into the meal. She was feeling thoughtful at the moment, and remained silent while she ate. Not ignoring conversation, but just being comfortable in the moment.

Zane started cleaning the few dishes, and tossed the kitchen towel onto the counter when he finished, leaning against the counter casually as he waited to retrieve the last dish from Ellyria.

Ellyria finished her food before looking over at him properly again. "I can't believe it's been more than a year." She smiled softly.

He nodded. "Yeah, and there will be many more ahead of us." He concluded.

Ellyria stood up and stepped into their magically warded backyard. She had her grimoire in hand, and looked at the sky as the moon started to slowly turn red. "Zane?"

Zangrunath quickly did the last dish, and followed her outside. "Yeah?" He asked her.

"I wanted you here for this." She smiled.

"Well," he smiled back, his arms stretched wise, "here I am."

She looked down at the book, and saw runes beginning to appear on the cover. She smiled for a second, but it quickly turned into a frown when she read the archaic language. "Shoot." She muttered.

He looked over her shoulder at the book. "I thought you knew your Latin better than this." He sighed, pointing to the page. "That is lesson one." He chastised.

"That does not look like normal Latin. That's," she looked at him, "how old is this book?"

"Old." He deadpanned, seeing demonic writing now appearing. "Where did your Dad get this book?" He asked himself.

She looked at him seriously. "They are passed from family member to family member, and, sometimes, are taken when things like what happened with Heather go down. Mine being blood bound means that someone in the family thought the information inside was worth protecting at some point."

"I can understand why." He replied in awe as to what he was looking at. "This is a copy of the demon code." He informed her quietly as he flipped through its pages. "This should not exist."

She looked at him. "What?"

"This book should not exist." He repeated a growl starting to rumble deep within his chest. "This book contains the codes of conduct between demons and how they operate. The bylaws, the order, the intricacies of deal making, and the very core of how to make demons." He told her seriously, a fire in his eyes. "You should not be holding that."

She looked down at it. "Well, I'm not giving it up." She told him. "Besides, I wasn't the one to put it there, and why are you growling at a page that isn't written in demonic?" She looked at the words. "It's just soul binding. Whatever that means."

He shook his head at that. "Soul binding is, in essence, a way for people to share everything." He explained dismissively as he pointed back to the other page "I am growling at that because humans possessing that knowledge could use it to their advantage. It could destroy everything." He let out a low growl, but did nothing. "There is nothing I can do to stop you." He told her simply. "That book tells you all the details."

"Fine, Zangrunath." She growled back at him with a little eye roll. She walked towards the house, and sat down on the couch. She started to carefully read the ancient language within. She struggled through several pages where the demonic looked so much different from the Latin, but she was smart enough that she could fill in the blanks of the parts she didn't understand. By the time she was finished reading over the passages, it was nearly midnight. "You can't disobey, and you can't harm me. So what? I already knew that."

Thursday, May 27, 2021

"Correct." He told her with a nod. "Until such time as the deal is complete, I must make sure all of your needs are met." He handed her a cup of coffee.

"I'm sorry, but this book is too important to destroy. When I'm done with it, I'll put a new blood binding on it." She told him seriously, taking a sip of the coffee.

He sighed. "If that is what you want to do, so be it. Just make sure I can't get near it." He told her seriously.

"It's already under several protections." She sighed. "You have to destroy it now that you know about it, don't you?"

"I am a general in Hell. I was tasked to destroy every copy of the code during the crusades. Clearly, one got away." He growled as he looked at the book with resentment and fire in his eyes. "Fuck." He grumbled turning away.

"You'll be punished." She stated.

"If I know where it is after this." He told her honestly. "I can't do anything about it now. It would break the code if I did so."

Ellyria sighed. She opened the book, and carefully unmade the binding that contained the pages he was concerned about. "It's just these. Right?"

Zangrunath meticulously went over the pages several times before he nodded. "Yes." He told her with absolute certainty.

She nodded, handing them to him. "Don't destroy them until the contract is through."

He looked at her, grabbing the pages as he did so. "I will do that." He nodded, letting out a sigh of relief as he took the pages.

"I might read them again." She admitted. "Not sorry."

He nodded. "You are going to be terrifying." He sighed deeply.

"I already am." She told him. She took another sip of the coffee, leaning into him. "I should've slept."

He rubbed her shoulder a little. "You should have." He nodded in agreement. "But, you are stubborn."

"I was honestly afraid for my grimoire otherwise." She chuckled; her eyes closing a little.

"After seeing the code, I understand." He responded, looking at the pages. He was still baffled that they even existed, but he set them aside for now, placing them down on the coffee table.

Ellyria put the mug down, and put her grimoire next to that. She turned to him. "Is my book safe now that the pages are yours?"

"Yes." He told her honestly. "As long as no readable copy of the code stays on earth, it is fine."

"Well, very few people can read that sort of Latin," she replied defensively, "but I get it."

"It could cause a lot of trouble if it were to get into the wrong hands." He told her. "Seemingly everyone could have the power to become nigh unstoppable."

Ellyria leaned in. "Good thing I already am." She stole his lips for a moment before sitting back down. "I've been waiting to do that sober for a while, but the time never felt right."

He looked at her for a moment, and shook his head in surprise. "You finally realized you had a thing for me?" He chuckled.

"Months ago." She smiled, leaning on his shoulder. "Even without the disguises."

"Well, at least, you know what you want, then." He grinned, looking down at her.

She nodded. "I do, but I'm not going to order anything out of you. The rest is up to you."

He looked at her for a moment, and leaned back. "You need sleep before anything happens." He told her simply. "I won't deal with an exhausted woman. It's all or nothing." He smirked.

She nodded, slowly standing up. "Don't let me ruin my sleep schedule too badly."

He grabbed her hand, and moved her back onto the couch. "Either you stay awake until a reasonable time or nap for an hour or so." He reasoned, resting her head in his lap. "Take a nap."

She yawned. "Yes, sir, general, sir."

"Don't do that. Just sleep." He told her simply.

Ellyria nodded as rest started to take her. "Night." She murmured.

"Morning." He quipped, shaking his head as she rested.

COMING SOON

Zangrunath and Ellyria will return in Terms and Conditions
Book Two:

Ex Gratia

After getting out from under the Vatican's thumb, Ellyria's life is looking up for the first time in years. Between her budding romance with the demon Zangrunath and college, she has never been happier. However, tragedy looms in the near distant future as she is constantly reminded of her magical contract with the demon that would leave her alone at its inevitable conclusion.

When an unexpected twist of fate leaves Ellyria disfigured and in agony, they seek assistance from an unexpected ally who holds their fates wholly in his hands. The Prince of Darkness has no compunctions or obligations to assist them except for his own agenda. With a thought, he could crush them both, but, if they could somehow convince him otherwise, they'll owe the devil himself a debt of gratitude that has yet to be seen in all of history.

Earning a favor from Lucifer makes blackmail, politics, and misogyny look pathetic by comparison.

ABOUT THE AUTHOR

Terms and Conditions Book One, Covenant, is M. W. McLeod's first book in The Veil setting. They currently reside in Arizona, and enjoy playing Dungeons & Dragons with their friends. After years of writing fanfiction, they branched off from borrowing a spark of others' worlds to casting their own type of spells. They are fascinated with tall ships, and are a self-proclaimed caffeine addict, flavored coffee being the poison of choice.

www.beyondtheveilauthor.com

Twitter: @MWBeyondTheVeil

CPSIA information can be obtained
at www.ICGtesting.com
Printed in the USA
BVHW091635230621
610215BV00008B/1546